RELEASE

STINGRAYS HOCKEY
BOOK 4

MARI CARR

Cover Photography: WANDER AGUIAR PHOTOGRAPHY LLC

Cover Design: Qamber Designs & Media

Editor: Kelli Collins

Final Line Editor: Nan Mabbitt

RELEASE

He's her PR nightmare. She's his forbidden fantasy. Falling in love was never part of the game.

Tank Phillips is used to scoring—on and off the ice. But after a scandalous night with two puck bunnies makes headlines, the cocky star of the Stingrays is benched in more ways than one. His only shot at salvaging his career? A squeaky-clean image makeover…starting with a fake girlfriend.

Enter McKenna Bailey—nerdy, no-nonsense, and painfully new at her job as the Stingrays' social media manager. Tasked with taming Tank's wild reputation, she'd rather be buried in data analytics than babysitting the team's notorious playboy. He calls her mouse, barely remembers her name, and flashes that infuriating grin like he owns the world. But the more time they spend together faking a romance, the more the chemistry between them feels dangerously real.

McKenna has her own secret—one that could blow everything up: she's the estranged daughter of Coach Fields. And when the truth comes out, Daddy Dearest gives Tank a hard warning—stay away from my little girl.

But Tank's never been one to play by the rules…especially when the one thing he wants most is finally within reach.

CHAPTER ONE

BUZZ.

Buzz.

Tank Phillips groaned as he slapped in the direction of the nightstand, not bothering to open his eyes. Rather than wood, he hit bare skin...and grinned.

Buzz.

Buzz.

"Make it stop," a sleepy female voice mumbled next to him.

He blearily attempted to open his eyes, snapping them shut again quickly as sunshine from the window burned across the bed.

"Too bright," he grumbled.

Another female voice sounded *behind* him, twisting away to pull the pillow over her head. "It's too early," she whined.

Tank drew in a deep, somewhat unsteady breath, covering his eyes with a hand before trying to open them again.

No more tequila, he vowed—not for the first time in his life.

Last night's celebration ran into overtime and then some.

Buzz.

Buzz.

Tank managed to keep his eyes open this time, though he

was squinting hard against the bright light. Pushing himself up to sit, he took a moment to admire the two shapely bare asses on either side of him.

Buzz.

"Fuck," he muttered, reaching over Lara to grab his phone.

Glancing at the screen, his eyes widened in shock because his phone was literally blowing up with texts and calls. For a moment, his chest tightened in fear, wondering who had died.

He clicked onto one of the six or so texts he'd gotten from his best friend, Blake.

> Wake the hell up.

Tank looked at the time stamps, discovering Blake hadn't given him more than a minute or so between each text before sending the next. So Tank read through the entire thread, somewhat amused by his friend's increasingly irate comments.

> Seriously.
>
> Get your ass out of bed.
>
> Shit is hitting the fan.
>
> Where the fuck are you?
>
> I'm serious, man. Call me. This is bad.
>
> Management is losing their shit over your escapades last night.

Tank frowned, confused. His escapades? What the hell did that mean?

Clicking off Blake's text thread, he glanced at the countless others. No less than seven other teammates had texted, their comments running along the same theme as Blake's.

Then he checked the missed calls; there were as many of those as texts. His teammate and buddy, Victor, had called four times—no voicemails, of course, because Victor fucking hated leaving messages. Then there was a call from his coach, one from the head of HR for the Stingrays, and one from—*fuck*—the general manager.

Tank climbed over Lara's slumbering form and grabbed his boxers, heading toward the bathroom. Shutting the door, he pulled them on as he listened to the voicemail from the GM. It was short and to the point.

Tank was being summoned to the administrative offices for a meeting. At eleven o'clock this morning.

He glanced at the time on his phone and cursed under his breath. It was just after ten now, which meant he didn't have time to go home and change into clean clothes. Emily, his other date for the evening, had spilled red wine on his jeans at some point last night, and God only knew how wrinkled his shirt was. Or…*where* it was.

Tank needed a shower. But more than that, he needed fucking answers. Clicking on Blake's number, he put the phone on speaker and placed it on the counter of the sink, so he could splash cold water in his face. He didn't have to wait through one ring before his best friend was on the line.

"Where the fuck have you been?" Blake demanded, by way of greeting.

"Sleeping it off," Tank answered, clearing his throat, which was gruff.

"Jesus. Go to YouTube, type in your name."

Tank snorted. "Highlight reels from yesterday's game? In case you forgot, I was there, so I'm totally aware I scored an amazing hattrick."

"That won't be the first video that pops up," Blake muttered.

Tank clicked on YouTube and typed in his name.

The first video was titled, "Tank Phillips Scores Again." It took him a second before he figured out what he was looking at. When he did, he laughed.

"You think this is funny?" Blake shouted through the phone.

"It was a crazy night," Tank said. "Me and the girls decided to celebrate in style, so we got a suite at the Pendry." Tank loved the hotel because it was situated on the waterfront in Fells Point. Which was actually pretty close to where he lived, but he had a hard and fast rule about never bringing women back to his place. "We were in the middle of—"

"I know what you were in the middle of," Blake interjected.

Tank snorted and skipped ahead. "When the fire alarm went off."

"Yeah, I figured out that much. Actually, I think I've managed to piece out everything that happened last night. So did management."

"I don't see why this is a big deal."

Blake sighed heavily. "Tank, you walked outside in your boxers, drunk off your ass, with two half-dressed women, one of whom had handcuffs dangling from her wrist."

Tank chuckled. "We couldn't find the key." Which reminded him, he was going to have to pay for the damn bed he broke, trying to get Emily free so they could evacuate. Maybe if they hadn't been three sheets to the wind and laughing hysterically over the damn alarm, they might have tried harder to find the key. Especially since, upon their return to the room after the hotel determined there was no fire, they realized the key was in plain sight on the nightstand.

"Do you know who Lara's uncle is?"

Tank wasn't entirely sure what Lara's last name was, so it was safe to say he knew nothing about her family. "No."

"Charles Steele. Of Steele Industries. One of the Stingrays' biggest sponsors."

"Ooookay," Tank drawled.

"He's not amused by the attention this video is garnering, especially considering Lara was wearing your shirt and nothing else, and the three of you were clearly under the influence. The views are astronomical. The thing is going viral."

Tank looked at the video again. He didn't think it looked that bad. The three of them were laughing and having a good time, even if it was a bit heavy on the PDA, and while they weren't completely dressed, they were covered enough. It wasn't like they were running around stark naked.

"I've been out with Lara several times in the past few months." Last night had been his fifth booty call with Lara, and the second time, her bestie Emily, who was always down for a good time, had joined them. "Her uncle has never bitched about me going out with Lara before."

"You've never made it quite so public before, so he's bitching now. Loudly."

"How do you know all this?" Tank asked.

"I came in early to work out with some of the guys. Coach asked if I knew where you were. Apparently, the general manager is pissed and looking to put your head on a stake. If this had been an isolated incident, maybe—"

Tank growled. "That Mindy bullshit was *not* my fault. She followed me into the men's restroom and started taking off her clothes."

"I know," Blake said. "But your fault or not, it didn't help that a sports reporter walked in on the two of you and told everyone in the world a very different tale. Between that and the pictures of you and that model in Turks and Caicos in the hot tub at that resort—"

"That was last summer and off-season. Besides, I took Lara and Emily to the team's fall gala, and no one complained," Tank pointed out.

"Maybe not, but I also heard the marketing department couldn't use any of the pictures of you with your *two dates* because they didn't want the bad press that could bring. Instead, they got ahead of things and minimized the damage on that appearance."

Tank raked his fingers through his hair, aware he was looking pretty rough, and he had zero time to change that state. "I got called in by the GM."

Blake—good friend that he was—cursed. "When's the meeting?"

Tank looked at the time. "In forty minutes. I'm still at the hotel, and I don't have time to go home for clean clothes. My jeans are…"

Blake had been at Pat's Pub with them when Emily spilled the wine. "You can't go to the meeting in last night's clothes. Come to the locker room first," he said. "You can wear my clothes. I'll go home in my workout gear. All I have are jeans and a sweatshirt, but I figure it'll look better than going in smelling like a bar."

"Thanks, man. I'm grabbing a quick shower. Should be there in thirty."

"See you then," Blake said, disconnecting the call.

Tank hopped in the shower, washing away the smell of sex, beer, and tequila. Today wouldn't be his first time getting a slap on the wrist for his behavior, and if he was being honest with himself, it probably wouldn't be the last, either.

He chuckled, unconcerned. The team management, HR, and especially that stupid PR department, always thought the sky was falling when it wasn't.

Hell, as far as Tank was concerned…this was just another weekend.

Tank tugged on the sleeves of Blake's sweatshirt, sorry he hadn't had time to grab his own clothes from home. He and Blake were relatively close in size, but Tank was larger, so he was currently squeezed into clothing that was one size too small.

He gave Gertrude, the general manager's secretary, a charming smile, and she flushed just as she always did. Her reaction amused him because she was pushing sixty, had been married for nearly forty years, and had three grandkids.

"They're waiting inside for you," Gertrude said, glancing at the clock.

Tank didn't have to look to know he was ten minutes late. Traffic had not been on his side.

"Thanks, Gertie," he said, tapping the top of her desk lightly. "That blue is your color," he said, gesturing to her blouse. "Really makes your eyes pop."

Gertrude waved him away. "Go on, you big charmer," she said, smiling briefly before her expression sobered. "Best not to keep them waiting any longer."

Tank nodded, knocking twice on the GM's door before opening it and stepping inside. He'd expected this conversation would consist of him and maybe the coach. That was who'd been in attendance the last couple of times he'd been called in for one of Hugh's "come to Jesus" meetings about his extracurricular activities.

Today, instead of sitting behind his big desk (definitely overcompensating), Hugh was at the head of the conference table that filled the left half of his large office. Also seated were two assistant general managers, Coach Fields, Kendra Kingsolver, who was the head of HR, Benny Truman, who ran the PR department, and—fuck him—James Finnigan, the President of Hockey Operations.

"Mr. Phillips," James said, gesturing to the empty seat—the hot seat—at the end of the long table. "Please join us."

Tank walked across the room, claiming his spot. "I apologize for my tardiness. Traffic was—"

"You know why we're here today, Mr. Phillips, yes?" James interjected.

Tank nodded. "Yes, I do. I understand that—"

James continued as if he wasn't speaking. "There's a video of you that's creating problems for us, both with our fans and our sponsors."

"With all due respect, sir, I'm not sure the video was really that—"

"It *was* bad," James stressed. "You were drunk in public, half naked, and one of the women was wearing chains."

"Handcuffs," Tank corrected, aware the second he opened his mouth it was a stupid thing to say.

"The other woman is a relative of one of the team's largest sponsors. To say he was less than pleased to see his niece half dressed and intoxicated with one of our players would be an understatement."

"He's calling for your head on a platter," Hugh snapped. "And I'm not so sure we shouldn't give it to him." Hugh was a hothead on a good day, and this was clearly not one of those. His complexion was red with anger, his body so rigid, he was in danger of breaking in two. "Dammit, Tank! How many times do I have to call you in here about your behavior off the ice?"

In the past, his slaps on the wrist had come from the coach and Hugh, and to be honest, they never felt like more than a "boys will be boys, just do this shit where there aren't cameras" kind of speech.

Today was something more.

Probably because money was involved, if the sponsor was threatening to pull his support.

"I can ask Lara to speak to her uncle," Tank suggested.

"No. You and your girlfriend have done—"

"She's not my girlfriend," Tank clarified.

"Jesus, Tank," Coach Fields muttered, shooting him a "shut the hell up" look.

"You are not going to do anything that we don't tell you to do. Charles Steele doesn't want you anywhere near his niece." James gestured toward Benny, who'd been quiet thus far. Which was probably a good thing, considering the "if looks could kill" glare he was shooting in Tank's direction. "The PR department is in the process of writing up an apology that you will read at a press conference."

"Apology?" Tank was struggling to figure out what he was supposed to be sorry for. He'd been celebrating one hell of a win, and if the stupid fire alarm hadn't gone off, no one would have been the wiser about his private party. It wasn't like the three of them were having an orgy in the street.

Benny scowled. "Yes. An apology. For your poor lack of judgment. And you will read it word for word. No straying from the script. We've scheduled a brief press conference for three o'clock today." Benny looked him up and down. "You will need to shower, shave, and dress appropriately for it."

James leaned back in his chair, staring him down hard. "We have spent a great deal of time and money on creating a specific family-friendly brand for this team, and your actions have damaged it. We've already heard from several outraged groups who've spoken out about your treatment of women, and how you're setting a bad example for the young boys who look up to you."

Tank started to defend himself, wanting to assure his boss that those women were there because they wanted to be and everything they did was consensual, but a quick glance toward his coach had him shutting his mouth.

"In addition to the apology," James continued, "you will be suspended for the next two weeks."

At this, Tank shot up from his chair. "You can't do that!"

James narrowed his eyes. "I *can* do that. And I have."

Tank looked toward Coach Fields, expecting him to fight the suspension, but the man just looked resigned.

"Furthermore," James said, but Tank didn't want to hear *more*. He wasn't finished fighting the first battle.

"That's six games," he said, more to his coach than to James. "I'll be out for *six games*."

Coach Fields remained silent, but that was only because he didn't have a chance to reply before Hugh banged his fist on the table.

"This isn't your first offense, dammit! We told you the last time you were called into this office that there would be serious consequences if you didn't rein in your behavior off the ice. The partying, the women…it's all too much."

"Furthermore," James repeated, louder and with more force, annoyed at being cut off, "you will work closely with the PR department from now on as they attempt to repair your reputation."

Tank sank back down in his seat, aware he wasn't here to defend himself but rather to take his punishment like a good boy.

Fuck that, he thought bitterly.

"For how long?"

"For as long as it takes," Benny said.

"Through the end of the season at least," James added, pausing when Benny leaned closer, murmuring something Tank couldn't hear in the president's ear. "That's a good point," James said in response to Benny, before turning back to Tank. "You made quite a name for yourself in the off-season last summer."

If partying his ass off in Turks and Caicos was wrong, Tank didn't want to be right.

"You'll work with the PR department until training camp begins next season. At that point, we'll reevaluate," James added.

"Six months seems like an unnecessarily long time," Tank muttered, pissed they were trying to curtail his off-season fun as well.

James narrowed his eyes. "We are in danger of losing one of our biggest sponsors. If this was your first offense, maybe we could be more lenient, but you've made it very clear that you're incapable of reining yourself in. So we'll do it for you."

Tank crossed his arms, fighting to calm down. This punishment did not fit the crime as far as he was concerned, but it was obvious the jury had already handed down their decision.

"The PR department has been in the office since the wee hours this morning, working on strategies to salvage your reputation," James said. "You will do everything they say, follow every edict they issue to the letter. Do you understand?"

"Tank," Coach Fields said, the first to speak to him in a gentle tone. "Do what the president says. Do what the PR guys say. Take your punishment and then let's learn, grow, and move on from this. Your primary focus should be on the game anyway. Keep your nose clean for the rest of this season and start next year fresh."

Tank clenched his jaw, pissed as fuck. He was being treated like a naughty schoolboy, even though he hadn't done anything wrong.

When he didn't respond, the coach forced the issue. "Tank."

"Fine," he muttered through gritted teeth.

Coach Fields lightly tapped his hand on the table. "Good. During the suspension, you'll be banned from games, practice, and workouts, so I'll expect you to keep up with your conditioning on your own."

Tank nodded once, his body vibrating with anger.

"One more strike," James said, lifting his pointer finger. "Do one more thing that reflects poorly on the Stingrays' program, and I promise, you will find yourself off the team."

Off the team.

What the fuck?

"I have a contract," Tank pointed out, his anger quickly morphing to panic. He'd dedicated his whole life to hockey, fighting tooth and nail for his shot in the NHL. And now that he was here, he refused to give up his spot, determined to break all the records and hoist the Stanley Cup over his head.

"With a standards-of-conduct clause that gives us every right to terminate it." James looked all too pleased to put that final nail in Tank's coffin.

Rising, the president nodded at the others in the room before leaving without saying goodbye to anyone. Hugh dismissed his assistants and Kendra, none of whom had said a word, but they still managed to speak volumes with their disapproving glares. They filed out as well, leaving Tank alone with just Hugh, Benny, and Coach Fields.

Hugh looked at his watch. "The press conference is at three.

From now until one o'clock, I want you to go with Benny and meet with the PR team. After that, go home and clean yourself up. Be back here by two-thirty, ready to act a hell of a lot more contrite than you are right now."

Tank blew out a long, slow breath, not that it helped to calm him down.

"There will be no more second chances," Hugh said, reiterating James's warning.

Tank stood, as did Benny and the coach. The three of them walked out of the GM's office together.

Coach Fields put a hand on Tank's shoulder and gave it a squeeze. "See you in two weeks."

Tank got a lump in his throat as he watched his coach walk away. The idea of missing six games and letting his teammates down hurt...bad.

"This way," Benny said, pointing in the opposite direction. "The rest of my team is waiting for us in our department's conference room. In addition to me, you'll also be answering to my assistant, Roger, and McKenna Bailey."

Tank knew both Roger and McKenna. Roger was perhaps the biggest Stingrays fan on the planet, something that served the team well, considering the guy did a lot of their publicity. His press releases were always glowing and practically likened him and his teammates to gods.

McKenna was also familiar, though definitely less of a fan— at least of him. She was a nerdy woman, with an awkward sense of fashion and glasses that never managed to stay on the bridge of her nose. Tank had started calling her Mouse, which probably hadn't helped endear him to her.

The nickname was the result of her appearance during their first introduction. He'd been on his way to Hugh's office for one of his usual slaps on the wrist. Benny had been showing McKenna around, and he'd stopped Tank to introduce them. McKenna had been wearing a Mickey Mouse T-shirt, her hair pinned up in two high buns that had reminded him of those Mouseketeer hats with the ears that people got at Disney World. Between that and the fact she was a tiny little thing, he'd taken to calling her Mouse.

Despite her small size, McKenna was a hell of a lot better at her job than the team's former director of social media marketing, an out-of-touch woman who thought TikTok was the sound a clock made.

Since that first meeting, McKenna had made it clear she didn't approve of him and his playboy ways with more than a few sideway scowls—which was, of course, a red flag to someone with his personality. So he tended to go full-on Tank whenever she was around, because her narrowed-eye glares amused him.

Tank followed Benny into yet another conference room. He'd expected the atmosphere in this room to be less tense, but damn, was he wrong.

The pressure was even thicker, as McKenna and Roger turned and looked at him with the bleary-eyed expressions of two people who hadn't gotten much sleep—and they were grumpy about it.

"Hey, Rog." Tank claimed the empty chair next to the affable guy.

Roger offered him a tired smile. "Hey, Tank."

"Mouse," he said to McKenna, who was sitting directly opposite.

McKenna blinked twice, before flat-out ignoring him, turning her attention to Benny, who sank down in the seat at the head of the table.

"Tank's been apprised of the press conference at three," Benny said. "Have the lawyers looked over the statement he's making?"

Roger nodded and slid a piece of paper over to Benny. "They made a couple of suggested changes." He pointed to them as Benny scanned the paper.

"Those work." Benny handed the paper to Tank. "Familiarize yourself with this."

Tank glanced at the paper and sighed. "Fine." He had a feeling that was going to be his standard response to all this bullshit.

"You'll need to shower and put on something more appropriate," McKenna said, taking in his too-small clothes as she pushed up her glasses.

"I know how to dress for a press conference, Mouse," Tank retorted with more heat than he intended. He shouldn't be taking things out on her, but he was literally at the end of his rope as far as patience was concerned.

McKenna bit her lip. Tank got the sense her response wasn't driven by nerves, but because she was trying to hold her tongue. She managed to swallow back whatever she wanted to say by rising to walk to the coffeepot in the corner. She refilled her cup, adding creamer and a shit-ton of sugar.

He took a moment to study her outfit, amused despite his bad mood. She was younger than him, probably no more than twenty-four or twenty-five, yet she dressed like she was a fifty-year-old crazy cat lady. She was wearing mom jeans, Chucks, and an oversized graphic T-shirt that had three cute big-eyed cartoon cats peering over a wall. She complemented that outfit with a long navy-blue cardigan with huge pockets and a hole in one sleeve. Because she'd been yanked from bed in the wee hours, her hair was pulled into a messy bun on top of her head. She also hadn't bothered with makeup, not that she ever wore much to begin with.

When she returned to the table, she took off her glasses, rubbing her closed eyes. As she opened them again, her gaze clashed with his. He couldn't help but notice the dark circles under her eyes, which were surprisingly a bright, light blue, framed by long dark lashes. He'd never noticed how pretty her eyes were, but that was hardly surprising, since they were always hidden behind those thick-framed glasses of hers.

Tank had never really paid a lot of attention to McKenna's looks, beyond the entertainment value of her wardrobe. He was attracted to feminine women, a sucker for high heels and legs that went on for miles, preferring women with a healthy helping of flirty playfulness blended with sex appeal. Oversized cat T-shirts and a judgy attitude just didn't do it for him.

Tank rose when the smell of her coffee hit him. He helped himself to a cup, needing the jolt if he was going to get through the next few hours. He should still be in bed nursing a hangover, not dealing with all this shit.

Once he returned to the table, Benny, who'd been flipping through several pages in a file folder, closed it and leaned back.

"As you know, we're in charge of repairing your reputation. The three of us will be working together on this. Mac's going to spin a more positive picture of you. Her social media posts help drive public perception of the players, and she's proven herself very capable when it comes to influencing fan opinions."

While Tank used Mouse, everyone else in the Stingrays organization simply called McKenna "Mac."

"So you're gonna make everyone believe I'm some choir boy in a bunch of Facebook and Insta posts?" Tank asked her, chuckling. "Good luck with that."

McKenna didn't share his humor, opening the folder in front of her. "We've scheduled several appearances for you over the next two weeks, since you'll have some time on your hands."

Tank took a couple seconds trying to figure out if McKenna's quip was meant as an insult or if she'd just chosen unfortunate wording. When she met his gaze and held it, he saw a spark in her eye and found his answer.

Tou-fucking-ché, Mouse.

He could count on one hand the number of one-on-one conversations he'd had with McKenna Bailey that weren't work related and still have all his fingers left.

Apparently, she had claws.

"The appearances range from a photo shoot with a local Pee

Wee team that just won a state tournament, visiting veterans at the VA, and a ribbon-cutting for a new sporting equipment shop opening near the Inner Harbor," Roger added.

Tank was no stranger to those types of appearances, but they ranked hella low on his list of what he considered a good time. He'd much rather be out on the ice with his teammates, practicing and playing hockey.

However, if there was one thing he'd learned today, there was only one appropriate answer.

"Fine."

"Also, once the suspension is over, you'll be expected to…" McKenna paused for a moment. "Curtail your victory celebrations."

Tank scowled. "Curtail how?"

"We know the team occasionally goes to a local pub after games. You can go out if you choose, but only for a beer or two," McKenna explained.

"No more drunken orgies," Benny muttered. "And stop bringing two dates to team events."

McKenna chimed in, glancing down at some printout in her hands. "A lot of the comments on that viral video of yours involve fans' concerns that perhaps you're an alcoholic or an addict. The word 'rehab' has been bandied about by more than a few people."

"I'm not an alcoholic," he snapped.

McKenna shrugged. "Public perception is what matters here. Not the truth."

"Oh, really," he replied, his patience all but gone. He didn't mean to keep snapping at the woman, but dammit…this whole fucking thing had been blown out of proportion.

"Yes, really," Benny responded angrily. "While you were tucked in a warm bed, sleeping off last night's revelries, Mac, Roger, and I have been in the office since five a.m., reading comments on social media and coming up with a plan to restore your reputation."

Tank was slightly chastened by that. "How the hell did this get so big, so fast?"

McKenna answered. "TikTok's algorithms pushed it out hard when it got uploaded around nine-thirty p.m."

Yesterday's game had a two p.m. start time, which meant he and the girls had started their celebration earlier than normal.

"The video got well over a hundred-thousand views in the first hour," McKenna explained.

"Jesus."

"And that number continues to grow," she pointed out. "You've pissed off several Christian mothers' groups, who are calling you everything from a bad influence on young boys to an amoral misogynist who abuses women."

Tank suddenly felt ill. "That's not true."

"Perception," she said, reminding him again that no one cared about the truth.

"And you think a bunch of photo ops are going to restore my reputation?" Tank asked.

"It's a start," she replied softly. "Are you, um," she paused, "dating one of the women from the video?"

Tank shook his head.

McKenna seemed disappointed by that. "So, *neither* of them is your girlfriend?"

"No." He grimaced. "They're just hookups."

Roger rubbed his eyes wearily. "That's a shame."

"Why?" Tank asked, confused.

"Mac and I were talking while you and Benny were in with the GM, thinking that it would be easier to restore your reputation if one of them was your steady girlfriend. If you were in a relationship, it would help us overcome your current playboy status."

Benny perked up. "That's a good point."

Roger nodded. "But since you aren't seeing either of the women…"

Tank got an uneasy feeling when Benny's gaze rested on him

consideringly. He had a good idea where this was headed, and he was not down for it. "I'm not interested in dating Emily or Lara."

Benny raised his hand, cutting him off. "None of us is suggesting you date one of them. Especially not Lara, because if that went south… You know what, stay far, far away from that woman, because if her uncle pulls his financial support, I'm not sure there's anything we can do as a department to save you."

"I guess we can assume there's no one else you're seeing?" Roger asked.

"No one." Tank enjoyed his bachelor lifestyle. Hell, he was only twenty-seven and way too young for a committed relationship. In truth, he'd never seen himself as the dating type, determined to sow his wild oats all the way until he retired from hockey—at which point, he'd *consider* settling down.

"That's a shame. If you were dating someone respectable, responsible, more serious," Benny started. "Not a puck bunny—"

"That's not exactly my wheelhouse," Tank joked.

Benny rolled his eyes.

"We'll make the social media campaign work, Benny," McKenna reassured her boss, before flashing Tank another of those disapproving looks he enjoyed so much. "If he takes it seriously."

He scowled. "I'm taking all of this seriously."

Benny tapped his pen on the table. "Tank, I'd like to take you at your word, but given the fact you're a repeat offender, you have to understand our skepticism. That shit with the model last summer—"

"We were just having some fun in a hot tub," he interjected.

"It wasn't a *private* hot tub," Benny countered. "There were families staying at that resort with their kids."

Roger shook his head. "How many team meetings have we had in the past year where we discussed our new family-friendly branding and our goals for the future?"

Tank rolled his eyes because as far as he was concerned, there'd been way too many of those stupid-ass boring meetings.

McKenna crossed her arms. "You know what? If you want to be a playboy asshole, talk to your agent and see if he can get you traded to Florida."

Tank barked out a laugh. Jesus, the woman didn't just have claws; she had fangs as well. He might have to rethink her nickname. He was suddenly leaning toward Dragon. God knew she was shooting all kinds of flames in his direction.

Roger covered his mouth, trying to hide his smile, and Benny looked amused as well. For a moment.

Then his attention turned away from Tank and toward McKenna. "She's right. It's time to take this seriously."

"I'll do as many publicity ops as you need, sign a million fucking autographs and pose for two million pictures. All I want to do is get back on the ice," Tank reassured them.

Benny rubbed his chin, and Tank got the feeling the guy was trying to decide if he was sincere. Guess he really did have some work to do if he wanted to prove he wasn't a screwup.

"You," Benny finally said, pointing at McKenna.

She frowned, confused. "Me, what?"

"You're in charge of the Tank overhaul."

McKenna looked genuinely horrified. "I thought we were working together as a team?"

"We are, but you're going to be our boots on the ground. Tank's keeper."

"Keeper?" he and McKenna said in unison, clearly neither fans of Benny's suggestion.

The PR director never cracked a smile. "Keeper," he reiterated.

McKenna shook her head. "But, Benny, he's, uh, he's a…"

"Horny bastard?" Tank supplied helpfully, perfectly aware that McKenna's list of descriptors for him would not be flattering. "A womanizer? A manwhore? Or would you prefer to stick with the ones you've already listed. Addict. Misogynist. Asshole."

McKenna bit her lower lip again, something Tank wished she would stop doing, because he was just now realizing she had very plump, pretty lips.

"Well?" he prodded.

"Those weren't my words. They were comments from the fans," she spat out.

"Asshole was all you," he reminded her.

Benny ignored their interchange. "You know exactly what we're up against here, Mac, and you're well-versed in how to spin things in our favor. So you'll go to all the promo ops with him, control the situation, make sure everything goes well."

"Benny," she started again, but her boss was on a roll.

"You're the best person to handle the task. We need you on the frontline with Tank, guiding him as far as what to say and how to behave."

Tank scowled. "Hey. I'm not an idiot."

Benny shot him a look that said he disagreed wholeheartedly with that statement. "This isn't the first time we've had to clean up one of your messes, Tank. Hell, it's not the fifth or sixth time. You're in my office more than I am."

That was an exaggeration.

But not as big a one as Tank might have liked.

Benny turned his attention back to McKenna. "You're dedicated to your job, Mac, but more than that, you love this team and the brand we're building, and it shows."

"I appreciate you saying that, but even so...this is..." McKenna rubbed her forehead, acting as if Benny was suggesting she donate a kidney.

"It won't be easy," Roger chimed in.

"Won't be easy?" Tank asked, aghast. "You guys do realize I'm still in the room, right?"

"He's a loose cannon on a *good* day," McKenna said to Benny.

He agreed. "I know. He speaks hours before his brain kicks in."

Tank turned to Roger. "*You* can see me, right?"

Roger chuckled.

Benny didn't.

"I have a lot of other duties, Benny," McKenna said, still fighting the good fight. "And the schedule we've created for him, even beyond the next two weeks, would take up a lot of my time."

"I'll reassign some of your tasks to that new intern we just hired."

McKenna deflated. "I'm not sure I'm comfortable with that."

"It's only until training camp begins next season. Then we'll reevaluate."

"Six months!" McKenna gasped, though Tank wasn't sure if she was more upset about the time or the task.

"You really don't think I can change?" Tank asked hotly. Then he saw a glimmer of something in her eyes, and he realized—not for the first time today—he would have been smarter to keep his mouth shut.

Because why was he asking that question?

He didn't *want* to change.

He fucking loved his life exactly the way it was.

McKenna leaned back in her seat, chewing on her thumbnail as she considered him.

"Fine," she replied, using his word.

And Tank suddenly felt as if he'd found a kindred spirit. At least he wouldn't be suffering alone with his punishment. Because apparently he was taking McKenna down with him.

"I'll do it," she muttered, sounding like she'd just agreed to put her dog down.

Benny turned his attention back to Tank, crooking a thumb in McKenna's direction. "She's in charge. If she says jump, you do it without question. Got it?" Benny raised one impatient eyebrow.

Tank sighed, aware there was only one right answer. "Fine."

CHAPTER TWO

MCKENNA HIKED her bag on her arm and pushed her glasses up as she rode the elevator to Tank's fourth-floor apartment. Today was day one of Operation Tank Overhaul, and she was not looking forward to it.

Of all the players…why did it have to be him?

She'd managed to forge decent working relationships with most of the other Stingrays during her eight months as the director of social media marketing. Part of her duties included traveling with the team, so she'd spent a lot of time with the guys, and she'd been touched by how readily they'd welcomed her into their midst. Most of them were always happy to give her sound bites for her posts, pose for pictures, and they'd even gotten the hang of sharing photos and tidbits from their off-ice lives, whenever something happened they thought was worth a post.

She loved every minute of the job, coming to work each day excited and energized. The only somewhat sour note had been Tank, who had a way of driving her up the damn wall.

The man seemed to take pride in pushing all her buttons, which, to be fair, she probably made easy for him. She was typically better about not letting cocky guys get under her skin, but

Tank was the exception to that rule. She was completely incapable of schooling her expressions around him, something that only served to egg the man on.

The man was sex-on-a-stick hot, like drop-dead gorgeous, and boy did he know it. She'd seen him nearly hurt himself to cross a room or a restaurant to flirt with some big-boobed, big-haired, sexy woman. He was so transparently shallow it wasn't even funny. And while she'd known and ignored other men like that in the past, Tank's actions annoyed the hell out of her for some reason.

If she was actually susceptible to guys like him, she'd think she was attracted. But, despite his stunning good looks, Tank wasn't her type. Period. He loved the spotlight and leaving chaos in his wake, simply because he didn't give a shit.

McKenna, on the other hand, preferred routine and control. She started each day with a well-thought-out agenda and a solid plan of all she needed to achieve. Her mom accused her of being a workaholic, something that wasn't wrong.

She'd never been great about achieving a good work/play balance, but she blamed that on the fact she genuinely loved her job. And unlike Tank, she didn't need to be front and center. Instead, she preferred to be an observer, comfortable hovering on the edge of any room, reading it and the people around her. It was her observational skills that allowed her—much like Lady Whistledown in the *Bridgerton* books—to create insightful, interesting posts about the team, the players, the fans, and the games.

But ever since getting that phone call from Benny yesterday morning—and by morning, she meant four a.m.—she'd been flying by the seat of her pants, unable to maintain her typical daily routine.

All because Tank Phillips couldn't keep it in his goddamn pants.

To make matters worse, Tank clearly thought her meek, given that silly nickname he'd bestowed on her. Though she couldn't for the life of her figure out where he'd gotten the impression she was timid. Sure, she didn't talk a lot, but it wasn't like she cowered or retreated from conversations.

If she hoped to have a snowball's chance in hell of getting on top of this situation he'd created, she needed to set some very firm boundaries right from the start.

This wasn't the first time she'd had to clean up a Tank mess because he wasn't shy about expressing his opinions of players from other teams or past games played. Tank didn't hesitate to speak his mind, even when it might piss off others, so she'd had to do some fancy footwork in terms of spinning his words, or attempting to hide them by inundating social media with a ton of positive comments from him—some things he'd actually said; others, shit she'd made up.

McKenna hadn't been shocked to see Tank with the two women in the video, because she was sure they were the same women he'd brought to the team's charity fundraiser in the fall. He'd swaggered around the entire night with a woman under each arm, introducing them to everyone as his dates, which made it challenging for her when it came time to find "family-friendly" pictures of him to post online.

The viral video, however, was in a league of its own. Rather than die down, the thing was still gaining momentum. McKenna wished someone would hurry up and create some new scandal so everyone could turn their attention away from Tank's ménage à trois, complete with a bondage element.

Jesus. H.

While she appreciated the fact that no one would have been the wiser about Tank's threesome if that fire alarm hadn't gone off, he sure as hell could have minimized the damage by putting on some damn clothes and taking the handcuffs off that woman.

Benny called this morning to let her know the hotel had added their own fuel to the video fire, telling reporters there had been significant damage to the suite, mentioning a broken bedframe.

So that was fucking awesome.

Just what they needed.

More negative press to counteract.

When the elevator reached the floor, she stepped off and girded her loins, so to speak. With any luck, the publicity tour would do the trick—hopefully quickly enough that she wouldn't be tied to Tank full time for the next six months.

The man didn't strike her as the type to respond well to a keeper, which meant he was bound to be one gigantic pain in her ass the entire time.

Ugh.

Tank had done a great job yesterday during his press conference, sticking to the script while managing to portray genuine contrition. Luckily, the media soaked it up, even though *she* hadn't bought the act. She hadn't seen a whole lot of regret on Tank's part during their initial meeting. At least not in regard to the video. The only thing he seemed sorry about was the suspension.

Taking a deep breath, she knocked on his door. Following the press conference yesterday, she'd made plans to meet Tank here. She'd passed at least half a dozen sports reporters on her way in, and Benny said there were twice that many camped outside the Stingrays' headquarters, all of them hoping to score a scoop from Tank, despite his statement yesterday.

Her concern was that, if left unsupervised, Tank would *give* someone a scoop and God only knew what he would say. They were meeting here, privately, so the two of them could go over the schedule her team had prepared for the next two weeks. It was an ambitious tour, with something on the books for nearly every single one of the fourteen days of his suspension.

When he didn't open the door immediately, she knocked again, a litany of curses flowing through her mind. If the asshole stood her up, she would lose her shit.

Then another thought came to her, and she got even angrier. Because…what if he wasn't alone?

Finally, Tank opened the door, giving her that signature

cocky smirk of his. He was shirtless with a towel wrapped around his waist, and it was obvious she'd caught him in the middle of a shower, as water droplets slid down his very lickable skin.

Nope. Not lickable.

"Mouse," he said.

"McKenna," she said, correcting him for the thousandth time, not that she expected it to work.

Now, as always, his gaze slid down as he took in her outfit, and she felt oddly self-conscious. She wasn't a girlie-girl. While she owned one pair of high heels, the same couldn't be said of a curling iron or a blow dryer. Her makeup bag consisted of mascara, tinted Chapstick, and a tube of cover-up for the occasional zit concealing. Her wardrobe was basic at best—jeans, work pants, plain blouses, sweaters, and a huge pile of cute graphic tees because what was life without a little whimsy.

Since today was destined to try her patience, she'd worn her most comfortable pair of jeans with a T-shirt that said, "I'm silently creating a spreadsheet for that," and her favorite cardigan.

"Nice shirt." His lips quirked at the edges, as if he was amused by what he was seeing. Then he opened the door wider so she could walk in. "Sorry for making you wait. Lost track of time during my workout."

"That's okay," she said, trying—and failing—to hide her expression as she took in his apartment. "Oh. Wow."

Tank shut the door behind him, chuckling at her horrified look. "I have a housekeeper who comes in every other day to put the place back together. She missed yesterday due to a doctor's appointment."

"You did all this in just three days?"

Tank crossed his arms, completely unoffended. "It's not *that* bad."

McKenna took in the dishes with caked-on food on the coffee table, the trails of dirty clothing leading in countless directions, empty bottles of Bodyarmor scattered around, and the pile of shoes by the front door.

"I'm not great at keeping the place tidy."

"Not great would be one way to describe it," she said, picking up a sweatshirt from the couch and tossing it to the side to clear a spot for her to sit. "Another way would be to admit you're a slob."

Tank laughed at her comment, which she hated to admit strangely pleased her. She wasn't typically considered the funny one in any group, always the serious one. Making Tank laugh felt better than it should. Especially because Tank—who drove her crazy with his smug, swaggering ways—had the sexiest smile she'd ever seen in her entire life.

Everything about the man was hot, charming, breathtakingly attractive. No doubt he had women throwing themselves in his direction left and right. McKenna was proud to say she had no intention of ever tossing her panties in his ring—she had too much self-respect for that—but she had to admit he was good-looking.

"You're not the first to make that observation," he said. "Blake Mills and I tried the roommate thing when he was transferred to the Rays. It didn't last long."

She was sure it didn't. Since the holidays, she'd been invited to Blake's apartment a couple times for game nights, and his place always looked immaculate.

McKenna had recently been adopted into what she called the "Girlfriends Club" by Blake's significant other, Erika. The other women included in the group were goalie Coulton's girlfriend, Ainsley, and Chelsea, who was co-parenting the most adorable little boy with left winger, Preston. Chelsea's best friend, Allyson, was also part of the newly formed social group, and like McKenna, she wasn't dating a player.

McKenna had been delighted to be included in the occasional happy hour and shopping excursions, because all the women were super nice and a lot of fun. She hadn't had a lot of girlfriends in her life. She was the type of girl who only seemed to manage one friend at a time. She'd had a high school bestie, and then a college one, but both those friendships faded after they graduated and moved on with their lives, taking jobs in different cities.

Tank picked up the sweatshirt she'd just moved, as well as several other articles of clothing, tucking them under his arm. The man was seriously built and no stranger to the gym. McKenna had never seen honest-to-God six-pack abs in real life. Then she counted again…

Tank had an eight-pack.

"Well, I guess I should go get dressed. Unless you prefer me in the towel."

McKenna quickly averted her eyes, aware she'd been staring. "You should get dressed. We have a lot to go over." She reached into her bag to pull out the schedule she'd just finished finalizing this morning. "It's going to be a busy couple of weeks."

Tank growled low in his throat, but that was the only sign he gave that he wasn't looking forward to his penance.

She watched as he walked down the hall to his bedroom, admiring his bare back. McKenna was a big fan of a muscular back, finding it just as sexy as a man's chest, and damn if Tank didn't look as good going as he did coming.

She quickly erased the word "coming" from her mind because it sent her thoughts down very inappropriate paths.

Tank turned, catching her in the act of ogling his ass. He gestured to the towel. "You sure?"

She shot him a dirty look and flipped open her notebook, pretending to read something, breathing a sigh of relief when he entered his bedroom and shut the door.

She really needed to keep her wits about her. She refused to let Tank get the upper hand on anything. Benny had reiterated this morning that he wanted her to take the lead on *everything* concerning Tank. She wasn't sure if her boss had stressed that point because he wasn't sure she could manage the guy, or because he wanted to make sure she understood she really *did* have carte blanche. She hoped it was the second.

She'd been successful in her new job thus far, so she didn't want to fail now, given this was the first time Benny had trusted her with something other than making posts on social media. McKenna had only been working with the Stingrays since June, so she knew she had a long way to go as far as proving herself, but this still felt like a good indication that Benny would be open to expanding her role within the department at some point down the road.

Tank returned after only a few minutes, dropping down on the couch next to her. "Want something to drink?"

She shook her head, holding up her tumbler of coffee. "I'm all set."

He leaned back, resting his arm along the back of the couch. "Okay, so what's the plan?"

"Community outreach, family-friendly content about your personal life, and zero scandals."

Tank grimaced. "Sounds boring as shit."

"Exactly."

He'd pulled on a pair of jeans that looked new and an army-green button-down. She had no idea how he managed to make such a conservative outfit look so freaking sexy.

Concentrate, Mac. Stop looking at the hot man.

"We thought it best to let the dust settle on the video and your apology for a couple of days. The hotel's statement this morning didn't help."

Tank scowled. "I told them about the bed when we were checking out, and I paid to replace it right then. I can't help but notice they didn't manage to mention *that*, or the fact that was the only thing damaged in the room."

McKenna shrugged. "That makes for a less-interesting story, and right now, people seem determined to paint you as the bad boy. Hence, our plan. Today and tomorrow, we're going to focus on generating wholesome, positive content about you for Instagram, TikTok, and Facebook."

"Not sure what the hell I can offer that's wholesome," he said, wiggling his eyebrows suggestively.

She drew in a deep breath, refusing to be baited. "What did you do for the holidays?"

"What, or who?" he joked.

Yep. This was going to be a long damn day. She didn't take the bait; rather, she attempted to pin him with an annoyed look.

"You're taking this way too seriously, Mouse."

She narrowed her eyes. "McKenna. And you're not taking it seriously enough."

For a moment, she thought Tank was going to argue. But in the end, he relented. "I spent Christmas Day at Victor's house."

Victor Reed was a defenseman for the Stingrays, as well as a native of Baltimore. As such, each Christmas, he opened his home to players who didn't have time to travel to their hometowns for the holidays.

"Oh," she said. "That's nice. I tried to get Victor to share a few pictures from the day, but he's overly private about his personal life." Which was putting it lightly. While most of the other Rays were happy with the publicity, Victor went the opposite direction, offering her nothing because, as he'd told her on more than one—or five hundred—occasions, his personal life was "nobody's fucking business."

"Yeah, he's super private. He probably didn't want to share any pictures because his niece, Pip, was in a lot of them. And he's protective as fuck over that girl."

McKenna was grateful to Tank for explaining. Victor had simply said "fuck no" to her request and walked away, which honestly had been no surprise, but, given her job, she felt like she had to keep trying. She'd learned not to take offense over Victor's gruff nature and language very early on. Mainly because she'd gotten a few glimpses of him with young Stingrays fans, and the man was an absolute softie when it came to kids. So, she no longer jumped at his sharp tone and constant use of the F word. "That makes sense."

Tank opened his phone. "I have a few pictures without her." He scrolled through his photos, then showed her a shot of himself standing next to two of his teammates, Andrew Thomas and Lucas Wilson, whom everyone called Rook. They were all three holding brightly colored Nerf guns, Tank dressed in full camo and Rook wearing a beanie and protective eyewear.

"We had an epic Nerf gun battle. It was Rook's idea."

"That sounds awesome."

Tank grinned. "It was, even though we got creamed. We divided up into teams. Andrew, Rook, and Vic's sister, Vivian, were on my team. Victor, Kostya, Anatoli, and Pip were on the other."

"It's nice that Victor opened his home to so many of you. I'm wondering how your Nerf team lost, though. You, Rook, and Andrew are seriously competitive."

"Victor failed to mention that Pip had gotten an Elite Blaster for Christmas."

When McKenna tilted her head, confused, he explained. "A Nerf machine gun. Plus, Pip is still pretty young, so we were careful with her. Even though she was pummeling us."

She laughed. "That sounds like so much fun."

"It really was. We've already planned to do a rematch next Christmas, and we've talked about it so much, I swear some of the other guys on the team are ready to bail on their own family celebrations, just so they can come too. I've already started shopping for my gun for next year."

He scrolled through his pictures, showing her a screenshot of a bright blue Nerf gun he'd saved. "Check this out. Mega barrel, seventy-two darts. I'm not going down without a fight next time."

McKenna was suddenly jealous and wishing she could go. "I love this. Would you mind sharing that picture of you with Andrew and Rook, as well as the Nerf gun you want to buy?

Even though it's well past Christmas, I can still write a fun post telling that story, building on your camaraderie with the team, the strong friendships."

She heard the swoop of his phone, hers pinging a second later as the photos hit her messages.

"Thanks. So I'm assuming since you were at Victor's, you didn't get to spend any time with your family?"

"I didn't."

"Not even around Thanksgiving?"

Tank shook his head. "Nope."

For a man who never seemed at a loss for words, he was definitely giving her short answers regarding his family. McKenna tried to remember what she'd read of Tank's bio yesterday, but it didn't say much. His mother died of a stroke when he was twenty, right at the end of his first year playing professionally. His dad currently lived in Buffalo and had been a hockey player as well, though he'd never made it out of the AHL.

She decided to give it one more try. "Your dad was a former hockey player as well, wasn't he?"

Tank nodded. "Yep. And all of that's been discussed and covered before. Nothing new to share."

Okay. Well, that was clearly a dead end for some reason.

McKenna wanted to press but decided to change the subject for now, covering more superficial topics in the hopes Tank would eventually become comfortable sharing personal stuff with her.

"Fine. Then what about your climb to the NHL?" she asked. "Tell me about the first time you strapped on a pair of skates."

By the end of two hours, she had a decent list of topics to work from, as well as quite a few accompanying pictures Tank shared from his phone. More than that, he'd started to relax, telling her a lot of funny stories from the locker room and the road. Here in his own home, without anyone to show off for, he'd shed his over-the-top personality and instead let her see what she was coming to realize was the real him.

Without his swagger, cocky grins, and disgusting locker room talk—which she was sure was for her benefit, meant to either make her blush or scowl—Tank was pretty chill, and he had a wicked sense of humor. He was popular amongst his teammates, and for the first time, she began to understand why.

"This a good start," she said, closing her laptop and tucking it into her bag.

Tank leaned forward, resting his elbows on his knees, drawing her attention to his muscular arms. Welcome to the gun show.

"You got a boyfriend, Mouse?"

"I'm not here to talk about me."

Tank grunted. "You've been swimming around in *my* personal life for the past two hours."

McKenna pierced him with a look. "And whose fault is that?"

"Dammit, Mouse! I'm not going to apologize for having consensual sex with two women. I know you made me read that stupid lawyer-approved statement, but I'm not sorry about that night. I enjoyed being with Emily and Lara, and there's nothing wrong with the things we did together."

"I'm not saying there is, and I'm also not judging you, Tank," she replied calmly. "But you have to understand that you are a public figure, and for better or worse, your actions reflect on the team and even on the city, because as a Stingray, you represent Baltimore. There are a lot of people in the world who *will* judge you for that video, for all kinds of reasons, based on what they believe. Those conservative mother groups are inundating TikTok with videos condemning you. As a professional athlete, you live under a microscope, so you're not going to be able to fly under the radar the way the rest of us can."

Tank sighed. "I get it. I don't like it…but I get it."

"Since becoming president of the organization, James has been very definite about how he wants the team branded, and your lifestyle doesn't exactly fit the family-friendly vibe he's going for."

Tank snorted. "I happen to think I'm very friendly."

"You're impossible," she said, with no real heat. Ordinarily, Tank drove her up the wall with his brash attitude, but today, she felt like she'd gotten a small peek at the man underneath the obnoxious charmer.

"I'm starting to win you over, aren't I?"

She shook her head, refusing to give him an inch. For all she knew, he was playing her, attempting to sneak in and steal her upper hand. "I haven't gotten much sleep the past couple of nights."

"Sorry about that."

She studied his face, sensing he was sincere about that apology.

"So…got a boyfriend?" he asked, repeating his question.

She shook her head, deciding the quickest way to shut this conversation down was to just answer. "No."

"Dating anybody?"

Again, she shook her head. "I'm new to Baltimore, and my job is demanding. I'm focused on proving myself at the office, so that doesn't leave a lot of time for a social life. I haven't met many people outside work."

"There are plenty of single men in the organization. Hell, you're surrounded by a whole team of hot hockey players every day."

McKenna huffed out a loud "ha," followed by a "no thanks."

Tank frowned, confused by her response.

Before he could question her, she raised a hand and lifted one finger. "I will never date a hockey player." She added a second finger. "And I will never date someone from work."

"Never is a long time."

"And yet, still not long enough." She was aware her tone had gotten way too forceful, so she turned away from him, packing up her notebook so he'd know that subject was closed. "Well, I think we're done for the day. I want to get back to the office, make notes on what we discussed, and start building some of those posts. Then I need to grab dinner before the game."

Tank's face fell when she mentioned the game. "Gonna suck not being there."

"It's only two weeks," she said, hoping to cheer him up.

She failed.

"Six games," he muttered. "I've never missed six games in a season. Ever. Not even when I was a kid and had the chicken pox. That only took me out for four."

McKenna didn't know how to make him feel better, so she went for distraction instead. Picking up a copy of the publicity schedule she'd printed out for him, she pointed to it. "The day after tomorrow, we'll meet here again and go to the VA hospital together. I'll have some swag for you to sign and hand out. And no need to dress up. I think it would be cool if you just wanted to wear some Stingrays' apparel."

"Okay." He glanced at the paper.

"I didn't want to schedule anything right on the heels of the video, so there's nothing public for tomorrow. I'll stop by in the morning again and show you some of the posts I plan to create this afternoon. I'll start scheduling them to release, one every few days to start out with, though I'll slow that down eventually and put you back in the normal rotation with the other guys on the team.

"In the meantime, maybe you could come up with a list of other positive stuff we can include. What we've generated today is a good start, but I'd like to keep the posts coming out consistently for the rest of the season. So we need a lot more," she said. "I was hoping... I would like..." She took a deep breath, recalling she was the boss right now. "Don't leave your apartment until the VA visit. If you need food, get it delivered. I suspect the handful of reporters outside will give up sooner rather than later, especially since the temperature's not supposed to crack the teens tomorrow. I'm not sure your scandal is big enough for anyone to risk frostbite."

"Hope you're right, Mouse."

She pushed up her glasses, the damn things always sliding down her nose. "Why do you call me that?"

Tank's grin widened as he stood. "I've been waiting for you to ask me. The first day we met was in the hallway outside the PR department, remember?"

She nodded, because she did recall that. She remembered being blown away by Tank's size and his charming smile, and she'd made a mental note right then and there to steer clear of the man, because she could tell he was trouble with a capital T.

"You were wearing a Mickey Mouse T-shirt," he explained, "and you had your hair pinned up in these cute little buns on the side of your head. You reminded me of one of those Mouseketeers. You one of those big fans of Disney World or something? Because I've noticed you've got a Mickey key chain, and you seem to have more than a few Mickey Mouse T-shirts."

While McKenna refused to admit it, now that she knew his reason for the nickname, she hated it a lot less. "Oh. The Mickey thing is my mom's doing. Apparently when I was a one-year-old, I absolutely loved it whenever Mickey came on the television. I'd start laughing and clapping my hands. My mom started calling me Mickey after that. He and I share a lot of the same letters…M, C, K. The nickname stuck, and so did the gifts. Mom is always on the hunt for unique Mickey Mouse stuff. I own way too much of it for someone who doesn't even particularly like Disney. I tried to put my foot down a few years ago, told her enough was enough. It didn't work. She still gives me a new Mickey Mouse T-shirt or pajamas every year for Christmas. I guess it's too hard for moms to break traditions like that."

"Mickey, huh? I like it."

McKenna pointed a finger in Tank's face. "My mother is the only one who calls me Mickey."

Tank chuckled as he reached out to toy with one of her "Mouseketeer" buns. "That's not a problem. I've already got my own nickname for you, Mouse."

McKenna rolled her eyes, though she was a hell of a lot less annoyed now that she knew he didn't call her that because he'd mistaken her for some timid creature. "You and everyone else. It's very rare when anyone calls me by my full name."

Tank nodded. "Yeah, I noticed you're Mac at work."

"And my dad calls me…K-Kenny." McKenna stumbled, shocked she'd shared that with Tank. Her relationship with her father was beyond complicated, so it was rare for her to even mention the man. "I guess I just have one of those names that work a million different ways," she added hastily.

"I'm no stranger to nicknames myself, though everyone uses the same one. Funny, but now that I think about it, my mom gave me my nickname, too."

"Really?" she said. "I would have thought the Tank nickname was one you picked up over the years from playing hockey."

"Nope," he said. "My mom started using it when I was three. I've always been a bit of a brute. I used to rearrange the furniture in our house, moving really heavy-ass shit whenever Mom wasn't looking. Said she left me alone in the den once for a few minutes and when she got back, I'd pushed my dad's recliner all the way across the room. Thing weighed a ton. Started calling me her little Tank."

McKenna enjoyed his story. "I love that. You know what? Nicknames would be a great series of posts for social media. A lot of the guys have them. I'm going to start asking them where they got their nicknames from."

"That's a fun idea," he agreed.

The two of them walked to the door. Tank leaned on the doorjamb as she turned to say goodbye.

"Thanks for all your help," he said, with a sincerity that caught her off guard.

She shrugged. "No problem." Then she realized she probably should have put stricter parameters on his short-term house arrest, especially since he didn't put up much of a fight.

"When I say stay in, I mean alone. You got that, right?"

Tank reached over, gently pushing her glasses up on her nose before bopping the tip of it. "You starting to get jealous, Mouse?"

She tilted her head. "I'm being serious, Tank."

Tank chuckled. "So am I."

McKenna started to come back at him, but he quickly threw his hands up in surrender. "Okay, okay. I'll be good," he said, drawing a cross over his heart. "No sleepovers, no fun. I know the drill."

"Great. See you tomorrow morning."

Tank remained in the doorway until she got to the elevator and pushed the button, and he was still there when she got on. Just before the doors closed, he gave her one final wave, and while she knew he was sleeping in the bed he'd made, the glimmer of true sadness in his eyes almost had her going back and offering to watch the game with him, even though she was needed in the press box.

She resisted that tug.

Breathing a sigh of relief when she reached the lobby, she walked to her car, proud of her first day's efforts.

Now, she just had to stay the course, keeping Tank out of trouble while resisting his gorgeous face, eight-pack abs, and charming smile.

Piece of cake.

Ha ha.

CHAPTER THREE

TANK WAS DRESSED and ready when McKenna picked him up for yet another evening of schmoozing the fans, talking hockey, shaking hands, and working overtime to convince them he wasn't some degenerate womanizer.

Good fucking times, he thought sarcastically.

They had officially reached the final day of his redemption tour yesterday, but tonight's excursion had been included anyway, because it hit on a night when the team didn't have a game.

He'd returned to practice this morning, and while it was great to be back with his team, he had actually missed seeing McKenna today. The two of them had been in each other's faces for fourteen days straight, which, to be honest, was way more than he could stand of most people. Surprisingly, he didn't feel that way about her. Over the course of the past two weeks, he felt as if he and McKenna had forged the beginning of a friendship—despite how unlikely that seemed.

The trip to the VA hospital had gone well, as had the ribbon-cutting at the sporting goods store, and the other five million "positive" promo opportunities McKenna had arranged to help clean his reputation. Not that there hadn't been people at some of the various places hoping to stir up shit or provoke him into giving them more ammo to use against him. McKenna referred to them as trolls and hecklers and said the best way to shut them down was to ignore them.

If she knew him better, she'd know how much remaining quiet went against the grain for him. Regardless, he'd managed to keep his damn mouth shut, because he was bound and determined to play by the rules. All that mattered to him was getting back out onto the ice with his teammates. Well, that and protecting his contract.

The first thing he'd done following those initial meetings with team management after the video went viral was to call his lawyer *and* agent, certain James had been bluffing about breaking his contract. Both had informed him the president was within his legal rights to terminate Tank's contract if James felt he was doing anything to damage the reputation of the club.

Then they both told him the same thing Coach Fields had: do what he was told, keep his head down, and stay out of trouble.

"Hey, Mouse," he said, as he climbed into the front seat of McKenna's VW Golf. The damn thing felt like a clown car to him, given his long legs. He'd already pushed the seat back as far as it would go, but he still had to fold himself in half to get inside. Tank had offered to drive every single day, but McKenna had set up the trunk of her vehicle like a mini-Stingrays' swag shop. She'd continued to reject his invitation to drive, claiming there would be too much stuff to transfer over, so eventually he stopped bothering.

"You realize this car is ridiculous," he said, feeling like a jackass with his knees pressed against the dash.

"You've gotta stop hating on my poor car," she retorted, stroking the steering wheel affectionately. "She's my baby."

"I guess you need a car this small so you can reach the gas pedal and brake," he teased.

McKenna rolled her eyes. He was becoming very familiar with her eye rolls, because he managed to provoke them no less than twenty times a day. "Wow. You managed to work in a comment about my height," she glanced at her phone, "in less than three minutes. That might be your personal best."

In addition to giving her shit about her car, Tank also teased McKenna about her tiny stature.

"I'm just stating facts. You are a tiny human being. So small, in fact, I could probably tuck you in the pocket of my jacket."

She narrowed her eyes. "I'm not *that* tiny."

He laughed. "Seriously, Mouse. How tall are you?"

"Five-four," she replied haughtily, as if her tone could make her appear bigger.

He snorted. "Compared to my six-three frame, I assure you, that's tiny."

She huffed but didn't continue to argue. Because how could she? She *was* vertically challenged. And the fact she was petite as well as short only made her look even tinier. Tank bet she didn't weigh one-ten soaking wet.

"I have to admit, when I first started this job, it took me some time to get used to how big you guys are. At my last job, most of the men I worked with were regular-sized."

"What was your last job?" he asked.

"I worked in the marketing department for a small sporting goods chain. Pete's. They have seven stores in Ohio," she said. "With plans to expand into a couple more states eventually."

"I think I've heard of Pete's," he said. "Why did you leave that job?" It occurred to Tank that while he'd become an open book to McKenna, she shared considerably less with him. He didn't like that after two weeks, he still didn't know much about her. Part of that was simply because they'd been busy, focused on salvaging his reputation. But also because McKenna, like Victor, was proving to be a very private person.

She didn't answer immediately, and for a moment, he wondered if she was going to blow him off.

"I, um… There wasn't a whole lot of room for advancement there," she finally said.

Tank wasn't sure why, but he was damn sure that was a lie. For one thing, a company of that size would have plenty of room for advancement, especially if they were planning to expand. For another, she wasn't looking at him, focusing on the road more than she needed to—*and* she was blushing.

McKenna was a true ginger, possessing dark auburn hair, a pale complexion, and a freckled nose. As such, she was prone to blushing, something she'd admitted hating a few days earlier. Tank had been amused, then pointed out that she should've known better than to confess something like that to him, because he would take making her blush as a challenge. And he had.

"Were you into sports in school?" Tank asked, deciding to continue digging.

"Not in the playing sense but as a spectator, yeah. I was on my school's yearbook staff, and senior year, I was made the editor of the sports section. I can't begin to count how many nights a week I spent at school, sitting in the bleachers of the gym or the football stadium, taking pictures and interviewing the fans and athletes."

"Sounds like you knew what you wanted to do for a living right out of the gate."

She nodded. "Yeah. I guess I did. I like writing. Not just about sports but about the players and the way a game like hockey can bring people from all different walks of life together."

"Were you always a hockey fan?" Tank asked.

McKenna nodded. "Oh yeah. It was impossible to live in my house and not be one. My mom literally lives and breathes hockey."

"Your mom?" Tank asked, amused. "Not your dad?"

His question was met with another one of those pregnant pauses. Only this time, she didn't bother to lie. Instead, she just flat-out ignored the question.

"Why are we talking about me? We're wasting valuable time."

McKenna was incredibly efficient when it came to planning promotional opportunities, always going the extra mile to make sure he knew everything he needed to going in. Hell, most of the time, he knew *more* than he needed to.

Like right now, as she changed the subject to give him the names of not only the coaches of the Pee Wee team they were going to see but also the name of the head coach's wife, with whom she'd spoken while setting up the appearance. She followed that with all the details of the celebration the parents had held for the kids following their big win. Tank had to admit, the parents had gone all out. He'd won countless tournaments on God only knew how many teams when he was young, and the parents had never congratulated him and his buddies with a bouncy house, laser tag, all-you-can-eat pizza, and two giant ice cream cakes—one chocolate, one strawberry—in the shapes of a hockey stick and a puck.

But he figured the over-the-top celebration made sense when he learned that the team went from dead last the previous year— never winning a single game—to top of the heap this season.

Because it was a Monday, they'd scheduled their meet and greet for four o'clock, as that was when all the kids were out of school. When they pulled up outside the ice-skating rink, he watched as McKenna opened her trunk, pulling out a box of swag she'd obviously packed prior to picking him up. He tossed his duffel bag over his shoulder, grabbed his hockey stick, then took the box from her.

He was surprised when she pulled her own skates from the trunk.

His were in his bag, since today's photo op didn't just include him posing for pictures with the team. He was also slated to skate around with them, do some fun drills, stuff like that. Of all the things the PR department had scheduled for his penance, this was the thing Tank had been looking forward to the most. He loved getting to slap the puck around with young players.

"Skates?" he asked, when she hung them over her shoulder by the tied laces.

"I'm taking pics of you with the kids. I figured I'd get some big group shots in front of the net. It's easier for me to skate than to try to walk on the ice in my street shoes."

"You skate?"

"Why do you ask that like you're surprised? Of *course* I skate."

Tank wasn't sure why he was shocked. Maybe it was as simple as he'd never seen her in skates before, which was a stupid reason, considering she'd have no reason to wear them around him.

They walked into the rink together, and within seconds, Tank was surrounded by young fans, all the boys and girls jostling for position. He smiled, promising to sign all their stuff as they slowly made their way to the side of the rink. The stands were filled with parents and grandparents, all excited to see their kids spend time with an NHL player. This was the best part of his job, Tank decided…after playing games, of course.

The coach walked over and introduced himself.

"Jason Burrows," he said, shaking Tank's hand effusively. "Really nice of you to take time out of your day to help the kids celebrate. I thought my wife was pulling my leg when she said someone from the Stingrays had called and Tank Phillips wanted to come meet the team. I swear it took her a good twenty minutes to convince me it was really happening."

Tank chuckled, waiting for the man to take a breath so he could enter the conversation. Right now, he wasn't sure who was more excited. The kids or their coach.

"I'm glad to be here. After all, winning a state tournament is no small feat." While he was talking to the coach, he was aware the kids and parents were hanging on his every word, so he spoke up. "Told my boss I needed to meet the team that pulled off such a big win, especially after struggling last year." McKenna's shared wealth of information was helping him win back any fans he might have lost in this group with that video.

McKenna smiled and played along, then did what she'd done on all their other press stops. She took charge.

"It's very nice to meet you, Coach Burrows. I was the one who spoke with your wife, Janet. Tank and I thought it might be fun to start with a little bit of skating. He's offered to teach the kids some of the drills they do in the NHL."

That comment was met with lots of oohs and aahs, and more than a few kids started high-fiving each other, saying "all right!"

Tank walked over to the metal bench to quickly pull on his skates. He'd dressed appropriately in athletic gear. McKenna sat next to him, placing her own skates on the floor.

"I'll stay on the sidelines for this part and take pictures and videos while you drill. Then, I'll join you on the ice, and we'll set the kids up for the photos. I suspect they'll all want a picture with you on their own, along with the group photos."

"That sounds great."

"Cool. I also told the coach's wife you'd sign one thing for each kid, as well."

"You didn't have to put a limit on it." Tank got the sense McKenna expected him to balk at what she'd set up, though he wasn't sure why. He hadn't grumbled about any of the other things they'd done, genuinely enjoying the time he spent with the veterans at the VA, the cancer patients at Hopkins, as well as chatting with the fans who'd shown up at the sporting goods store. "This sounds like a lot of fun."

McKenna tilted her head. "Really?"

"Of course. I love playing hockey with young kids. Figure when it's time to hang up my skates, somewhere way, way down the road, I'll see about volunteering to coach my own Pee Wee team."

"That's sweet," McKenna said. "I'm totally including that future goal in one of my posts about today."

Tank tapped McKenna on the nose, enjoying the way that

silly touch always made her blush. Rising from the bench, he faced the kids and gestured toward the ice. "Who's ready to tear this thing up?"

The kids cheered, clambering to the ice, clad in helmets, sticks in hand. Tank joined them, and for the next hour, he ran the kids through a whole series of drills before initiating a quick game of pickup.

McKenna was the one to guide them to the photo shoot portion of their plans, even though Tank and the kids still weren't finished playing.

The parents laughed when Tank complained to McKenna the loudest, begging for "just five more minutes."

McKenna played along, putting one hand on her hip, assuming a motherly tone. "We still have pictures to take and things to sign," she said, "and it's a school night. We need to make sure they have time for dinner and homework."

Tank led all the kids in a bit of playful booing over homework, then McKenna herded them—as best she could—toward one end of the rink. She was a natural on skates, gliding across the ice with ease as she organized them for the group picture. Quite a few of the parents joined them on the ice, standing near McKenna with their phones, grabbing their own photos of Tank and the team.

He cheesed it up, then McKenna had the kids grab the items they wanted signed. Tank autographed them, then took the individual photos. More than a few parents—clearly Stingrays superfans—asked if they could pose in the pictures with their kids. One mother exclaimed the shot of him with her entire family was going to be included in her Christmas card next year.

The signing took longer than it probably should have, but everyone was having so much fun they didn't seem to care.

Once he posed for the last picture, he pointed to McKenna. "Isn't McKenna great?" he asked the kids, who cheered for her.

McKenna brushed off Tank's compliment, laughing when he

skated over to wrap his arm around her shoulders. "Look how tiny she is," he joked. "Like a little mouse."

The kids laughed.

McKenna played along. "I'm not tiny. You're just a giant."

"He *is* a giant!" one of the younger kids yelled out.

"A giant?" Tank held his hands over his head, like he was a giant from a children's book, playfully chasing McKenna around the ice. She skated around the kids, some of whom got into the game, chasing *him* as he continued trying to capture *her*. When he caught her, they tussled, Tank messing up her hair as she tried to bat his hands away, much to the amusement of the kids.

"Bad giant!" she chastised, laughing. "Behave yourself."

"Never," he retorted, giving her a quick, impromptu kiss on the cheek.

McKenna flushed bright red, and Tank caught sight of more than a few of the mothers grinning at them, as if they were the cutest couple ever.

Tank didn't have a clue what had prompted him to kiss her, because that sure hadn't been his intent. It was just…she looked so adorable, rosy-cheeked in the chilly arena, grinning widely at him. Then he caught a whiff of strawberries in her hair, and he'd felt a stirring of something…

Something he had no business feeling for McKenna Bailey.

He chalked up his lack of judgment to the fact that he wasn't used to abstaining from sex.

Slowly, the parents began to collect their kids, everyone heading home. He suspected at least fifty percent of the families would be stopping at McDonald's to grab dinner on their way.

Coach Burrows walked out with McKenna and Tank, his wife and their two sons already waiting for him in the car.

"I can't thank you enough for tonight," Coach Burrows said, shaking Tank's hand again. "Suspect half the team now wants to play hockey professionally after that."

Tank chuckled. "Nothing wrong with that. Given what I saw out on that ice, quite a few of them have what it takes." That wasn't completely true, though there were two kids on the team who were absolute brutes, with the skills and mindset to go far if they applied themselves.

The coach shook McKenna's hand next, then said good night.

He and McKenna climbed into her car. Before she started it, she turned to him. "You were great in there, Tank."

"I really love playing hockey with kids. It's fun. There's no stress, and it makes me remember why I fell in love with the sport to begin with."

"It shows. I'm sort of sorry we didn't line up more promotional opportunities like that one for you. I didn't realize you were such a natural with kids. I don't think a single person who was here tonight isn't now officially a Tank Phillips fan for life."

"Are you included in that group?" He wasn't sure what made him ask that question, but after spending the last two weeks with McKenna, Tank hated that he'd made such a shitty first, second, and thirty-eighth impression on her. There had been plenty of opportunities for him to welcome her to the Stingrays organization the way his teammates had, but instead, he chose to act like a swaggering ass rather than get to know her.

McKenna didn't reply to his question immediately, and he started to fear she'd tell him no.

Finally, she put him out of his misery. "Yeah. I think I am."

Strangely relieved and pleased, Tank leaned back—as much as he could in this damn small car. "You think, huh? Guess I'm going to have to go the extra mile until you're sure. Let me take you to dinner," he said. Quickly adding, "Since I kept you out so late on a school night."

McKenna started to shake her head.

"Do you have other plans?" he asked.

"No."

"What do you intend to eat for dinner tonight?" Tank wasn't going down without a fight. He was riding high from the fun afternoon, and he wasn't in the mood to go home and eat alone. He'd done that too much since the video, not in the mood to deal with the damn hecklers, trolls, and reporters. It was easier to toe the line if he wasn't out and about, but there was no way in hell he'd manage to keep this up for six months. Unlike McKenna, Tank was a very sociable person, who fed off crowds and attention.

"I subscribe to a meal delivery service. I think tonight's easy-prep meal is maple Dijon salmon."

Tank reached over, playfully tugging on her ponytail. "I can do way better than that. How do you feel about fish and chips?"

"I love it," she admitted.

McKenna had joined the team at Pat's Pub a few times for victory drinks after big wins, but she typically sat with the wives and girlfriends. "Pat's Pub has the best in the city."

Her eyes lit up. "Oh. I love that place, though I'll admit I've never eaten there. I've only ever gone for drinks after the games."

Tank shook his head. "That's shameful. You've lived in Baltimore what? Six? Seven months?"

"Almost nine," she corrected.

"Those fish and chips should have been one of your first meals in Baltimore."

McKenna grinned slightly. "Well, I guess we'd better correct that wrong."

She started the car, the two of them rehashing some of the funny things the kids had said and asked. McKenna had a memory like a steel trap, and he suspected a lot of the silly comments would find their way into posts, and she'd find a way to make him look great and the kids adorable. Miss Efficient had also made sure every parent signed a media release form, allowing her to share the pictures and videos she'd taken of the kids.

Tank had never paid a lot of attention to the team's social media pages because they hadn't felt particularly important. With so much time on his hands lately, he'd decided to check out McKenna's work, and he had to admit, she was really good at building a positive image of not only him but his teammates as well. She made them sound less like hockey stars and more like approachable, friendly people, and it obviously resonated well with the fans, if the comments were anything to go by.

When they arrived at the pub, she parked by the curb across the street. Tank got out quickly, walking around the hood and wrapping his arm around her shoulders, tucking her close, pretending it was his attempt to provide warmth from the chilly February wind coming in from the harbor.

The truth was, he was hoping to sneak another whiff of her strawberry-scented hair because *damn*, she smelled good.

"Tank," she warned.

"It's cold out. Don't want you to catch a chill."

She snorted. "Yeah, sure. FYI, you and I are going to talk about that kiss in front of the kids."

"It was just in good fun," he said, trying to minimize his actions, mainly because he still wasn't sure what had prompted him to do it. He kept trying to tell himself it was just a platonic kiss on the cheek, but that didn't console him much…as he now wanted a *real* kiss that was a hell of a lot less innocent.

McKenna didn't step away or force him to lower his arm. "I *am* cold."

Tank grinned, keeping his arm right where it was, not wanting to admit—even to himself—it felt nice holding her like this.

"Tank!"

They weren't two steps inside the pub before the bartender loudly called out his name. Tank smiled and waved at Padraig Collins.

McKenna shot him a raised eyebrow, her gaze sparking with mirth.

"I'm not an alcoholic," he said, getting her unspoken joke. "You know the team celebrates here."

"I know, but the bartender calling out your name doesn't really help our case."

Tank pulled her closer. "Hush. Padraig is a huge Rays fan."

Padraig followed them over as they claimed a booth in a quiet corner. Tank had been going stir crazy in his apartment, so it felt good to be out like this.

Sure, he and McKenna had been out and about pretty much every single day for the past two weeks, but their promo ops and his independent workouts hadn't come close to filling enough hours in the day for him. He was used to being on the go pretty much nonstop during the season, so the lull had hit him hard. Eating take-out meals alone while sitting in front of the TV, watching his teammates play without him, had been brutal.

This wasn't a game night, as the team had traveled home from Carolina late last night after a crushing loss in overtime. Ordinarily, McKenna would have been on the road with them, but Benny had sent Roger instead, claiming it was more important for her to focus on what the PR department was calling the "Tank Project," which made him feel like he was some goddamn science experiment.

Padraig started to hand each of them a menu, but Tank waved them away. "McKenna has lived in Baltimore for months and never had Riley's fish and chips," he explained, mentioning the chef's name—and enjoying Padraig's horrified face as he played along.

"You're kidding? How the hell did that happen?" he asked.

McKenna laughed. "Tank has insisted we correct that oversight."

"He's a wise man." Padraig kept the menus, tucking them under his arms. "I'm assuming you want the same, Tank?"

"Do bears bear? Do bees bee?" Tank joked.

"And to drink?" Padraig asked with a chuckle.

"I'm good with water." Ordinarily, Tank would have gone for a Guinness, but there was a small part of him that felt like he needed to prove to McKenna he didn't have an issue with alcohol.

"I'll have an unsweetened iced tea," McKenna ordered,

smirking in such a way that said she wasn't fooled by his good behavior.

"You've got it. Sure have missed seeing you play," Padraig said to Tank.

"Suspension officially ended yesterday," he said, grimacing as he spoke. "I'll be back on the ice again tomorrow night."

Padraig placed a hand on his shoulder. "Good. The team is better with you out there."

"Hate how last night ended, and that shit went so fucking far sideways with that video." Tank hadn't seen Padraig since the suspension, but Blake had filled in the bartender, who'd become a pretty good friend over the past few years.

Padraig had texted to tell him to keep his chin up, saying, "This too shall pass."

Tank had appreciated the support.

"My family's dealt with enough drama that I know for a fact, most people have very short attention spans," he assured him.

"Thanks, Paddy," Tank said. "I appreciate that."

"Let me go grab those drinks for you." Padraig walked away to put in their orders, as McKenna frowned, looking confused.

"His family's had a lot of drama?" she asked, curious, and Tank realized McKenna had missed out on more than just Pat's Pub's delicious fish and chips.

"Padraig's got some very famous relatives."

"Really?"

"Yep. His aunt is Teagan Collins."

McKenna's jaw nearly hit the table. "Shut up. She is not!"

Tank chuckled, recalling he'd had nearly the same reaction when Padraig told him about his illustrious family ties. Teagan Collins and her husband, Sky Mitchell, were rock icons, their names often included with legends such as Sting, Billy Joel, and Cher. Even as a professional athlete, Tank had been more than a little bit starstruck when he'd learned about Padraig's family connections.

"And his cousin Ailis is married to Hunter Maxwell. In fact, Hunter was discovered in this very pub."

"No way!" McKenna began looking around the pub, and he noticed when her gaze landed on photographs of the very people he'd mentioned, posing with other members of the family. "How did I miss all of this?"

"When we're here, we're celebrating with the team. I'm sure you're not checking out the pub's décor."

"Even so," she said.

"The Collins family is a big one, and they've lived in Baltimore for all their lives. Padraig joked once that he couldn't turn around twice without bumping into someone he's related to."

"I'm sure Teagan and Hunter have probably had to deal with bad press from time to time. Stuff like that is a curse of being so famous."

Tank agreed. "It is, but I think the drama Padraig was referring to just now was a viral video involving his cousin Sunnie and her husband. Maybe you've heard of *Hot Cop Saves Sexy Nurse*."

McKenna must have hit Collins overload, because she leaned back, shaking her head in disbelief. "He's related to them, too? You know, that video is still one of the most viewed ever, near the top of every viral list out there. I can't believe all these people are related."

"I've become friends with quite a few of the Collinses. Landon—the hot cop—texted me a few days ago, assuring me the heat from my video would die down eventually."

"That was nice of him," McKenna said.

"The entire Collins family is very nice."

Padraig returned with their drinks but didn't have time to chat, as a large group arrived, and he walked away to help them pull a couple tables together.

He and McKenna talked about—and analyzed—last night's game until Padraig returned with their food. McKenna was well-versed when it came to the finer points of the actual game, impressing him with some of her insights.

Tank took a sip of his water before digging in. "So, we are officially finished with the promotional penance part of my punishment, right?"

McKenna nodded. "For the most part. Though I've got some interviews scheduled for you over the next month or so. A few sports podcasts and one magazine."

As they ate their fish and chips—which she agreed were the bomb, as she liberally poured vinegar on her fries—she walked him step-by-step through potential interview questions, assuring him that she'd made certain the interviewers knew the viral video was off the table as a topic. Then she stressed that if they tried to bring it up, he was to stonewall by saying nothing more than the same contrite "poor judgment, won't happen again" bullshit he'd had to read at that initial press conference.

The conversation flowed easily between them, and they even stuck around a little longer, splitting a piece of Bailey's cheesecake.

Several people in the pub tried to surreptitiously sneak photos of him, and a couple of the more forward ones had approached him for autographs, which he'd gladly given. Other than that, the two of them had been left alone. Tank had kind of liked having McKenna all to himself during his suspension. It would suck having to share her with the rest of the team from now on.

He paid for dinner, even though McKenna tried to split the check with him. The meal had ended too quickly for Tank, who really wasn't looking forward to going home.

"What do you say to a walk along the waterfront?" he asked, when they left the pub.

"It's kind of cold."

McKenna had unwittingly given him the opening he'd been hoping for. No stranger to working in chilly environments, Tank wrapped his arm around her, once more pulling her against him. "I know how to take care of that."

She didn't push away, which he was counting as progress.

"Put your arm around my waist, Mouse. I'll keep you warm."

She considered his request long enough that he thought she'd dig her heels in and insist on going home. He was relieved and pleased when she did as he asked, wrapping her arm around him under his jacket, stealing as much warmth as she could.

They headed across the cobblestone street, walking toward the Inner Harbor. The lights along the shore sparkled, the clear sky and bright full moon creating a beautiful, if chilly, evening.

"Do you miss Columbus?" Tank learned early on that McKenna had been born and raised in Ohio, but apart from that fact, he knew very little else.

He could tell from her shrug, she was about to give him yet another unsatisfying answer.

"Sometimes," she replied. "I mean, apart from college, I lived in Columbus my whole life."

"Your family is still there?"

She nodded.

"Do you go home very often?"

"A bit. I went home for the holidays, and my mom usually makes her way to Baltimore at least one weekend a month to visit."

Hot damn. She actually offered up a crumb he didn't have to beg for.

"Just your mom?"

McKenna nodded. That was it. Just a nod.

Tank sighed. "You're quite the conversationalist, aren't you?"

McKenna laughed quietly. "Fine, Nosy Nelly. I was raised by my mom, who's also my best friend. She was upset when I decided to move away, but she understood this job was a great opportunity for me."

"No dad in the picture?" he asked, slightly confused, because he recalled her mentioning that her father called her Kenny.

"I was an oopsie baby, the result of a summer romance."

Tank grinned. "I'm suddenly hearing 'Summer Nights' from *Grease* in my head."

McKenna giggled. "That probably would be an appropriate theme song for my parents. When summer ended, my dad had to move for his job, and he broke things off with Mom. She's never really said, but I think she was hurt when he decided he didn't want to keep seeing her. At that point, neither of them realized she was pregnant. When Mom found out, she was still pissed at my dad for ending things, so she decided she was going to do it on her own. She blamed pregnancy hormones and sheer stubbornness for not telling him about me right away.

"I was six months old when she stopped being mad and hurt, and guilt kicked in. She called to tell my dad he had a daughter. Apparently, he flew to Columbus the next day. They talked, and my father said he'd help her financially, but that he wasn't in a position to be part of my everyday life. His job was one that kept him traveling a lot. So, Mom did what she'd planned all along and raised me alone."

"Strong woman."

McKenna smiled. "One of the strongest."

"Did your dad keep his promise about the money?"

She nodded. "He did. He sent Mom child support faithfully every month, and he never missed a birthday or Christmas—always sending a ton of 'overcompensating' gifts." She finger-quoted the word "overcompensating."

"Good for him, I guess," Tank said, glad her father hadn't completely abandoned her and her mom, though he couldn't help but wonder if McKenna was really as cool with her dad's decision to basically become a bank rather than an active part of her life.

"The money he sent meant Mom didn't have to work two

jobs. It allowed us to live comfortably and gave her plenty of time to spend with me. I had an awesome childhood."

Tank thought it sounded like she was trying to convince *herself* of that, as much as him.

She gave him a wicked grin. "So…how was that for conversation? Up to your standards?"

"Not too bad. A good first effort," he replied, playing along with her joke.

McKenna lowered her arm from his waist as she tucked her coat around herself more securely. "It's getting colder. Maybe we should consider heading back to the car."

The temperature hadn't dropped a bit, which proved what he'd already figured out. She wasn't comfortable talking about herself. So, he decided to let her off the hook on sharing personal details because he wasn't ready to call it a night.

Tank glanced around. There were more people than he might have expected braving the cool February weather, and like the patrons in the pub, a few had recognized him—not that that was a hard thing to do, considering he was a giant and he was in Stingrays apparel. More than a few phones were pointed in their direction. One group of three businessmen looked like they were debating whether they should approach.

McKenna suddenly noticed the attention they were attracting as well, and he felt her stiffen briefly before attempting to step away from him.

"People are taking pictures," she murmured, when he refused to release her.

"So what? I'm not doing anything scandalous," he said. "Just taking a walk along the waterfront with a pretty girl."

"I'm not one of your puck bunnies, Tank. I know you're a natural-born flirt, but this really isn't appropriate." McKenna tried again to step away, but he didn't let her, tightening his grip and turning her to face him.

She had to lean her head back to look up at him, her expression serious and maybe even a little confused.

"I know you're not a puck bunny. And this isn't flirting, Mouse. I'm just making a factual statement. You look very pretty tonight."

McKenna blinked several times, and he could see her trying to replay his words, as if she'd misheard him. "I look the same as I always do."

She absolutely did, right down to the cardigan with the hole in it and the Chucks. He wrapped his hand around her ponytail, looping it over his hand. "You should wear your hair down sometimes."

"I, um…" She reached up, tugging her hair out of his grip. "I need a haircut."

Tank chuckled at her sudden embarrassment, then ran the back of his fingers over her soft cheek. "You blush real easy, Mouse."

"We've already discussed that, as well as the fact that I hate it. Yet you seem to go out of your way to make me blush."

He chuckled. "Because it's cute." Then he cupped her cheek, looking deeply into her eyes.

"What are you doing?" she whispered, when he merely held her gaze.

"Honestly?" he said. "I have no idea."

"This isn't part of the plan."

Tank lifted one shoulder casually. "I'm shit at following rules, Mouse, but I've done everything you told me to. I haven't strayed, haven't done anything that would bring bad press."

"I know that," she whispered. "So don't ruin it."

He wanted to pull those glasses off and kiss her. Wanted it more than he'd wanted anything in a long time. But she was right. Kissing her in front of the cameras would be a step backward, and he wasn't going to risk his career for an ill-advised kiss.

Protecting his contract was why he'd gone the extra mile at every single one of the promo ops, why he'd remained secluded in his condo, alone, night after night. Why he hadn't replied to any of the countless texts—sexts—from Lara, who was now convinced that viral video was some sort of sign they should change their status from booty calls to proper dating.

Regardless of all that, he kept thinking about how things between him and McKenna were going to return to normal. After spending so much time with her, he hated that, with the suspension over, their time together would be limited. He'd gotten used to having her around, and he genuinely enjoyed her company.

"I'll behave on one condition."

McKenna attempted to give him a stern look, but she was too flustered by their close proximity to sell it. "You remember that I'm the one calling the shots."

He merely chuckled in response, then waited her out. Because if he'd learned anything about McKenna, her curiosity always got the better of her.

"What condition?" she asked, just as he knew she would.

"You have dinner with me before the Tampa Bay game on Friday."

She gave him a funny look. "You always eat with your team-mates when we're on the road."

"Yeah, well, on Friday, I want to eat with you."

"Why?"

He shrugged. "I've gotten used to you. Going to be weird not talking to you every day."

Mercifully, she accepted that answer. "Yeah. As much as it pains me to admit, I've gotten used to you, too. I should prob-ably consider starting my therapy again."

He wrapped his arm around her shoulders, messing up her hair playfully. "Minx," he teased, while she laughed and tried to bat his hand away.

Tank couldn't recall exactly when the two of them started touching each other so much, but somewhere in the midst of the past two weeks, the personal space between them shrank as he frequently pulled her ponytail or tickled her, while she touched his hand as she talked or punched his arm whenever he made a smart-ass comment.

"I really am cold," she said, as she finally broke free, turning away from him and heading back in the direction of her car.

Tank caught up to her in three long strides, amused by her low growl when he wrapped his arms around her shoulders again.

Now though, like before, she didn't push him away.

They returned to the car and the ride back to his place was made in silence, though it wasn't awkward. Instead, they listened to the radio, lost in their own thoughts.

When they got to his place, she pulled in front of the entrance and put the car in park. She didn't turn it off, so he figured it was pointless to see if she wanted to come in for a nightcap.

"If I don't see you before tomorrow night's game, good luck," she said.

He bopped her nose playfully. "Thanks. Night, Mouse."

"Night."

He got out of the car, turning around to watch as she pulled away from the curb. Simply because he couldn't resist the desire to steal one more look at her.

At McKenna Bailey.

What the hell was going on?

CHAPTER FOUR

MCKENNA LAUGHED at a joke Tank made, the two of them sitting together in a corner of the hotel restaurant. The rest of the team, as well as the coaches and everyone else who traveled with the Stingrays, were scattered around the same place, all of them waiting for dinner to be served. The hotel they were staying in had a decent restaurant, so whenever they traveled to Tampa, they simply ate there. The kitchen had been amenable to preparing a high-carb meal, low on fat. Tonight's fare was salmon and wild rice, McKenna noticed, as the servers began delivering plates to the other tables.

"Thanks," Tank said to the server when she dropped off their meals, asking if they needed drink refills.

"I'm good," McKenna said, pointing to her still-full water glass.

"Me too."

The two of them started digging in as the server moved on, delivering the rest of the food.

"This is good," McKenna said, pleasantly surprised by the light lemon flavor of the flaky fish. Dinners on the road tended to be hit or miss.

"It really is."

Ordinarily, McKenna ate with Benny, Roger, and a couple of the team's trainers, so she wasn't surprised by the curious look her boss gave her when she said she was joining Tank tonight.

It was unusual for a social media director to travel with the team, but Benny had discovered early on that she was a wonderful photographer, so he expanded her role to include covering away games in that capacity. Initially, it was supposed to be a short-term thing, lasting only until the team's photographer returned from maternity leave. Then, because the new mother was breast-feeding, it was decided that McKenna would continue traveling until the baby was older, at which point the photographer would return full time.

McKenna loved the travel, so it worked well, both for her social media posts and for Benny, who was starting to rely on her as much as his right hand, Roger. Her boss had mentioned on their last road trip that he'd like her to *continue* traveling with them, even after the photographer's return.

Tank got a few sideways glances as well, when he told Blake and Rook he was eating with her. The guys had offered to make room for her at their table, and McKenna was more than ready to pull up a chair, but Tank said no, claiming he needed to talk to her about an upcoming interview.

"What interview are you worried about?" she asked, after a couple minutes of eating in silence.

Tank gave her a funny look. "What?"

"You told the guys you wanted to talk to me about an interview."

His expression cleared. "Oh. I lied. Just wanted you all to myself."

McKenna wasn't sure what to make of that statement because...*what*?

Unable to come up with a suitable response, she merely said, "Oh," and tucked back into her food. Glancing around the restaurant, she caught more than a few people casting looks in their direction. Which was unsurprising. She was sure it must look strange for the quirky social media girl to be sitting alone with the team hottie.

"I like your shirt," Tank said, grinning at her Mickey Mouse shirt that said, "I'm not arguing. I'm explaining why I'm right." As always, it was a gift from her mom, and probably an accurate one, as McKenna was headstrong and vocal when it came to things she was knowledgeable about.

There were a couple of hours between dinner and the time she left for the game, so she'd change into her official Stingrays attire after they ate, just in case she spilled food on herself, something she did too frequently. Her mom always joked that even at twenty-four, she was still as messy as a toddler at mealtimes.

Tank's phone pinged for the tenth time since they'd sat down. He glanced at the screen, then flipped it face down on the table again without replying.

"It won't bother me if you want to text back."

He shook his head. "No response necessary."

"Are all those texts from the same person?"

Tank grimaced. "They're from Lara. She and Emily are apparently doing happy hour at some country club. They keep texting me pictures of their sexually suggestive cocktails, wishing I was there."

"What's a sexually suggestive cocktail?" McKenna asked.

"First round was Sex on the Beach, second was Buttery Nipples, this time they're having Blowjob shots."

McKenna winced. "Don't envy them the headaches they're going to have tomorrow."

"Oh yeah. They're definitely wasted."

"Have you seen them since that video went viral?" McKenna asked, hating that she cared about his answer more than she should. Tank was a coworker, so who he slept with—as long as it wasn't in public and in front of a camera—was none of her business.

He shook his head, and she felt an instant wave of relief. She told herself it was because she didn't need to deal with any more bad press surrounding Tank and his ménage à trois partners, but that was a lie.

He'd been on his best behavior since that stupid video, so it was easy for her to forget what a cocky playboy he'd been prior to his suspension. Discovering that he was still hooking up with those two women would tarnish her new impression of him. Because *this* version of Tank was a good guy, someone who was great with kids, respectful of veterans, and someone she was starting to consider a friend.

She wasn't sure he'd say the same thing about *her*, because the two of them were opposites from the word go. Part of her wondered if he was just hanging around her because he thought it might get him out of hot water quicker.

She hated to dash his hopes on that, if so. It hadn't even been three weeks since the video hit TikTok, and while the hubbub was starting to die down, there were still a lot of negative comments flying around. She'd overheard Benny telling Roger just yesterday that Hugh hadn't landed yet, temper-wise. The general manager was still pissed as hell, so one misstep and the house of cards they'd been building could collapse.

McKenna had hoped Hugh and James were bluffing about breaking Tank's contract due to his behavior off the ice—after all, he was one of their best players—but she'd done some research and learned that other hockey players had lost their jobs for a variety of reasons, ranging from drug and alcohol abuse to domestic violence to extremely controversial remarks in the media.

She didn't think Tank's behavior in the video was quite that bad, but considering the recent poor publicity was just one offense in a long list, she could understand Hugh being at the end of his rope.

"They weren't bothered by the video?"

"No. Lara's the type of woman who craves constant attention, so I'm not surprised she found the whole thing funny. I haven't heard from Emily, who's a bit more reserved. I don't have a clue what she thinks, though usually it's whatever Lara *tells* her to think. Lara's very open about her bisexuality, but Emily's first foray into both a threesome *and* sex with a woman was what the three of us did together."

McKenna held up a hand. "Let me stop you right there. I don't need any more details than that. What happens between you and your girlfriends can stay between the three of you."

He grinned, and she wished his smile didn't have such a strong impact on her libido. The second he flashed those pearly whites, her body woke right the hell up. So much so, she'd considered packing her vibrator on this trip. She'd quickly dismissed the thought, but now she was suddenly regretting leaving it behind.

She'd never been an overly sexual person. She liked sex fine with her previous lovers, but she wasn't the type of woman who needed sex regularly. It was kind of rare for her to pull out a vibrator. As a single woman, her horniness was usually driven by a sexy movie or steamy romance novel, and given the fact she worked constantly, who had time for either of those things?

One thing that had *never* prompted a need for her vibrator was a simple smile flashed her direction by an oversexed, cocky, gorgeous hockey player.

Until Tank.

Dammit.

Lately, her vibrator was getting a regular workout. So much so, she'd gone online to look for different models. because she was feeling the need for some variety after using her tried and true so many nights in a row.

"I told you. They aren't my girlfriends. In fact, I have a confession to make," Tank said, leaning closer, lowering his voice. "I've never had a girlfriend."

McKenna waited for him to add some clarifier to that. Like, he hadn't had one in several years or since high school or something. But he didn't. He let the statement stand on its own.

"As in *never*, never?"

He shrugged. "When I was in high school, I lived and breathed hockey, always skating, drilling, playing. Much as it might surprise you to hear, girls took a backseat to that."

"I don't believe you."

Tank laughed. "I swear. I was solely focused on making it to the big leagues, and then when I did…" He let the suggestive wiggle of his eyebrows fill in that blank for her.

"You discovered puck bunnies."

"I was nineteen years old and had beautiful women throwing themselves at me left and right. Who was I to deny them a night with a hockey god?"

His question was a throwback to the Tank she'd known pre-suspension. An arrogant, swaggering boast meant to annoy her. And if he'd said it a month ago, his comment would have done just that. Had her rolling her eyes and dismissing him as a shallow manwhore.

But tonight, she could see the twinkle in his eyes, which were crinkled at the edges with laugh lines.

"You're regressing," she muttered, even though she knew he was joking.

"Nope. Just stating facts. Or at least the way I saw things. It's pretty easy for a nineteen-year-old guy wearing an NHL jersey and making bank to start believing his own press."

"Apparently, it's just as easy for a twenty-seven-year-old man," she said, pointing out that he hadn't changed much. At least not until lately.

"Touché, Mouse." He lifted his glass of water in a playful toast.

"So are you planning to hold on to your bachelor status forever?"

"Nope," Tank said, shaking his head. "Just until I hang up my skates."

"You realize you can play the game and be in a relationship, right?" McKenna gestured toward the table of his friends. "Blake, Coulton, and Preston are all making that work."

"It's not a question of ability. Just desire. I like my life the way it is. Like my freedom and being unencumbered."

She snorted. "What you like is the ability to remain a slob without some woman telling you to pick up your dirty socks."

Tank chuckled. "You read me like a book, don't you?"

"It's not hard when it's more primer than great literature," she joked.

Tank laughed so hard and loud, more than a few heads turned in their direction.

"So what about you?" he asked, once he settled back down.

"What about me *what*?

"Have you left a long string of broken hearts in your wake?"

McKenna put her fork down, too full to eat any more. When Tank realized she was finished, he reached over and snagged the last bit of her salmon. "No," she replied. "My dating history isn't much bigger than yours."

Since day one of his redemption tour, Tank had been asking her questions about herself. At first, she was determined to remain professional and keep her distance. She hadn't been thrilled about having to work so closely with him, given his obnoxious attitude. She figured anything she told him would be twisted and used against her somehow, so she'd kept her mouth shut.

She was kind of shocked when she starting viewing him as someone she wouldn't mind having as a friend. Which meant she didn't mind sharing some personal details about her life.

"I've had a whopping three boyfriends," she admitted.

Tank's eyes widened as if in surprise. "Why so few? Did you go to all-girl schools growing up or something?"

McKenna blinked a few times, trying to figure out if he was kidding. Because if not, that was a sweet compliment. "All my schools were co-ed."

"Were they long-term relationships?"

She lifted one shoulder. "I started going out with my first boyfriend, Camden, toward the end of junior year of high school.

He was on the yearbook staff with me and one day after school, we were both talking about how neither of us had a date for prom. He suggested we go together, and I agreed. We had a great time at the dance, so we kept going out. Right up to graduation."

"When you say first boyfriend…"

She rolled her eyes. "Not everything is about sex, you know."

"I'm just asking if he was the one to pop your cherry."

McKenna pretended to vomit. "Jesus, what are you? A high school cheerleader?"

Tank winked, making it clear he'd chosen his words specifically to irritate her. He had way too much fun teasing her. "Just answer the question, Mouse."

She crossed her arms, huffing out a breath, then decided fuck it. She was enjoying this conversation. "He was."

"I didn't lose my virginity until I was seventeen either."

McKenna hadn't expected him to reciprocate, or for him to be so old. The guy was a total hound dog these days, so she'd assumed he'd started having sex two minutes after he hit puberty.

"Really?"

"Refer back to my earlier comment. I was all hockey, all the time."

"So who was the girl?"

Tank leaned back in his chair, wiping his mouth after cleaning off his plate—and hers. "She was a girl on my hockey team. Kayla. Girl had a wicked slap shot, hot as shit. One night after a game, I offered her a ride home. We found a quiet country lane and took a different kind of ride in the back seat."

"Of course you did."

"Turned out she was hot for my crossovers. We hooked up a few more times before the season ended, and that was that," he said. "So what happened to your first love?"

"I went off to college and he didn't. We said we'd do the

long-distance thing, but in the end, I guess he got tired of being alone. He started going out with one of my friends."

Tank nodded when the waitress came by with a water pitcher. She filled their glasses before moving on. "That must have hurt."

She took a sip of water. "At the time, I was devastated because I found out from a girlfriend that he was cheating on me with another friend of ours, who didn't realize we hadn't officially broken up. When I called him, he confessed and said things were never going to work out with us being so far apart. I begged him to change his mind, which makes me cringe when I think of it now. Hindsight really is twenty-twenty. Because all those tears, while claiming I'd never find anyone else, wasn't because I was genuinely devastated but because I was nineteen, and teenagers feel things way too deeply and stupidly."

"Isn't that the truth? So who was boyfriend number two?"

McKenna tilted her head. "Do you really want to hear all of this?"

He frowned. "Of course, I do. I wouldn't ask otherwise. Besides, this is the first time you've answered my questions with some details. I'm getting tired of playing twenty questions with you."

She narrowed her eyes. "Our time together has had a purpose," she reminded him.

He raised his hands. "I'll concede on that point if you tell me about guy number two."

McKenna sighed. "Camden was very sweet, and even romantic, but the second guy, Dale, was…" She shrugged. "I think every girl in her life has to date the asshole. Just so they learn what they *don't* want in a guy."

Tank's brows furrowed. "What kind of asshole are we talking about?"

McKenna wasn't sure what to make of the sudden change in his tone of voice. It was deeper and even a little bit angry. She was strangely touched by the idea that Tank Phillips might feel protective of her.

"He was a nice guy at the beginning. We met my sophomore year in college. He was a junior. For the first year, it was a decent relationship. We went to parties, hung out in his apartment with his roommates, did all the typical college life stuff. Somewhere around the beginning of his senior year, there was a shift. He was suddenly wildly jealous—like, irrationally so—and he started this very subtle campaign of emotional abuse. Making sly comments meant to make me feel self-conscious or bad about myself. Eventually, it was a lot less subtle."

"What did he do?"

"He started accusing me of being a slut, either because of what I was wearing or because he thought I was looking at some other guy. It took me some time to wiggle out of his web because his earlier, more subtle digs had taken root and my confidence was at an all-time low."

"Guy sounds like a prick."

"He was," she agreed. "A total prick. One night, I hit my limit and finally woke up, finally realized I wasn't the problem. He was. I dumped him. That was followed by a firestorm of drama because he didn't take it well. Spent hours beating on my apartment door, demanding we talk. He blew up my phone for weeks. All the things."

"He didn't physically hurt you, did he?"

She shook her head. "No. It took some time, but I guess he figured out I meant it when I said we were done. After him, I wasn't in any hurry to date anyone else, so I spent the rest of my college career single."

"I can see why. So, if I'm counting correctly, there's one guy left to go."

McKenna toyed with her fork, cursing herself for being a fool. She should have foreseen where this conversation was headed, but she'd dived in anyway.

The last thing she wanted to do was talk to Tank about Eddie, because try as she may, his rejection still stung, even after more than a year. Probably because, while Dale had revealed himself to be a total douchebag, Eddie had been more like Camden…a good guy. Or at least, she'd thought so.

Her confidence had rebounded after Dale because she could see their issues had been driven by his jealousy, not by her actions. Which was why Eddie's punch had blindsided her and knocked her out. Now, no matter how many pep talks she tried to give herself, no matter how many times she looked in the mirror and told herself she was pretty and smart and any guy would be lucky to have her, she still couldn't quite believe that was true.

Because Eddie, whom she'd genuinely loved, hadn't believed it enough to stay with her.

More than that, he'd felt the need to look elsewhere.

Mercifully, before she had to come up with some way to change the subject, Benny and Roger arrived at their table and changed it for her.

"Hey, sorry to interrupt," Benny said, pulling a chair over to join them, "but I wanted to have a quick chat before you head back to the rooms."

Roger remained standing, hovering slightly behind Benny's chair.

"What's up?" she asked, never so grateful to see her boss.

"Roger and I were just talking about the black-tie event the Stingrays Foundation is putting on next weekend."

"What about it?" Tank asked.

"In the fall, you brought two dates, as I recall."

Tank grimaced. "Emily and Lara."

Benny sighed. "Yeah. You weren't planning on bringing them again, were you?"

Tank shook his head. "No, Benny. I'm not an idiot. I know that would go over like a lead balloon."

"Good," he said. "Roger and I think it would be best if Mac went with you as your date."

McKenna instantly panicked. "*Me?*"

Benny nodded.

"But I can't. I *work* the event," she reminded him, shooting Roger a what-the-hell look, since he was clearly in on this idea.

Roger, who'd become a good friend to her, grimaced, which let her know she was probably fighting a losing battle. Not that she planned to stop trying. She was struggling enough with her misplaced attraction to the last man on the planet she should be fantasizing about. Going on a date with him would be the equivalent to throwing gasoline on a fire. Her vibrator wouldn't be able to withstand it.

"I need to be there in my official capacity, Benny, walking around, taking pictures, talking to people for my posts," she insisted.

Benny crooked a thumb over his shoulder. "Roger offered to cover the event for you."

McKenna narrowed her eyes, hoping her friend could read the words—"*Et tu, Brute?*"—she was thinking.

She shook her head. "Benny," she started again, but her boss talked over her.

"Mac, there are going to be a lot of sponsors at the event. Not to mention the big-time fans, who are dropping a mint for the tickets just so they can meet their favorite Rays players. I'd feel a lot better if you were there to guide the conversations."

"Do you seriously think I'm going to do or say something wrong?" Tank asked the table in general.

"No," McKenna said. At the same time, Benny replied, "Yes."

Unlike McKenna, Benny hadn't been a witness to his redemption tour, so it was obviously going to take Tank a little longer to convince the PR director that he was walking the straight and narrow.

McKenna, on the other hand, had had a front row seat to all the promo ops, and she'd seen how well Tank had handled himself.

"Tank." Benny leaned forward and rested his elbows on the

table. "Last year at this event, you told a dirty joke in the hearing of the president's wife."

"I didn't know she was standing behind me."

"And at the one this past fall, you and your," Benny paused, drawing in a deep breath, "dates were on the dance floor most of the night. And let's just say…you weren't leaving much to the imagination."

McKenna winced as she recalled Tank bumping and grinding with Emily and Lara, the dancing so sexually charged, she might have thought they were actually fucking if they hadn't been fully clothed.

Benny tapped one finger on the table. "The only reason all this shit with Lara didn't blow up back then was because Charles Steele had been out of town on business and couldn't attend. We didn't make any photos of the three of you public, so you got away with it that time. We're not pushing our luck this time around, so I think it's in everyone's best interest if Mac attends the gala with you."

McKenna closed her eyes, aware nothing she said was going to change Benny's mind. She glanced at Tank, hoping he would pick up the battle. Maybe he could find some way to persuade Benny it would be fine if he attended alone.

Their gazes locked—and she realized he wasn't going to fight. Instead, he gave her a crooked grin and casual one-shoulder *whatever* shrug.

McKenna sighed. "Fine. I'll go with him."

"Great." Obviously, now that Benny had gotten his way, he was making a quick escape lest she tried to change her mind. "Good luck tonight," he said to Tank, as he and Roger left the hotel restaurant together.

"Looks like you and I are going on a date," Tank said, kicking back and stretching his legs out under the table. His feet brushed against hers.

"It's not a date," she pointed out. "I'm going to this thing as your keeper."

Tank grinned. "You know, I'm starting to think you don't want to date me."

McKenna couldn't help it. She laughed. "What was your first clue?" she joked, but Tank didn't take it that way, which was wildly out of character for the man who never seemed to take anything seriously.

"Why not?" he pressed, frowning. "What's wrong with me?"

McKenna got the sense his question was a sincere one, and that she'd even hurt his feelings.

"There's nothing wrong with you," she said, diplomatically. "You're just not the kind of guy I date."

"What kind is that?"

"I just told you. I've only dated three guys, Tank. And I was in love with all three of them. I'm not interested in sex without strings. Unlike you, I want committed relationships. So when I sleep with a man, it's because I have feelings for him. Meanwhile, you just admitted that your sole purpose for dating is to hook up."

Tank didn't reply to that, and she knew why. They'd gotten way off base.

"This is a pointless conversation, because next weekend is not a date. It's just an extension of the work we started a few weeks ago. Okay?" she asked.

Tank sighed, and for a moment, she got the sense he didn't agree, though she didn't have a clue why not.

Finally, he nodded slowly. "Fine."

"Great." With his agreement, McKenna decided to take a card from Benny's playbook and make a quick escape. For one thing, she was afraid Tank would want to resume their previous conversation about her dating history, and for another, she needed to get away from him so she could get her thoughts in order.

While she'd just insisted that the gala wouldn't be a date, and that he wasn't her type, she wasn't so sure she believed either of those things. And she desperately needed to.

Fantasizing about the sexy hockey player while she got herself off at night was one thing.

But there was no way in hell she could let that attraction bleed over into the real world or her job. She'd made that mistake once before, and it had resulted in her moving away from home and starting a new job in a new city.

She liked Baltimore, so she wasn't about to make the same mistake twice.

Which meant she needed to double down on her "rules to live by."

No hockey players and no one from work.

Tank was both.

Fuck.

CHAPTER FIVE

TANK DROVE past McKenna's house, searching for parking on her narrow street. She'd texted him the address that morning reluctantly, initially insisting she could meet him at the gala, but finally relenting when he pointed out there would be lots of opportunities for him to say the wrong thing if left alone on the red carpet. Obviously he wouldn't, but he decided to use Benny's lack of faith in his intelligence to his own benefit.

Because he wanted to see where McKenna lived.

While Tank had bought a large condo on the waterfront after signing with the Rays, McKenna was currently renting a small townhouse on a narrow side street much farther away from the Inner Harbor. Tank had lived in Baltimore for six years, but he'd never been in this part of the city. He had to admit, he was impressed. Obviously, the townhomes housed people living on budgets considerably smaller than his own, but it was still a nice area with well-kept houses and tree-lined sidewalks. What wasn't great was the parking. He'd gone nearly a full block past her house before he found a spot where he could parallel park.

There were plenty of sections of Baltimore where Tank wouldn't even consider leaving his baby—aka, his Audi R8—but he'd be fine to park it here for a few minutes. He stepped out and engaged the locks, walking back in the direction of McKenna's house.

It had been two weeks since his return to the ice, and it felt amazing to be back in the game. His teammates had been very supportive throughout his suspension, but that didn't help the fact he felt like shit for missing six games.

McKenna's positive promotional posts had been making the rounds, and he'd started to see less negative comments circulating. In addition to her posts, several pictures of him and McKenna had hit social media, as well. One of the parents from the signing with the Pee Wee team had filmed him chasing McKenna around the ice. She'd even gotten the impromptu kiss on the cheek. The mom had uploaded it to TikTok, including the hashtag #cutestcouple. Because TikTok apparently had a hard-on for him after the damn viral video—McKenna explained it was the algorithms—the mother's video had gotten quite a few views itself.

McKenna hadn't been thrilled when he'd pointed it out to her, but Benny hadn't seen it as a bad thing, which was a surprise and a relief. Then Benny reminded him—a-fucking-gain—that a lot of the Stingrays' biggest sponsors would be in attendance tonight and Tank should be on his best behavior. He got pissed every time Benny said shit like that, because it made him feel like he was some naughty toddler. He wasn't a fucking idiot.

Of course, the second he thought that, he recalled that he'd taken Lara and Emily to the last fancy fundraiser he'd attended in the fall...and after way too much champagne, the three of them had given new meaning to the term "dirty dancing." So he begrudgingly decided that maybe the reminders were justified.

Tank climbed the three steps to the small front landing in front of McKenna's townhouse, but before he could knock on the door, it swung open.

Tank's eyes widened because…

Holy.

Fuck.

"Mouse?"

McKenna frowned, confused by his tone. "Who else were you expecting?"

Tank couldn't stop himself from blowing a low whistle. "Jesus Christ. You look gorgeous."

Her cheeks instantly grew pink, which only made her look even hotter, as far as he was concerned. Tank had had no idea before her that blushing was a total turn-on for him. The women he usually dated were experienced, confident, and oozing with sex appeal, so blushing wasn't something they did.

He wouldn't have thought McKenna ticked any of those boxes until a few weeks ago, certain that she was just what his first impression had told him.

Awkward introvert.

Now, he knew better. He'd seen her confidence up close and personal…at least as far as her job was concerned. She knew her shit when it came to work, and she didn't cower or remain quiet about her thoughts and opinions.

As for sex appeal…

His gaze slid along her body once more, taking in the visual feast.

She might be the sexiest woman he'd ever seen. And that was saying something.

"You have a waist."

If Tank could have swallowed those words back he would have, because what kind of stupid line was that?

McKenna, however, didn't take offense. Instead, she rewarded him for idiocy by treating him to one of those eye rolls of hers.

"Ha ha," she said.

"Seriously," he said, taking one of her hands in his, playfully spinning her around.

McKenna's work wardrobe consisted of baggy shirts—either blouses or her funny graphic T-shirts—loose-fitting pants or mom jeans, and always topped by one of what had to be a million oversized cardigan sweaters she owned.

He'd never—NEVER—seen her dressed in anything that told him she had a body that looked like *this*. She had a legit hourglass figure with decent-sized tits—where the hell had *those* come from?—and hips that offered a man plenty to hold on to.

And while her figure was mouth-wateringly gorgeous, he didn't take as much time to admire it as he normally might because he was too fixated on her face.

"Where are your glasses?" he asked.

She pointed to her eyes. "Contacts."

"Why don't you wear those all the time?"

McKenna shrugged. "My eyes tend to dry out too quickly with them in, especially if I spend a lot of time in front of a computer screen. Which, FYI, is ninety percent of my job. Plus," she grinned, "I'm usually too lazy in the morning to bother with them. It's easier to just slap my glasses on and go."

Tank chuckled. As good as McKenna looked without her glasses—her bright blue eyes sparkling—he realized he preferred her in them. The thick frames gave off sexy librarian vibes.

"This hair," he said, aware that with each passing comment, he was coming off as an even bigger buffoon.

She pushed the dark auburn waves over her shoulders. "It's already driving me mad. I never wear it down because there's just too much of it and somehow it always ends up in my face."

Tank couldn't come up with an intelligent reply to that, because he was too busy imagining himself closing a fist around the wavy tresses as he took her from beh—

Brakes screeched in his brain, because *what the fuck*?

Why did his mind keep going there with her?

McKenna was not his type. Period.

"Should we go?" Mercifully, she didn't seem to be suffering from the same case of the stupids he was.

She stepped out onto her porch, and he waited as she locked the door.

It was then that he realized she was taller tonight. Glancing down, he spotted the heels.

"I'm afraid I couldn't find a spot on the street to park. My car's about a block away. I can go get it if—"

"Oh, that's okay," she assured him, smiling when he offered his arm, the two of them walking down the steps to the sidewalk. "While I rarely dress up, I'm actually pretty good at walking in heels."

He tightened his crooked elbow to his side, her hand nestled between as they walked down her street.

"Parking is always bad around here, I'm afraid," she explained. "There's only room in front of each townhouse for two smallish cars, and my neighbors on both sides are couples in their mid-forties with older teens still living with them. So they're four-car families. Fortunately, they're super nice and they know I'm a single woman living alone, so they've told their kids to always leave one of the spots right in front of my house clear for me."

"That *is* nice."

"It's a great neighborhood," she continued. "I was a little worried about living on my own in the city, but this street's quiet, with a lot of working families, and everyone looks out for everyone else."

Tank was glad to hear that, because he knew there were plenty of other parts of the city where he'd worry about McKenna living.

Worry?

Jesus.

Tonight was going to be way too challenging if he kept thinking about McKenna as anything more than a work colleague.

"That's a pretty dress," he said, when they reached his Audi and he opened the passenger door for her.

"Thanks."

He closed the door behind her, quickly crossing around the front of his car to climb behind the steering wheel.

When he started the vehicle, McKenna said, "Blake's girlfriend, Erika, invited me to go shopping with her and Ainsley when she learned I was attending the gala with you. I was glad she did, because I wouldn't have had a clue what to wear. Ainsley was in the same boat. We're both new to attending fancy parties like this."

Blake and the Rays' goalie, Coulton, had been the first of Tank's friend group to fall hard and fast for their ladies, both guys shedding their bachelor statuses in the fall. Tank hadn't been surprised at all when Blake fell for his long-time neighbor and best friend, Erika. In truth, he was shocked it had taken them so damn long to figure out they were perfect for each other.

Coulton had the reputation as being the team's gentle giant, the quiet guy who'd never shown much interest in women at all. Which Tank could never understand. Because why be a professional athlete if you weren't going to take advantage of the perks? And in Tank's opinion, puck bunnies were a sweet perk.

Coulton had never agreed, perfectly fine with spending his nights alone until he found "the one." Which he had after walking into a dive bar in Cherry Hill on a whim and spotting the tough-as-nails bartender Ainsley behind the counter.

Tank never imagined his quiet friend would fall for a tatted-up, curses-like-a-sailor woman, but damn if she and Coulton didn't fit together perfectly.

"Erika's great," Tank agreed. "And she obviously has amazing taste if she helped you pick out that dress, because you look..." He shook his head as he snuck another peek at her in her curve-hugging, sapphire-blue dress. "God, you look fucking hot."

McKenna flushed again, but her expression told him she was pleased by his compliment.

"You might look *too* hot," he murmured, suddenly thinking about all the men who were going to see her tonight. "I probably should have brought my hockey stick along to beat off the guys who're going to try to steal my girl."

McKenna pressed her lips together, trying not to smile, but he still saw it. "You're ridiculous," she said, before laughing. "Also, not your girl, remember?"

He ignored that assertion, because he didn't want to hear her call herself his keeper again.

"Whenever I attend in my official capacity," she continued, "I just wear black slacks and a muted-color blouse so I blend in with the background."

Tank found it hard to believe she could ever fade into the background, no matter what she wore. Then he recalled that, until a month ago, he'd been one of those blind idiots who'd failed to see her…and her true beauty.

They passed the drive to the party in quiet conversation, talking about their favorite parts of the city.

The gala, which included dinner and dancing, was being held at the Baltimore Museum of Art. Tank pulled up to the entrance, stepping out of his car and handing the keys to the valet before opening McKenna's door for her.

While it wasn't an official red carpet, quite a few reporters and fans had gathered near the entrance, hoping to see their favorite players, as well as the elite of Baltimore's high society, all dressed to the nines. Tank held McKenna's hand, smiling and waving. A few people yelled out questions about the season and the previous night's game, which he answered charmingly. Surprisingly, no one mentioned the video, which he was taking as a sign McKenna's redemption tour was working.

McKenna was less comfortable with the attention, attempting to stand in his shadow. Apparently, she really was well-versed at fading into the background.

Which was a shame for her, because he didn't intend to let her do that tonight.

"Smile," he murmured, wrapping his arm around her shoulder. "Say hello to my beautiful date, McKenna," he told the cameramen, a few of whom played along, affably saying hi.

Tank signed a half dozen autographs for fans before leading her away from the crowd.

"That was a lot of cameras," she said softly.

Tank grinned. "Isn't that the point of shindigs like this, Miss Social Media? To draw publicity."

"It is," she agreed.

Once they entered the museum, a woman was there, pointing them toward the Fox Room, where tonight's event was taking place.

"People are probably going to try to figure out who I am," McKenna murmured, as much to herself as him.

"Is that a bad thing?"

McKenna looked up at him. "Not really. I'm sure it won't take them long to find out I work in the PR department. Given that viral video, it won't look all that strange that you're here with someone who's basically your publicist." She glanced back toward the entrance. "I'm not sure how you can stand all those cameras being pointed at you all the time."

"Are you kidding me? That's the best place on earth," he joked, because front and center of any crowd was his preferred position.

"Of course, you would think so." She flashed him a smile so genuine and bright, he forgot to breathe for a second. "But I can tell you right now, I prefer to be on the other end of the camera. I could never get used to that."

Tank shrugged. "All the photographers are really hoping for is a bit of a show. Paparazzi are looking for the best or the worst in celebrities."

"Well, tonight you gave them the best," McKenna said. "Thanks for that."

"Can't give my gorgeous date a hard time at her first gala, can I?"

"Gorgeous, huh? Smooth."

Tank winked, then continued toward the ballroom.

Once inside, he spotted the bar, where quite a few of his teammates were already standing in line. "Why don't I get us a drink while you find our table? What would you like?"

"A glass of Chardonnay would be great. Thanks."

He nodded, lifting her hand to kiss her knuckles, perfectly aware there were at least half a dozen cameras capturing images of people as they entered. Fortunately, McKenna hadn't noticed, so the way she flushed and smiled sweetly was certain to set the gossip pages aflame as people started to wonder who she was.

Tank reluctantly let her go and headed over to the bar.

"Hey, man," Blake said, fist-bumping him as he stepped into line with several of his friends. "You clean up good."

Tank chuckled.

"Nothing worse than a night spent in fucking monkey suits," Victor grumbled, tugging at his bow tie, which was askew.

"It's not so bad," Tank said—aware that was the wrong response when Victor, Blake, Preston, and Coulton all frowned at him.

"You're usually the first one to bitch about having to wear a tuxedo," Preston pointed out.

It was true. Tank's preferred attire was loose-fitting athletic gear or nothing at all, a joke he'd made countless times with his buddies, claiming he did his best work naked. Usually after that jest, he'd make a crude gesture to drive home his meaning, not that it was necessary.

Tank shrugged. "Please tell me we're all sitting together."

Blake grimaced. "Of course not. They've got us all split up so we can schmooze the guests and talk them into contributing big tonight."

"It's for a good cause," Coulton pointed out, just as he always did. The Stingrays Foundation raised money for several causes, but their pet project was one that spoke to Coulton's heart. Funds made tonight would provide money to foster children so that they could participate in school and community athletics. The foundation paid for equipment, registration fees, and even provided transportation to practices and games, if necessary.

"Yeah, man, I know," Tank said, agreeing. Coulton volunteered for Big Brothers Big Sisters and he'd grown incredibly close to his Little Brother, Slade, who Tank had to admit was the bomb. The kid was fucking hilarious and cool as shit.

"So you really brought Mac to the gala?" Preston must have seen Tank and McKenna walk in together. "Blake said you were, but I figured he was joking."

"What's wrong with me bringing her?" Tank asked, even though he knew the answer.

"Not a damn thing," Preston quickly assured. "We all love Mac, you know that. It's just that you usually bring a puck bunny—or two—to these kinds of things."

"Speaking of," Blake said, leaning closer. "Lara is sitting at her uncle's table tonight."

Tank groaned. He should have anticipated Lara's presence here, as Charles Steele was one of the Rays' biggest sponsors, but since embarking on "Project Tank" with McKenna, he'd pretty much forgotten all about the woman.

Which was surprising for two reasons.

One, she was part of the reason he was in trouble at work to begin with; and two, she was constantly texting him. He'd gotten to the point that whenever her name popped up on his phone, he deleted the message without even reading it. He kept telling himself to just block her damn number, but there was a tiny part of him waiting to snap out of…whatever this thing he had going with McKenna was.

"Thanks for the warning," he murmured to his best friend.

Tank glanced around the room. He told himself he was just curious who else was in attendance, but the truth was he was looking for McKenna. They'd been apart all of five freaking minutes and yet, he felt the strong need to check on her, see her.

He spotted her in the far corner, talking to Coach Fields. He didn't have a clue what they were talking about, but it looked like a serious conversation.

Probably about him and his reform, he thought begrudgingly.

Dean Fields had come on as the Stingrays' head coach at the end of last season. It had been a return home for the guy, as he'd ended his hockey career as a Stingray thirteen years earlier, after several injuries sidelined him for good. He'd played with Victor and Preston back in the day, and they were delighted to have their old teammate back as their coach.

Dean had become an assistant coach in Vancouver a couple years after hanging up his skates, where he'd been until Baltimore hired him for the head coach job. They'd announced Dean in January, a few months after their former coach decided to retire, and he'd taken over in late April.

There was always an adjustment period whenever a new coach came into a program and tried to make it his own. Tank had decided to withhold judgment—as he'd really liked their previous coach—and give Coach Fields a chance to prove himself. So far, he was impressed with most of the changes the man had brought to the team. Coach had been cool about Tank's after-hours shenanigans, alluding to the fact he'd gotten into more than his fair share of trouble back in his player days, as well.

So he was surprised to see the coach looking so serious right now. Tank knew Benny, Hugh, and James were at the end of their ropes with him, but he really thought Coach Fields was more chill and understanding about it all.

When he finally got to the head of the bar line, he ordered McKenna's wine and a beer for himself, surprised to discover her still deep in discussion with Coach Fields. He started across the large event space, intent on joining them, but was waylaid several times by sponsors and fans, all wanting to meet him or snap selfies or grab autographs. Since tonight was all about promotion, he plastered on a smile and laid on the charm.

After fifteen minutes, he managed to break free and tried to spot McKenna in the crowd. The coach was now conversing with Hugh and James, so perhaps she'd managed to find their table.

He groaned to himself when he discovered McKenna had been cornered by Lara.

Fucking awesome.

Tank wasn't sure when McKenna's opinion of him started to matter so much, but he liked the friendship that was blooming between them, and he hated to think something either the coach or Lara might say would negatively impact that.

He crossed the room, somewhat covertly. There were more than enough people milling about that he could approach them unnoticed. He was hoping to overhear what Lara was saying, because it was obvious from McKenna's expression that she wasn't comfortable with the conversation.

"Wait, I know who you are," Lara said, snapping her fingers. "Don't you work in the PR department? You're like the social media girl or something."

McKenna nodded. "I am."

"Oh, well, I guess that makes sense, then," Lara said, as if she'd just figured something out. "You're keeping my man on a rather short leash tonight, aren't you?"

Her man?

The handful of times he'd hooked up with Lara, they'd met at a bar or nightclub, had a few drinks, dirty danced as foreplay, then went back to her place and fucked. No part of that meant he was *her* anything.

"Tank usually brings *me* to these events," Lara continued.

He'd only brought her to one event—the fall fundraiser—so her words were an outright lie.

"Given the video," McKenna started, but Lara cut her off with a loud scoff and an eye roll.

"I don't know why Uncle Charles is so up in arms about that video. It was all in good fun."

Tank decided he needed to cut this conversation short. "There you are, Mouse." He handed McKenna her glass of wine, then placed his arm around her shoulders. Turning, he faced the other woman and painted on a smile. "Lara," he said, nodding his head.

"Well, hello, stranger," she purred. "I've been waiting for you to make your way over here to see me." She put a hand on her hip, purposely jutting it out in what he knew was a practiced pose, meant to look sexy. Lara was a beautiful woman, and there was no denying it was her looks that had attracted him.

Tonight, however, he didn't find himself as drawn to her Barbie Doll features and statuesque figure. Glancing down at McKenna, who was looking at him with those large blue eyes, he found her a thousand times more beautiful.

That realization caught him off guard.

He'd been blaming this strange pull he felt toward her on abstinence; certain the occasional hits of desire were based on the fact he wasn't getting laid on the regular. But now, as he stood here between the two women, he was forced to admit it wasn't a lack of sex driving his needs...but a genuine attraction to McKenna.

What the fuck was he supposed to do with that?

"I have a bone to pick with you, Tank Phillips," Lara said, playfully. "Why haven't you been replying to my texts?"

"I've been busy. We're getting close to the end of the season, and I need to focus on the game," he lied, because he suspected it would be bad idea to tell Lara things between them were over with Charles Steele so close by. Tank knew a spoiled woman when he saw one, and given things Lara had said in the past, he'd learned early on there was nothing she wanted that she hadn't been given. She drove a Porsche 911, had a high-rise condo on the waterfront, and was always dripping in jewelry from Tiffany's and Chanel bags.

The crazy part was, Tank was pretty sure the woman had never worked a day in her life, though if anyone asked her, she claimed she ran her uncle's charitable foundation. Up until the video, he hadn't even cared enough to ask who her uncle was.

"I think they're getting ready to start serving dinner," he said to McKenna. "We should probably take our seats. Good to see you again, Lara."

He guided McKenna away, not bothering to give the other woman a chance to reply.

McKenna waited until they were out of earshot to murmur, "She's delightful."

Tank laughed because her tone was the definition of sarcasm. "Right?" he tossed back, as if he'd thought her comment sincere, because he couldn't help himself when it came to teasing her.

McKenna nodded her thanks when he pulled out her chair. "She's *still* texting?"

"Yes, and as you heard, I haven't replied," he said, uncertain why he felt the need to say that.

"I'm glad. I don't know that she'd make texts between the two of you public, but I don't get the sense she's very bothered by that video."

She wasn't. Lara loved attention, good or bad.

"What else did she say to you?" he asked.

"Not much. At first, she was kind of catty. Typical girl stuff. I'm here with you, and she doesn't like it. She pointed out I wasn't your usual type, probably hoping to make me insecure. God, some women are real bitches."

Tank chuckled. "Yeah. They are. Hope you didn't let any of the shit she said bother you."

McKenna shot him an "are you kidding?" look that made him laugh again.

"I wasn't born yesterday, Tank. And I've been a girl my whole life. I've been on the receiving end of crap like that before. There was this guy in my dorm freshman year who hung out in my room a lot—just as a friend—because we both loved the same video game. I didn't realize the girl across the hall had gone out with him a few times, and she didn't take it well when he broke things off. When she saw him coming out of my room late one night, she attacked me the next morning. Said a bunch of shit meant to make me feel bad about myself. Maybe if I'd liked the guy it would have mattered, but he was kind of an idiot, so I just laughed it off."

McKenna was so different from the woman he'd thought she was when they'd first been introduced. As he peeled back more layers of the onion, he kept finding more to like. She was confident, intelligent, and driven, and yet she hated being the center of attention. Every single thing he learned about her fascinated him, made him want to discover more.

As soon as they found their seats, dinner was served. They'd been placed at a table with four other couples, and conversation flowed easily. After the dessert plates were cleared, a band started playing popular dance covers. Several of his teammates and their dates were already out on the floor.

Tank glanced in McKenna's direction, lifting his brows and tilting his head in the direction of his friends shaking their booties on the dance floor.

McKenna shook her head. "No thanks. I don't dance."

Tank grinned as he took her hand. "You do tonight."

Part of him expected her to kick up a fuss, so he was delighted when she held on to his hand, rising. Tank took a second to let his gaze slide over her body in that sexy dress. She really was breathtaking.

As soon as they reached the floor, Tank tugged McKenna against him, her breasts brushing against his chest, her hands gripping his waist.

"Tank," she said, in a slight tone of surprise. He spun her away from him, his hands spanning her tiny waist.

He leaned down, his lips brushing the shell of her ear when he hummed, "Hmm?"

McKenna's head fell slightly to the side, though Tank was

certain that was unintentional. Regardless, it gave him better access to the side of her neck.

"You smell so good." He spoke the words against her throat, loving the slight shiver it provoked.

There wasn't a doubt in his mind, McKenna would be a very responsive lover. Even now, he could see her hard nipples pressing against the thin material of her dress.

He shouldn't be thinking about her that way, but he was done fighting with himself. He wanted McKenna Bailey. It was as simple and as insane as that.

Whatever McKenna's hang-ups about dancing, they weren't apparent right now. She pressed her back against his chest, her hips swaying in time to the music—under the direction of his hands. Her eyes were closed, but they opened quickly when, on one brush of her hips, she discovered he was hard.

She looked over her shoulder at him, her face flushed. He didn't have to be a genius to know her red cheeks this time were the result of arousal.

This dance had gotten out of hand very quickly.

He and McKenna locked eyes, and then she slowly turned around. He got the sense she intended to pull away, but he wasn't ready to let her go, so Tank retained his grip on her waist.

The music changed, a slow song beginning. The band did one hell of a great rendition of "Die with a Smile" by Bruno Mars and Lady Gaga. Tank slid his arms around her back.

McKenna went stiff, but only for a moment before giving in, lifting her hands to his shoulders. Tank might have thought the difference in their heights would make dancing hard, but the truth was they fit together perfectly. Granted, the heels were contributing to that.

McKenna wasn't what he'd call feminine. She didn't subscribe to so many of the things the women he slept with did. Things like makeup and fancy hairstyles, stylish clothing, and an abundance of shoes and handbags.

She wore tatty mom jeans, T-shirts, and cardigan sweaters.

The only makeup he'd ever seen her apply was Chapstick, and her long red hair was only ever pinned up in a messy ponytail or those adorable Mouseketeer buns.

So seeing her tonight, in her hip-curving sapphire dress, with her hair down and that smoky look lining her blue eyes, was a goddamn revelation. Now that he'd seen all that hair, he feared he'd be hard-pressed not to start pulling the bands out at every opportunity, just so he could run his fingers through the silky auburn waterfall.

He reached out with one hand, stroking her hair before holding it in a loose ponytail in his fist. He tugged it slightly, and McKenna lifted her head, tilting her face to his. Those heavy-lidded eyes of hers were going to be the death of him.

"Tank," she said.

He loved the sound of his name on her lips.

He lowered his face, moving closer to her.

McKenna blinked a few times, as if forcing herself to remember where they were. "We can't," she whispered.

"Oh, we definitely can," he murmured, closing the distance between them until he could feel the heat of her breath on his face, smell the sweetness of the wine she'd drunk.

He was just about to make landfall, about to kiss those plump, sexy lips, when someone tapped on his shoulder, clearing their throat loudly.

Tank turned around, frowning, ready to lay somebody out for interrupting.

He pulled up short. "Coach?"

"Got a couple of sponsors who want to meet you."

It took Tank a second to shake off the residual effects of his almost-kiss, then another couple trying to figure out why his coach was fucking cock-blocking him.

"Right this minute?" he asked, attempting to temper his tone.

"Yes," was all Coach Fields said, taking one step to the side while waiting for Tank to lead the way.

McKenna's cheeks were flushed, her gaze lowered as if

embarrassed. He did *not* like that. She'd been just as drawn to him as he was to her—and as far as he was concerned, there was nothing wrong with that.

Then he glanced around the room and reconsidered that opinion. Kissing her at a work function was a big fucking no-no. He should probably be grateful to his coach for intervening, but he was struggling to feel anything other than disappointment.

"I'll go back to the table," McKenna said, trying to walk away.

Tank shook his head and held out his hand. "No. Come with me. You're supposed to help, remember?" He didn't need help, but he wasn't above pretending he did if it kept her close.

She seemed reluctant as she glanced at Coach Fields, but in the end, she accepted his hand. The coach led them to a group of tuxedoed men who were obviously dripping in money. Coach Fields introduced them to only Tank, then took a short step back, leaving him to pick up the conversation.

Tank introduced McKenna as his date, then mentioned her role within the Stingrays organization.

As he talked to the men, he kept his arm around McKenna, who entered the conversation a few times, drawn in by their discussion of the latest Stingrays game. Eventually, talk turned to local concerts coming to the city within the next few weeks. Apparently, McKenna loved going to events at Lyric Baltimore, and she was quite animated as she discussed her excitement over going to see some comedian he'd never heard of.

Tank tucked that information away. Once the season was over, he'd get them tickets to a few of the summer shows. He figured he could convince her to go with him by reminding her that he was expected to be on his best behavior until training camp.

He wasn't the kind of guy who dated, not in any sort of conventional sense. Most—okay, all—of the women he asked out were perfectly happy to be wined, dined, and then taken to bed at the end of the night with zero expectation of a morning-after phone call.

Now, as he considered going out with McKenna, he realized sex wasn't his primary goal. He'd be just as happy spending time with her, even if their night didn't end up in bed. He wasn't sure what to do with that feeling, but he decided to roll with it. It was fruitless to continue trying to explain this unlikely attraction away.

While she wasn't his type, McKenna had wormed her way under his skin, and he had absolutely no desire to resist the pull.

When one of the men they were talking to continued stealing way too many peeks at McKenna's cleavage, Tank added jealousy to the list of new emotions he was experiencing.

Unfortunately, once they were off the dance floor, Tank was approached by countless other fans and team sponsors. Ordinarily, he found those kinds of conversations a grind, but with McKenna by his side, it wasn't so bad. Mainly because she was taking some of the pressure off him, the people they spoke to as taken by her as he was.

He was disappointed when the band played the last song, because they were too deep in conversation with local billionaire Lucas Whiting and his wife, Keira—another of Padraig's cousins —for him to pull McKenna out to the floor for another dance.

When the gala ended, he placed her shawl over her shoulders and tucked her close as they waited for the valet.

Once they were in the car, McKenna fiddled with the radio until she found a song she liked. When they arrived at her house, Tank was once again forced to park halfway down the block.

She tried to insist he could just drop her off, but there was no way he was letting her walk to her door alone after dark, no matter how safe she felt in her neighborhood.

McKenna didn't put up a fight and even let him hold her hand as they walked. Climbing the three steps to her small landing, he waited as she unlocked the door. Once it was open, she turned to face him.

He hoped she'd invite him in, even though he knew she wouldn't. While Tank was all-systems go on seeing where this thing with McKenna led, she was too much of a professional to give in to the pull.

Not that he wasn't determined to test—and break—all of her limits.

"Tonight was fun," she said, making it obvious they were saying goodbye right here, right now.

"It was. Although, there is one piece of unfinished business."

McKenna frowned. "There is?"

Tank nodded. "Mm-hmm." He cupped her cheeks in his large hands, tilting her head so he could see her pretty face.

The quick swipe of her tongue over her lower lip and the way her eyes started to drift closed told him all he needed to know regarding her willingness. Maybe she wasn't as committed to that professionalism of hers as he'd thought.

Hot damn.

Tank pressed his lips to hers.

His original intent had been to keep the kiss gentle, soft. That idea lasted for all of a second and a half.

Overwhelmed by her taste, her scent, and everything else about her, Tank ran his own tongue over her lips, encouraging her to open for him. The moment she did, he took her with a passion he'd never felt before.

One hand remained on her cheek, the other sliding through her hair, gripping it roughly and using it to twist her head, allowing him to deepen the kiss.

She whimpered hungrily into his mouth. Her tongue stroked his, her desire matching his own.

Tank started to push her inside the house, ready to expand on the embrace, but he'd obviously overplayed his hand, and she broke the kiss.

"We can't do this," she said, taking a large step away from him.

"Why not?"

"Because this wasn't a date. It was work."

The entire night had felt like a real date to *him*, so hearing that it hadn't to her bothered Tank. A lot.

But he decided maybe it would be smart to take things slower with her. Because starting a relationship with McKenna—hell, with *any* woman—had been so low on his list before tonight, it hadn't even registered.

The fact he was considering one with McKenna was throwing him for a loop. Not the desire—he was finished denying that he wanted her—but the how-to. He'd never had to woo a woman, never had to convince her to go out with him. McKenna was going to make him work for it, was going to fight him every step of the way.

On top of that, Tank was an impulsive guy. *Thinking* wasn't something he ever did. If he wanted something, he just took it. But that wasn't going to work with her.

So he'd take a knee—only for tonight—and make a goddamn game plan. But he wasn't going to lie and agree that tonight was just work, because it wasn't.

When the silence lingered too long, McKenna filled it. "I guess I'll see you tomorrow at the game."

Tank nodded.

"Good luck," she said.

He smiled. "Thanks." Then, even though he knew he shouldn't, he gave her another kiss, careful to keep it quick and platonic.

McKenna's cheeks were still flushed from their first heated kiss, so he ran the back of one finger over her soft pink skin.

"Good night, Mouse. Sweet dreams." He sent up a silent prayer that he featured heavily in those dreams.

Tank waited until she got inside her house and he heard the

dead bolt slide into place, then he walked back to his car, trying to grapple with all the new emotions flowing through him.

Climbing behind the steering wheel, he started the car, heading in the direction of his condo. He was decidedly grumpy and horny…until his brain kicked in, and he realized that while she might have pushed him away in the end, initially—and for several minutes—she'd kissed him back.

Which meant he wasn't the only one struggling from this unexpected attraction.

Yeah, he thought.

I can work with that.

CHAPTER SIX

MCKENNA SCROLLED through the team's Facebook page, making sure all her posts for today went live and perusing the comments from fans, particularly the ones on the posts that showed her and Tank together at the gala.

It had been less than a week since the black-tie affair. Just six days since Tank had walked her to her door and kissed her to within an inch of her life.

McKenna still wasn't sure how she'd managed to pull away from him, because God knew that was NOT what her body wanted. After saying goodbye and locking the door, McKenna had gone straight to her bedroom, stripped off her dress, and given herself four orgasms in a row with her new best friend— her vibrator.

Every single one of those orgasms had left her trembling and wrung out, with Tank's name on her lips and his handsome face behind her closed eyes.

Jesus H.

She was in serious trouble here.

Because lines that should be crisp and crystal clear were now blurry as hell.

Tank Phillips was literally the last man on the planet she

should be thinking of beyond a professional working relationship.

The guy checked off every single one of the boxes in her "avoid like the plague" category.

He was a swaggering, cocky hockey player. That's a big hell no.

They worked together. Another hell no.

And the word commitment wasn't even in his vocabulary. Put a big *fuck no* next to that bullet.

So why—WHY—was he consuming her waking thoughts and monopolizing her dreams?

She'd nearly let him kiss her on the dance floor…in front of God and everybody at the gala. She'd spent months regaining control of her life, setting reasonable career and relationships goals that wouldn't leave her with another broken heart, and building her confidence back brick by brick.

Tank didn't fit into any of that. Even worse was, she knew all too well he could destroy what she'd found here.

This was her job, dammit, and she refused to screw it up. She was still too new, with only ten months behind her. She'd worked her ass off during that time to prove that Benny had been right to hire her, that she was more than capable of doing the job.

Her attention shifted from the computer screen to her phone, which was propped up on a PopSocket, Tank's voice coming through the speaker. He was currently doing an interview with a popular sports podcaster, something she'd set up during the early days of his reputation rehabilitation.

Tank was killing it, though she wasn't surprised by that. He'd been playing by all the rules she and Benny and Roger had laid down for him right after that video went viral.

In the past, she typically held her breath during Tank's interviews and press conferences, because he had a habit of saying the first thing that popped into his head rather than giving the appropriate responses the rest of the guys were so adept at wielding. He'd pissed off opponents from other teams—as well as some of his own teammates—with his hard-hitting comments about dirty plays, tough losses, and bad calls.

Today, however, he was nailing it.

Ten out of ten, chef's kiss perfection.

Of course, the second she thought that, the interviewer strayed from the approved list of questions.

"It's been just over a month since a video featuring you went viral."

"Five weeks," Tank said, his tone just as smooth as it had been throughout this conversation.

"The video, which featured you and two women standing outside during a fire alarm at a hotel, caused quite a scandal, as you were all under the influence, underdressed, and one woman was wearing handcuffs." The interviewer chuckled, as if amused by his own words.

Tank, uncharacteristically, remained silent.

The interviewer continued smugly. "The fallout from that video caused you to be suspended from play for two weeks."

Tank paused for another moment, then asked, "Is there a question somewhere in this recap?"

The interviewer sounded less amused when he said, "We're nearing the end of the season, and the Stingrays are going to have to fight hard if they want to secure a spot in the playoffs. You're one of the team's top scorers, and there are a lot of fans who believe the Rays would be in a better position now if you hadn't been sidelined for those six games."

McKenna growled. The podcaster had promised her the interview wouldn't stray into anything personal, as his listeners were more interested in hearing their favorite players talk about the sport. But obviously, he'd been playing the semantics game.

More silence met the interviewer, until Tank cleared his throat. "Still not hearing a question, Chuck."

McKenna could practically hear the smirk in Tank's voice, and she loved it. "Make the fucker work for it," she muttered.

"Do the Rays fans need to be concerned about your…er… extracurriculars keeping you off the ice again this season?"

McKenna held her breath, waiting for Tank's response.

"No, they don't. As I said in the press conference immediately following the release of that video, I regret my actions that night, because I not only let myself down but my team and the fans, as well."

McKenna blew out a long, slow breath because his response had been good. Very good.

She sent up a silent prayer that the conversation ended there, but…it didn't.

And this time, Chuck, the fucker, didn't even bother couching his personal question in with game talk. "Could that be because there's a new woman on the scene?"

Tank didn't miss a beat this time. "Do you really think the listeners care about who I'm dating?"

It was a good answer, but McKenna could tell the interviewer took that response as confirmation there was someone new. "Sources report that your date for the Stingrays Foundation gala last week, McKenna Bailey, is the same woman you've been seen with on several occasions in the past few weeks."

"McKenna works in the Stingrays organization. We're friends."

"Those who attended the Stingrays Foundation gala seemed to think the two of you looked like more than friends."

McKenna made a mental note to blacklist Chuck's podcast.

"Didn't realize you were such a big fan of gossip, Chuck." Tank's tone was smooth as butter.

There was a pause for a moment, and McKenna expected Chuck to be the one to break it.

She groaned when Tank did.

"Listen, I've known McKenna for almost a year. She spends a lot of time with me and my teammates, even traveling with us when we're on the road. We've become good friends. She's bright and funny. When all the stuff with the video went down,

McKenna was the one I turned to for advice because I trust her. I'm not going to lie, I was feeling pretty low during that two-week suspension. The only thing that made it tolerable was McKenna. She's smart and compassionate and she helped me through a very rocky time."

He trusted her?

Chuck accepted that response, mercifully changing the subject, he and Tank talking about the upcoming game. McKenna listened with half an ear, her mind whirling over all of Tank's comments about her.

He *trusted* her?

The fact that she was starting to trust him, as well, sent her heart racing, her breath growing shallow, until she forced herself to do some deep breathing exercises to calm down.

Turning back to her computer, she stared at the screen, struggling to recall what she'd been doing.

Not that it mattered. Because twenty minutes after the podcast was over, Benny showed up in her office with Roger on his heels. They shut the door behind them—something they never did.

"Is everything okay?" she asked nervously. She was still new enough in her job that she couldn't help but worry she'd be out on her ass after any misstep.

Benny raked a hand through his hair, a sure sign he was uncomfortable.

What the hell did she do?

She started frantically going through the past few days in her head, trying to figure out what she could have messed up.

"That podcast was great," Benny exclaimed, walking in and sitting in a chair across from her desk. Roger followed suit, claiming the second seat.

She nodded. "Yeah. Tank did well. Though I'm not happy with Chuck. I made it very clear he wasn't to mention the viral video, and he agreed."

Benny shrugged, seemingly unconcerned about Chuck

straying from the script. "Tank held the line, sounded contrite for his actions. It feels like Chuck helped further our cause, because it reinforced what was said in the initial press conference."

McKenna could see that point, but she was still pissed, certain if it had been Benny who'd set up the parameters of the interview, rather than a wet-behind-the-ears newbie, Chuck wouldn't have mentioned the video.

She started to relax, assuming Roger and Benny were simply here to rehash the podcast.

"Roger and I were interested in Tank's comments about *you*."

McKenna felt her face flush. Not because Tank had said anything inappropriate but because she couldn't stop thinking about that kiss and the fact he trusted her. "I knew when I went to the gala as his date, people would start wondering who I was. I suppose we should have anticipated that and come up with a canned response. Not that Tank didn't handle it well," she added.

"He handled it very well," Roger agreed.

"And you're right. We should have anticipated questions. I think we assumed you going to all the promo ops and to the gala with him would have been viewed as 'other duties as assigned,'" Benny said, grinning as he finger-quoted one of his favorite phrases. There was a standing joke in the PR department about Benny's love of assigning random tasks that weren't exactly part of a person's job description. Her presence on the road taking photographs fell into that category.

"Tank did a good job clearing that up in the podcast," McKenna said. "He let them know I work here, so—"

"I'm not entirely sure he *did* clear it up," Benny interjected.

McKenna frowned, mentally replaying what Tank had said. Obviously she missed something, and she would have to listen to that part of the interview again.

Roger leaned forward, resting his elbows on his knees. "I've spent the last couple of hours combing through the comments attached to the photos and videos of you and Tank online."

McKenna picked up a pen from her desk, tapping it nervously. She'd read most of those comments as well. "Okay," she said, uncertain where Benny and Roger were going with this conversation.

She'd seen some of the comments from fans about her and Tank making a cute couple, as well as those from women who'd been somewhat cruel about her not being hot enough to keep a guy like Tank interested. McKenna had to admit some of those hurt, but she'd shaken them off and moved on because it wasn't like she was *trying* to keep Tank interested anyway.

Or at least, that's what she was desperately telling herself.

"James was impressed with the two of you at the gala."

McKenna glanced from Roger to Benny, confused by her boss's abrupt change of subject.

"I'm glad." McKenna and Tank had spent a good twenty minutes in conversation with the president of the team and the Stingrays Foundation Director Gigi Romero, the night of the fundraiser. Tank had been his most charming, and she'd been pleased by how well the two of them had managed to work together to entertain sponsors and fans alike.

Benny had assigned her to make sure Tank didn't say anything wrong, so she'd done her best to set him up with safe topics. And the clever man caught every pass she fired at him, taking the puck and slamming it into the net. On top of that, their sense of humors seemed to work in tandem, so they were able to weave funny stories or lob cute one-liners back and forth.

At one point, Gigi had been laughing so hard, she had to grab a napkin from a passing server to wipe tears from her eyes.

"Do you remember when we first started making our plans to salvage Tank's reputation?" Roger asked, once again switching topics.

She was going to get whiplash if they kept this up.

"Yes." It had only been five weeks ago.

"I think it was you who said it would be easier to repair Tank's reputation if he was in a relationship," Roger said.

She thought back. "Yeah. I did say that. But Tank still isn't interested in dating either one of the women in the video. And as far as I know, he's not seeing anyone at the moment."

"What if he *was* in a relationship?" Roger asked.

"Tank doesn't date. He told me that point-blank. He has zero interest in a serious relationship." McKenna had been slightly disappointed—yet unsurprised—when he said he didn't have any plans to change his single playboy status until after he hung up his skates. Of course, she'd wanted to kick her own ass for that feeling. Because she shouldn't give two shits about Tank's relationship status.

"He said he wasn't interested in dating either of the women from the video, and we all agreed that was for the best, but Benny and I were just talking, and we think maybe we should revisit that idea."

She frowned.

Benny leaned back and crossed his arms. "We think Tank should be in a committed relationship."

"With who?" she asked.

Benny leaned back, not answering, while Roger fidgeted with the cuff of his shirt.

"With me?"

"The comments, Mac, about you and Tank," Roger said. "Overall, they're very positive. Lots of people remarking that the two of you make a cute couple, how you seem to be a good influence on him. A steadying one."

McKenna remembered how she'd blushed when she saw that cutest couple hashtag on the mom's video of Tank chasing her around the Pee Wee team's rink. "I've read the comments too, Roger, and there are just as many negative ones."

Roger looked uncomfortable; he obviously knew which ones she was referring to. "There are always going to be haters, people who exist solely to tear others down. But the truth is, there were a lot fewer of those than the positive ones."

McKenna hadn't really kept count or done a tally. Mainly because once she'd read a half dozen of the comments cutting down her appearance, she'd started skimming as a way of preserving her feelings.

"So how would this work?" McKenna wasn't sure why she was pursuing this line of conversation.

"It obviously wouldn't be a real relationship," Benny said. "Hollywood puts together fake romances all the time, either for promotion or buzz or to do exactly what we're attempting to do —repair reputations."

"That's true." She suggested the relationship idea back at the beginning of all this because she was certain it would be the quickest way to clean up Tank's relationship. If she was being completely honest, she still felt that way. The positive promo campaign was a race run in inches. Putting Tank—one of the most popular Stingrays players with the fans—in a relationship would garner a hell of a lot more publicity. And if they controlled the narrative, it would be good promo.

"You know exactly what we're up against here, Mac. And you've proven you're well-versed in how to spin things. Plus, public perception of you is very positive."

"It is?" she asked.

Roger grinned. "You've got a girl-next-door kind of appeal that's going over big with the fans."

She wrinkled her nose because she and Roger had become good enough friends that he knew how much she hated being referred to as sweet.

"If you don't want to do it, Mac, then obviously, the conversation is over," Benny said, reassuring her this would be her decision.

McKenna, unable to turn her marketing brain off, started thinking the situation through. "We'd have to put a romantic spin on it. Especially considering the dust hasn't fully settled on that viral video."

Roger nodded in agreement, and she could practically see him playing through scenarios, the same way she was. "You spend a hell of a lot of time with the team, traveling to away games, so it would be easy to play it off as your friendship blooming into something more after Tank turned to you for advice."

She chewed on her thumb nail as she considered that. Then she did a mental headshake, shocked she was even contemplating taking part in the idea. This was the kind of stuff that happened in books and movies, not in real life. "Is it against the rules for the two of us to date?" she asked, unwilling to do anything—real or fake—that might put her at risk of losing her job.

Benny shook his head. "There's no workplace rule against relationships between players and team management. We've had a few former players marry women who worked in the administrative offices over the years."

"Tish and Bobby." Roger started naming some of those star-crossed lovers from the past. "Dennis and Mina. Evelyn and…" He snapped his fingers, thinking. "Dammit, what was the name of that right winger she eloped with? The guy who was only here one season."

"Rick," Benny replied.

There were times when Benny and Roger reminded her of some old married couple. The two of them had worked together for nearly ten years, and during that time, they'd developed a kind of hive mind. Most of the time, it amused her, but today… today, she couldn't concentrate on anything except the thought of dating—fake dating—Tank.

"You know, it was actually James who planted this relationship seed, though I didn't realize it at the time. He stopped by the office to chat a few days ago, and as we were recapping the gala, he said the two of you made a formidable couple," Benny said.

She frowned. "Formidable?" That didn't sound flattering.

Benny must have heard her tone, because he chuckled. "It wasn't an insult. You calm Tank down, in all the right ways. You know how he usually is, always showboating or swaggering. His behavior at that fall fundraiser was abysmal."

McKenna couldn't argue with that. Between Tank's two dates, the champagne guzzling, and the completely inappropriate dancing, he'd made a memorable—though not positive—impression that night.

Roger grimaced, clearly remembering the same things they were. "This time, though, he was charming and entertaining, and you were the perfect companion. I watched the two of you all night, Mac. You were a well-oiled machine, working well together. I swear, I think more fans and sponsors talked to Tank than any other player. Because for the first time ever, he was approachable and friendly, and having you there helped."

"I got a call from Charles Steele yesterday," Benny added.

McKenna held her breath nervously, concerned. "Tank and I didn't go anywhere near him that night," she said. "I swear. I was very careful to keep them apart." She'd intended to give a wide berth to Lara as well, but the woman had cornered her before McKenna realized she was even there.

Benny nodded. "I know, Mac. And while you didn't talk to him, that doesn't mean the man wasn't watching. I think he was counting on Tank to make an ass of himself, and he was ready to pounce when that happened. Instead, Charles begrudgingly admitted he was impressed by Tank's behavior."

She released her breath, her shoulders sagging in relief.

Benny rubbed his chin. "The man is aggravatingly old school. He doesn't have any kids of his own, and Lara's an only child. Apparently, he considers himself the patriarchal head of his family—which means he pulls strings when it comes to marrying off the *women* in his family."

McKenna's eyes narrowed. "I suddenly hate Charles Steele."

Benny's and Roger's quick nods proved they felt the same way. "The guy is a total douchebag, but he's got deep pockets and he's a huge Rays fan. The money Steele Industries contributes to the team is, well…Jesus. It's *significant*. Ticket sales only account for about forty percent of our revenue. The money Charles's business contributes helps bridge the gap so the Rays can compete in terms of players' salaries, arena expenses, and so on."

McKenna knew all this. "I get that."

"It sounds to me like Charles has his eye on some rich, successful businessman he wants Lara to marry."

"Sounds like a merger, not a marriage," she grumbled.

Benny shrugged. "Whatever it is, Tank's putting a wrench in those works, because Lara has set her sights on *him*."

"I'm not sure it's Tank specifically, as much as just a Stingrays star," McKenna amended. "According to my sources, she's also hooked up with a couple other players on the team." Erika had been the one to mention that Blake had taken a few of his infamous "victory laps" with Lara, back before they got together.

"Yeah, I know her type. Regardless… If Tank's off the market, it hopefully takes him off Lara's—and by extension, Charles's—radar."

McKenna supposed that could happen. After all, Lara no longer went anywhere near Blake because he—and Erika—had made it clear, they were a rock-solid couple.

McKenna knew if she said no to this idea, Benny would drop it. But dammit, she was determined to prove she was a team player, someone willing to go the extra mile.

But more than that…she didn't want to say no.

Which was the epitome of stupidity.

"Do we really think this step is necessary? The positive promotion has been working well. I'm not sure we need to go a step farther."

Benny sighed and pulled out his phone. One of Tank's former lovers had decided to get in on the "I slept with a bad boy" action by sharing an older video of the two of them frolicking in a hot tub in Turks and Caicos last summer. The video made the rounds back then, but it hadn't hit the same viral status as the one from a month ago. In the woman's video, she claimed Tank was the best lover she'd ever had, while also insinuating he was hung like a mule. TikTok—fucking piece of shit social media platform—had once again grabbed on and rolled with it.

"It's an old video," she pointed out, aware that didn't make a damn bit of difference.

"It is," Benny agreed, "but this is only going to encourage some women to try harder to catch his attention, and we can't afford to let them. I get that he's been toeing the line, but for how long? The guy's track record doesn't work in his favor, so we need to take him off the market. Now. Show them that he's in a committed relationship, really sell him as head over heels in love."

McKenna wanted to argue with that, but Benny wasn't wrong. "How long would we have to fake it?" she asked.

Benny looked slightly surprised she was going for it. She was tempted to tell him to join the club because she was fucking shocking herself too.

"We've been charged with keeping him in line through the summer, so…"

"So I would fake date Tank Phillips for five months?"

Roger nodded slowly. "I know you weren't a fan of the guy when this all started, but you seem to have gotten over that. It looks like you have fun with each other nowadays. At least, that's what the pictures and videos and you two hanging out when we're on the road suggest."

She couldn't debate that. She and Tank had started to gravitate to each other whenever they were in the same room together. Whether in team meetings or at game nights with their friends or when they were traveling, they were always sitting next to each other.

And if her feelings toward him were just friendly, she

wouldn't hesitate to say no to this suggestion because she had a lot of fun with Tank. But she was struggling to keep her thoughts in the professional realm because the guy didn't just make her horny; he made her…fuck…happy.

Something she hadn't felt in a long time.

Not since Eddie.

And while being happy should be great, it was also terrifying because it was proof she was not in control of her feelings in regard to Tank.

She couldn't go down this road again, and yet, she didn't seem able to stop herself.

She was an idiot, and she was going to pay the price for that.

"What do you say, Mac?" Benny asked, looking like a hopeful puppy dog.

Why couldn't she just hate her boss like most normal people?

"Fine."

"Great! We can start slow, but I think for the next few home games, you should move from the press box to the team's box."

"What?" she exclaimed loudly.

"It's a subtle move, but it would help us start to sell this," Roger explained. "We've got that amazing new intern, Vicki, who needs experience, so I'm going to work with her in the press box, sort of mentor her, while we establish you as Tank's girlfriend."

When she first started working with the team, one of the things she'd incorporated as part of the family-friendly branding was pictures and videos and interviews of the players' family members—mothers, fathers, wives, and girlfriends—all rooting from the team's box during home games. Those posts had become incredibly popular with the fans, consistently getting a high number of likes and comments.

"I really think it's important for me to be in the press box."

Benny shook his head. "I understand that, but let's just give it a few games and then we can revisit."

McKenna sighed, then realized they were putting the cart before the horse. "What if Tank rejects this entire idea?"

The second she asked the question, she hated knowing she'd be disappointed if Tank said no. Because it wouldn't feel like he was rejecting the idea, but *her*.

That thought alone should tell her how NOT over Eddie's betrayal she was, and how much she REALLY needed to stay away from Tank.

She was in deep shit here.

"He won't," Roger said with a certainty McKenna couldn't understand. "The three of us can present it to him on Monday. That'll give you the weekend to really think this over and decide if you want to do it."

"If you change your mind," Benny added, "then we'll figure something else out."

McKenna gnawed on her lower lip, then shook her head. "No. I think I should bring it up with Tank alone."

"We can do it together," Roger insisted. "After all, it was our idea. We're not trying to dump it all on you."

"I know, but I still think it's better if it comes just from me." If he rejected it out of hand, McKenna preferred that happened in private and not in front of her boss and Roger.

"You think you can convince him?" Benny asked.

She shrugged because she didn't have a clue how Tank would reply to this idea.

Benny rubbed his chin. "You know, you'd probably have the best chance of selling this to Tank. The past few weeks have proven that he listens to you and does what you say. That's more than the two of us have ever managed to do in all the years before you arrived."

"And he just said as much in that podcast," Roger added. "Said he trusted you."

"Okay, yeah. Fine," she said. "I'll talk to Tank."

"Wait until Monday, Mac. I still want you to take some time

and think this through. I swear this is not one of my 'other duties as assigned.'" Benny joked, smiling. "You say no, it's no."

"I'll think about it," she promised.

Benny rose. "Well, it's after quitting time, and my husband will kick my ass if I'm late for dinner again this week."

Benny was probably late for dinner ninety-nine percent of the time, but considering he and his spouse of fourteen years were still madly in love, she figured he was always forgiven. "Tell Kyle I said hi."

Roger added his goodbye and the two men walked out together, leaving her alone and trying not to spiral into another panic attack.

Unlike Benny, McKenna didn't have anyone waiting at home to have dinner with her, so she was free to work—and stress out—as late as she wanted.

Turning back to her computer, she intended to schedule posts for the coming week, write copy and edit pictures. She needed to get ahead because she'd be out on the road with the team for the next three days. While she was able to work on planes or buses, she preferred working on her desktop in her office because it was easier and quicker to lay her hands on the files she needed, and the screen was much bigger.

Unfortunately, all she managed to do was stare into space, wondering how in the hell she was going to convince Tank to fake date her.

"You realize quitting time has come and gone."

She looked toward the door, surprised to see Tank leaning on the doorframe.

"What are you doing here?" she asked, glancing at the time on her phone and grimacing. It was nearly seven p.m., which meant she'd just squandered an hour and a half, lost in her thoughts.

"I had a suspicion *you'd* still be here," he admitted.

That wasn't much of a suspicion, because everyone knew she

always worked several hours past quitting time. For one thing, she had a shit ton of work to do, and for another, she was never in a hurry to get back home to an empty house.

"So," Tank said, holding up a bag of takeout. "I brought food. Redeeming me is probably hungry work."

She grinned, her stomach growling as the smell of Thai food wafted through her office. "Redeeming you wouldn't lead to hunger. It would lead to starvation," she joked.

"Very funny, Mouse." Tank crossed the office, reaching into the bag to pull out several containers and popping off the lids. "I wasn't sure what you liked, so I got a variety."

McKenna's mouth watered as he opened containers of Pad Thai, Pad Krapao, Som Tum, green curry, mango sticky rice…

"There's enough here for six people," she exclaimed.

"That's not a problem. I don't cook, so my meal planning usually consists of a huge take-out order, followed by two to three days of leftovers."

McKenna shook her head, then decided that probably wasn't a bad plan. Cooking for one sucked.

"Truthfully, I'm here because I felt like celebrating."

McKenna was confused. "Last night's game with Boston was an honest-to-God spanking, Tank."

He winced. "It really fucking was, but that's not what I'm talking about," he said. "Didn't you listen to that podcast? I killed it."

She had to give praise where it was due, so she nodded. "You really did. Benny and Roger stopped by afterward, and they were impressed. Although Chuck wasn't supposed to bring up the video. You can be damn sure I'm firing off an email first thing in the morning."

Tank shrugged, his signature cocky smirk firmly in place as he sat in the seat Benny had vacated an hour or so earlier, pulling it closer to her desk. "He didn't ask anything I couldn't handle."

McKenna studied the food. While she was hungry, nerves were starting to take over. She debated whether or not she should bring up the fake dating idea now or wait until next week. The idea of stalling was appealing, but she also knew that she wouldn't sleep a wink until she got this over with, too worried about his response.

Tank picked up a fork and the container of Pad Thai, shoveling a huge bite into his mouth before putting it down. He hadn't brought any plates with him, so it looked like they were simply passing the food back and forth. The idea of that didn't bother her like she thought it should. In fact, it felt intimate and…well…like they were dating.

Oh my God, Mac.

Stop.

She reached for the Pad Thai container he just put down, scooping out a big bite for herself.

"You did great," she reiterated, once she managed to swallow the noodles. She put the container back down but didn't pick up another because, apparently, in addition to not sleeping, eating wasn't going to happen, either, until she told him about Benny's plan.

Tank worked his way around the Thai buffet, stealing a bite from everything before he realized she wasn't eating. "Do you like Thai? I didn't think to ask."

"I love it," she said hastily. "It just, um… There's something I wanted to run by you. Well, actually, it was Benny and Roger's idea, or maybe it was mine, but they, uh… I mean we, um…"

Tank put the mango sticky rice down, as well as his fork, leaning back and taking in her face, which was no doubt blood-red. "Must be one hell of an idea. Just spit it out, Mouse. No need to hem and haw with me."

She bit her lower lip, then drew in a deep breath. When she released it, a flurry of words flew out of her mouth. "They-thinkweshouldfakedateuntiltrainingcampstartsbackup."

Tank tilted his head, confused. "They what?"

McKenna took another breath, wishing it would steady her. It didn't. Regardless, she managed to speak more slowly. "They think it would help improve your image if you were in a relationship."

Tank nodded. "Yeah. You said that the morning after the video dropped."

"Right. Well, apparently, because we've been seen together quite a lot, people have remarked that, um…"

"That we're a cute couple?"

She'd never gotten the impression that Tank ever looked at the team's social media, but she'd learned otherwise. He'd been the one to show her the video posted by the Pee Wee hockey mom.

"Yeah," she replied.

Tank grinned. "Chuck obviously thought the same thing."

"It's a crazy idea," she said, ready to put an end to this nonsense. "I'll tell Benny and—"

"Now hold on. I didn't say it was a bad idea. I'm just curious." Tank's eyes twinkled with mischief. "You think you got what it takes to be my girlfriend, Mouse?"

Her nervousness vanished, replaced by a more familiar emotion. She crossed her arms. "I wouldn't be your girlfriend. It would be fake."

"Fake. How does that even work?" he asked.

"We'd just have to be seen together in public, maybe holding hands, and um…" God, McKenna's cheeks were on fire. At this rate, she'd spontaneously combust before they got out of this office.

"And?" he prodded, enjoying her discomfiture way too much.

"And I'd sit in the team's box for the next few games. Probably wear your jersey."

"And?" he repeated.

"And what?"

"Well, if you and Benny and Roger are asking me to take myself off the market for…"

"Five months," she said softly.

"Five months." He blew out a low whistle. "That's a long time."

She rolled her eyes. "Not really," she lied because that was a hell of a long time for her to try to resist this pull she felt toward the sexy hockey star.

"It seems to me that if we're really going to sell it, we'd have to do more than just hold hands. We're not in middle school."

"I'm not having sex with you just because you can't stay out of trouble and keep it in your pants."

Tank threw up his hands. "Whoa, whoa, whoa. Who said anything about sex? Damn, woman, what kind of man do you think I am?"

McKenna tilted her head. "I know very well what kind."

He smirked, giving her the same list he'd rattled off at their original meeting. "Manwhore, playboy, asshole…"

Five weeks ago, she agreed with every single descriptor.

Now…none of them seemed to fit. At least, not quite as well as they had.

She shrugged and returned a cocky grin of her own, refusing to let him get the upper hand. "Why don't you cut to the chase, Tank? Aannnnnd what?" she drawled, tossing his question back at him.

"If we're really going to convince people we're a couple, in addition to the dating, hand-holding, and team box photo ops, we'd have to kiss. And because I'm a PDA kind of guy, it wouldn't be PG and it would be *a lot*. You think you're up to that, Mouse?"

"I've been kissed before, Tank. And it's not like these would be real kisses. They'd just be for show. We'd be like…actors in a movie."

Tank didn't reply to that, but she got the sense he was really considering what she was proposing.

She thought Tank rejecting the idea would be the worst thing. She was wrong.

Because the thought of the two of them kissing—*a lot*—was more than her heart could take.

"Obviously, you can say no," she added hastily, suddenly hoping he'd go that route. "We can't force you to do this. If you'd rather stay the course with the current plan instead of—"

"I'm not saying no. I think this is a great idea."

She frowned, suddenly suspicious. "You do?"

"It's a stroke of genius, really. Who knows? We could become the next Taylor/Travis sensation."

She snorted. "Yeah, I don't think that's going to happen."

"You never know," he replied, his tone softer, more sincere than she was used to hearing from him, as he studied her face.

McKenna wasn't used to any man looking at her like Tank, whose gaze seemed to say she was pretty. But more than that... she mattered.

Which was a ridiculous *and* precarious thought.

Because he couldn't really be thinking that.

Could he?

The moment lingered, steeped in something too dangerous as the two of them looked deeply into each other's eyes.

McKenna managed to break the connection, but only just. A huge part of her wanted to dramatically clear the top of her desk, crawl over it, and kiss the hell out of the man.

She hastily picked the Pad Thai back up and shoveled a huge helping of the spicy noodles into her mouth.

"How soon does Benny think we should launch TanKenna?"

She covered her mouth, trying not to spit out the food as she laughed. When she finally managed to swallow, she said, "That's a horrible portmanteau."

Tank chuckled. "I didn't know there was a word for that, but I still like it."

"We're not using that." McKenna paused. "You're really willing to do this?"

Tank studied her face for a moment. "Why would you think I wouldn't?"

"Because we haven't given the positive promotion time to work. Because people have short attention spans, which means Padraig is right, 'this too shall pass.' And because I'm…uh…"

"Not my usual type."

She shot him a look. "If by that you mean a giggly, shallow, ditzy puck bunny, then yeah."

Tank laughed loudly. "Man, you don't think much of me, do you?"

She wasn't sure how to answer that. If he'd asked that question pre-viral video, she would have said she didn't. Because the guy had been a strutting narcissist with an overweening sense of self. But nowadays, he'd revealed there was more to him than she realized.

"I think you're a good guy, Tank, when you put away the Hockey God and act like yourself."

Tank grinned. "You think 'myself,'" he finger-quoted, "is a good guy?"

She nodded, slightly amazed by how happy her response seemed to make him. Since when did Tank care what she thought of him?

"So when are we starting this thing?" he asked again.

She sighed. "I'm sitting in the team box at tomorrow's game."

"Okay. You can borrow one of my jerseys."

She brushed off the offer. "I'm sure Benny will grab me a new one from the shop. One that fits."

Tank frowned. "No. I'd rather my *girlfriend* wear one of mine."

"I'll swim in it," she pointed out, not bothering to comment on his use of the term "girlfriend" because she liked the sound of it way more than she should.

"You'll look adorable in it." Apparently, Tank had decided things were settled, because he started repacking the food in the bag. He handed her the Pad Thai, clearly noticing that had been her favorite. "I'll leave that with you. You didn't eat enough."

Tank had eaten a lot—the man could freaking *eat*—but there was still a ton of leftovers.

"Sounds like you and I need to start planning some dates."

"Fake dates," she said, compelled to correct him. She needed that descriptor to help her keep her head in the game.

"What are you doing next Thursday night?"

She opened her calendar on her computer. "There's no game that night, so I'll probably curl up on the couch in my pj's and catch up on all my shows. I'm painfully behind on *Below Deck*, and I haven't even started the new *Bridgerton* yet."

"Think I could convince you to change your plans?"

"It depends. It would have to be a pretty good offer. I love *Bridgerton*."

Tank chuckled. "Padraig let me in on a little secret. His cousin Ailis is home.

"Ooookay," she drawled, because she didn't remember who Ailis was.

"She's the cousin who's married to Hunter Maxwell. I told you about her, remember?"

The light went on, and she nodded.

"Hunter's planning to do an impromptu performance at Pat's Pub. They're closing the pub to the public. The performance is invite-only. I scored an invitation for me and my plus one."

"You convinced me," she said excitedly. "Holy shit! I love Hunter Maxwell so much."

Tank stood, moving around her desk and giving her a scowl that looked out of place on his face. "I'm starting to think I might be a jealous boyfriend."

"Ha ha. Very funny."

"Am I laughing?" he asked, far too seriously. Then he leaned forward and brushed a strand of hair from her face. "Looks like I'm gonna have to stake a strong claim."

"This isn't real," she whispered, when he gripped her upper

arms, pulling her out of her chair, before perching her on the edge of her desk. It should be scary how strong he was, how easily he could move her where he wanted.

It wasn't.

"Then you can call this practice instead," he murmured, his lips a mere inch from hers.

Like the kiss after the gala, Tank took her lips with a passion McKenna never knew existed outside of romance novels. He wrapped his arms around her back, his large hands stroking up and down her spine, before looping her ponytail around a fist and giving it a tug.

That pull found a direct line to her nipples and her pussy, both reacting strongly.

McKenna gripped his waist, her fingers digging into his sides as she sought purchase, desperate for something to anchor herself. She went light-headed as the kiss dragged on, but air was no longer a necessity. All she needed to survive were his lips on hers and his arms around her, holding her, touching her.

All she needed?

McKenna broke away, gasping, trying to regain her breath. She didn't need a mirror to know she was flushed, the temperature in her office skyrocketing.

She wanted to congratulate herself on finding the strength to pull away, but she couldn't. Because now, just like the night of the gala, she'd left it too long, letting the kiss linger for minutes, not seconds.

"This isn't real," she said again.

Tank considered that for only a second before calling her out. "Are you saying that to me or to you?"

She opened her mouth, but no reply came.

Tank didn't bother to wait for her answer, giving her a knowing grin that was just as hot as all his other grins and smirks and smiles.

Why did he have to be so damn hot?

As if he could read every single one of her chaotic, out-of-control thoughts, Tank winked, grabbed his leftovers, and walked out of her office.

"This isn't real," she whispered to the empty room, even though he wasn't there to hear it.

Because she knew exactly which one of them needed that reminder.

If only it would sink in.

CHAPTER SEVEN

TANK TWIRLED McKenna on the sidewalk outside Pat's Pub as she giggled, her auburn hair spinning around her shoulders. God, he loved when she wore her hair down.

The woman had been smiling ever since he picked her up several hours earlier for Hunter's secret concert. Her cheeks had to hurt by now.

Not that he was going to ask.

McKenna was a very sweet, very pleasant, but *very* serious woman. Of course, he'd seen her smile plenty times over the past nine months, but he'd never seen her this…well, uninhibited and happy. She radiated pure joy.

"That was incredible!" she gushed, saying the same thing she'd said no less than a hundred times tonight.

Tank was thrilled he could show her such a good time, but he hadn't lied about his newly discovered jealous streak. He was suddenly greedy about McKenna's blushes, wanting her to save them all for him. So he'd felt his eyes turning green when Padraig introduced her to Hunter after the show, and she'd blushed and stammered and looked adorably awestruck.

Tank wasn't sure what to do with the misplaced anger he'd

felt toward Hunter, who'd been standing next to the wife he clearly adored at the time.

Maybe this emotion wouldn't be so strong if he'd had any experience with it in the past, but he'd never had a girlfriend. When he looked back, it occurred to him, that meant he'd also never been in love.

Funny how he'd never considered that a problem.

McKenna's first impression of him hadn't really been the wrong one, and now, he found himself wondering if his emotional growth had been somehow stunted or delayed due to finding success as such a young age.

Tank's hockey career had taken off when he was in his late teens, as his hard work and natural talent got him drafted by New York when he was just nineteen years old. Two years later, he was traded to the Stingrays, and he'd been one of their top scorers ever since.

All of that meant he'd been handed the life most little boys dream of and write down whenever their elementary school teachers ask them what they want to be when they grow up.

At nineteen, he'd been there, playing professionally, earning a fuck-ton of money, and having beautiful women throwing themselves at him night after night. It's no wonder it all went to his head.

However, his attitude had been slowly changing during this season, though he wasn't sure why. Maybe it was a combination of things.

For one, several of his best friends had fallen in love and settled down. He'd tried to dissuade Blake from taking himself off the market at the beginning of his relationship with Erika, telling him he was making a mistake, wasting some of the best years of his life by shacking up with just one woman. In the end, it felt like Blake had schooled *him*, because Tank was certain he'd never been as happy in his entire life as his buddy was right now. Blake was still living the dream, playing the game they loved and making bank, but he also had…

Shit, he also had stuff Tank never thought he wanted until Blake got it.

Stuff like someone to go home to every night. Someone to celebrate his wins and help him mourn the losses. Someone to adopt a puppy with, laugh with, tell all his secrets to.

Blake had opened Tank's eyes to new possibilities, and Coulton and Preston had reinforced the lesson. Preston, the new father, had even expanded on it…as, for the first time in his life, Tank realized that he wanted kids. That revelation had blown his mind, even shaken him for a bit, but there was no denying that every time he saw Preston with Lennon in his arms, Tank longed for something he'd sworn he wouldn't even think about before retiring from the game. Now…that felt like too far away.

And while Tank could shift all the blame for this new attitude toward life to his buddies, he also knew a lot of the changes he was undergoing were due to stupid decisions he'd made. He had gotten too cocky, too conceited and overconfident. Tank had been taking too many things for granted—his career at the top of that list—prior to that viral video, by partying too hard, drawing too much negative attention, and speaking his mind when it would have been better to shut up.

Originally, he'd approached McKenna's reputation repair as a hoop he had to jump through. He figured he'd play his part, get it over with, and move on with his footloose and fancy-free lifestyle. Then he started spending time with her, McKenna becoming—unbeknownst to her—his first female friend. Or at least the first who wasn't also the girlfriend of one of his buddies.

Suddenly, he started to understand Blake, Preston, and Coulton better, because he saw firsthand how much fun it could be to spend time with an intelligent, sweet, funny woman. And as the days progressed, he found himself wanting her to like *him* as much as he was starting to like *her*.

"It's been a great couple of days. First, last night's blowout," McKenna said, "and now tonight."

Tank grinned, because it *had* been great. Last night, the Rays had pulled off an upset, kicking number-one ranked Edmonton's ass to the curb in a four-zero shutout. Tank had contributed one of those goals, assisting on two of the others.

Though you wouldn't have known that, given the way Coach Fields continued to ride his ass. The man had been holding some sort of fucking grudge against him for the past couple of weeks. The other guys had even noticed, Victor pulling him aside a couple days ago to ask what the fuck he'd done to piss Dean off.

Tank didn't have a clue, unless Coach Fields wasn't as chill about the video as Tank had initially thought. But that didn't make a lot of sense, when Coach had admitted to him shortly after summer that he'd been just as wild as Tank in his younger days.

He wrapped his arm around McKenna's shoulders as they walked down the sidewalk. He'd spotted the paparazzi the second they left the pub. He wasn't surprised to find them there. No doubt word had gotten out that Hunter would be performing, so they'd swarmed.

Pat's Pub was no stranger to the press, however, so they'd enlisted the help of the police, who'd set up a perimeter, and also hired security to help maintain it.

"Hey, Tank!" one of the cameramen yelled.

Tank didn't acknowledge the guy but decided to take advantage of the free publicity. He pressed an affectionate kiss to the top of McKenna's head. She glanced at him, and he winked. "Smile at me like I hang the moon, Mouse, and we'll make the front page tomorrow."

It proved just how happy McKenna was that she laughed at his joke rather than remind him again that this relationship of theirs was just pretend.

Benny's suggestion that the two of them "fake date" proved just how much of a lucky star Tank lived under. Because he'd gone to her office with the Thai food last week with the intention of asking her out on a *real* date.

Maybe he should have confessed that to her, but he wasn't one to look a gift horse in the mouth. There'd been a chance—probably a very good chance—that McKenna would have rejected his invitation. After all, she'd told him early on that she would never date a hockey player or someone from work, so he was a double whammy.

This way, he got to take her out whenever he wanted to, all under the guise of work.

As far as he was concerned, it was the perfect opportunity for him to show her just how good dating him for real could be. Hopefully, it wouldn't take long for her to drop the word "fake" and agree to be his girlfriend.

Tonight was the first time they'd gone out in public together, though they'd planted the seeds of a budding relationship in other ways. Like her sitting in the team's box, front and center with the other girlfriends and wives, wearing his jersey. They'd also continued eating together—alone—whenever they were on the road. And he'd picked her up this past weekend to take her to the game night that Blake and Erika hosted at their apartment. He sat beside her the entire evening, arm loosely draped across the back of the couch so he could play with her ponytail.

Tank had gotten McKenna to agree to keep the true nature of their fake relationship a secret from their friends, convincing her there was a higher chance of discovery if too many people were let in on the ruse. Or at least, that's what he told her. In truth, he wanted everyone to think they were an item because if he got *his* way, they would be soon enough. As such, he figured there was no reason to confuse their friends.

When they reached his car, Tank opened the passenger door for her, the sound of cameras clicking in the background. The paparazzi were taking full advantage of tonight's A-list of Baltimore's who's who. He suspected Blake and Erika, along with Preston and Chelsea, who'd all left earlier, had also been photographed.

Unable to resist, Tank cupped her cheek, giving her a quick kiss before she climbed into the car.

"Milking it, aren't you?" she murmured, though the twinkle in her eyes told him that wasn't a complaint.

"Gotta strike while the iron's hot."

Closing her door, he crossed in front of the hood, giving the paparazzi a quick wave before sliding behind the steering wheel and heading off in the direction of her townhouse.

Dark clouds had rolled in during the time they were in the pub, the forecast warning of some nasty storms tonight. When he arrived on McKenna's street, he drove two full blocks away from her place before finding a spot. Once again, McKenna had insisted he could just drop her off, but he refused. He wanted to walk her to the door. Not only to ensure she got in safely but also because he fully intended to steal another kiss.

However, they'd only made it ten feet from his car before the skies opened up.

"Holy shit!" McKenna exclaimed, as the two of them took off running toward her house.

By the time, she got the door unlocked and they raced inside, they were both soaked to the skin and laughing their asses off.

"I knew it was going to rain, but that escalated fast," she said, gasping for breath as she pushed wet strands of hair from her eyes.

"You're not kidding. I figured I could at least get home before it unleashed." Tank pulled his wet shirt away from his skin. "That was an insane amount of rain. I don't get this wet in my shower," he joked.

McKenna laughed. "Seriously."

They looked down at the same time when the sound of dripping became evident.

"Shit, Mouse. I'm getting your floor all wet."

"Stay there. I'll grab us both some towels from the bathroom." She quickly left the room, racing upstairs and returning in less than a minute with two fluffy bath towels.

"Thanks," he said, as he took one from her, rubbing his hair before running the towel over his clothing—a fruitless endeavor. Nothing short of wringing his clothes out and putting them in the dryer was going help.

A bright flash of lightning briefly blinded him, immediately followed by a crash of thunder so loud, he swore the house shook.

McKenna jerked, then took a step closer to him. Tank wasn't sure if her response was instinctive or intentional, but he didn't care. He pulled her into his arms, both to offer comfort and warmth, though the second wasn't going to happen as long as they stood there in wet clothing.

The rain pelted against the windows as the wind picked up.

"I didn't think it was possible, but I swear it's coming down harder," she observed, still tucked within his arms, the sound of her voice slightly muffled from where her face was pressed against his chest.

"You're right. You should get out of these wet clothes, Mouse, or you'll get sick."

She lifted her head, though she remained in his arms. "Is that a genuine concern, or are you just trying to get me out of my clothes?"

He chuckled at what he was certain she meant as a joke. The laugh was fake because he'd love to get her out of her clothing. "Is it working?"

McKenna snorted. "Sort of. I'm going to go change. Maybe you should hang out until the rain dies down."

He nodded. "I think that's a good idea. Not keen on going back out in that storm right now."

"I'll grab you that jersey you loaned me," she offered. "It's probably the only thing I have that will fit you."

"That'll be fine."

"I can toss the rest of our clothes in the dryer while we wait for the storm to pass."

Tank watched her walk upstairs, delighted by the way things

had turned out. He'd offered to walk her to her door in the hopes of another kiss. Getting to spend more time with her—while half dressed—was an even better opportunity.

Tank slipped off his shoes and socks, both of which were soaked through, and then used his towel to wipe up the puddles they'd made on the floor.

When she returned, Tank had to take a second to compose himself...because his drenched jeans were too tight to conceal his reaction.

For one thing, he couldn't understand why his cock was reacting so strongly at all, since all she'd done was throw on pajamas. Bright red pajamas covered in Mickey Mouse's smiling face.

Tank grinned, and she shrugged good-naturedly.

"I told you. My mom goes overboard on the Mickey nickname. Like, *way* over."

"I like the pajamas." She probably didn't believe him, but he really did. While she was gone, she'd also pinned her hair up in those Mouseketeer buns on the top of her head, the entire look completely adorable and so her.

As much as he loved her hair down, he was also becoming a huge fan of the buns.

"Here." She offered him the jersey he'd given her last week. At the time, she'd thanked him for letting her borrow it, though Tank had no intention of taking it back. He hadn't lied about wanting to see her in his shirt.

He followed her to her living room, looking around. This was the first time he'd been in her house, never making it beyond the front door. The room looked like McKenna. It was neat and tidy but also screamed of comfort. There were colorful throw pillows on the couch, a soft fleece blanket folded and hanging over the back. There were countless books on the built-in shelves that surrounded her television. Placed amidst the books were keepsakes and photographs. Most were of McKenna and an older woman with auburn hair who looked just like her.

Tank started unbuttoning his shirt, amused by the way McKenna's gaze darted around the room, returning every few seconds to steal a peek. He took his time, giving her a show. While she flushed and tried to pretend she wasn't looking, he stared straight at her, wanting her eyes on him.

Once he peeled the wet shirt off, he glanced around for somewhere to put it down.

McKenna's hand reached out. "I'll take it. My clothes are already in the dryer. I was waiting to grab yours before I started it."

He handed her the shirt, then started to unbutton his jeans.

"What are you doing?" she asked.

"I can't sit here in wet jeans, Mouse."

"Yeah, but…"

"My boxer briefs are still relatively dry."

"Oh. Um…"

"You gonna be able to handle that?" He knew exactly how his question would land. McKenna was very susceptible to his dares, always determined to come off as strong and tough and unflappable. And while she was all those things, that didn't mean he wouldn't push her when it suited his purposes.

She responded just like he knew she would, crossing her arms and giving him an almost bored expression that he didn't buy for a minute. "Of course, I will."

It took a bit of work, getting his drenched jeans off. He pulled his wallet, phone, and car key out of the pockets, tossing them on the coffee table before handing the jeans to her. He hadn't bothered to put the jersey on first, so he was standing before her in nothing but his boxer briefs.

And McKenna, though blushing like a rose, wasn't looking away, her eyes widening slightly when she realized he was sporting an erection.

He considered teasing her, telling her to take a picture, but he liked that gaze on him, liked seeing the effect his body had on her. McKenna was one of those people who wore her heart on her sleeve, her expressions hiding nothing. She was an open book, and he loved reading her.

For a few quiet moments, he merely let her look her fill, amused when—at last—she seemed to realize what she was doing and her gaze flew up to meet his.

"Take your time," he joked.

She narrowed her eyes—goddamn, he loved when she did that—then turned away from him, heading back upstairs for the third time. He listened to her progress, hearing the dryer door close before she turned it on.

Tank considered remaining in just his briefs, not bothering with the jersey, but he changed his mind because the rain had been a cold one and he was chilly.

Drawing the jersey over his head, he plopped down onto her plush couch, smiling when McKenna returned and claimed the other end, curling her feet beneath her.

She only remained there a second before she popped up again. She was clearly nervous. "Do you want something to drink? I can make coffee or tea. I also have water and half a bottle of red wine."

Tank gestured for her to resume her seat. "I'm fine, girlfriend."

"This is just for work," she reminded him, as she sat back down. "Because as you know, I don't date hockey players or coworkers."

"Why not?"

She'd made that comment before, but he'd never questioned her reasons. Now, he could see that was a mistake. Because whatever her reasons, they were the roadblocks to his end goal— and he needed to find a way to knock them down.

"I told you that I've only had three boyfriends."

He nodded. "The guy from high school and the asshole in college. You never got around to filling me in on bachelor number three."

"Eddie was the last man I dated. I met him shortly after I started my first job."

"The one at Pete's Sporting Goods," he said.

"Yeah. Eddie is Pete's son, actually. He came by to introduce himself on my second day at work and we just sort of clicked. Two weeks later, he asked me out on a date. By then, I'd learned from my other coworkers that he was well-liked by everyone. The woman I shared an office with said he was a super-nice guy, and that more than a few of the females in the office had been trying to catch his attention. I think she'd been one of them, because she was a bit chillier toward me after Eddie asked me out."

"Was it a good date?"

"It was a great date. One that led to another and another and before I knew it, we were in a serious relationship, spending every night together, either at his apartment or mine. For one year, it was complete bliss. And then…"

"Then?" he asked.

"Then, the company hired a new receptionist."

Tank growled, because he knew how this story was going to end.

"Lisa was tall and blonde and curvy—all the right measurements," McKenna said with a grimace. "She wasn't vertically challenged like me."

Tank smiled at her attempt at a joke, though it was forced, because the woman she'd just described could have been Lara.

"Several times I walked by and would see him standing near the front desk, talking to her. At first I thought he was just being friendly, because that's his personality. After a few times too many, I asked him about her. He said she was struggling with a couple aspects of the job, and he was helping her. I bought that… for a while. Then, I found out they went to lunch together one day. I confronted him, and he said she was new in town and lonely and he was trying to cheer her up.

"Every time I questioned something, he had an answer,

spoken in a way that made me feel like I was being unreasonably jealous. Something I was sensitive about, given Dale's insane jealousy. Eddie's comments sort of made me feel like I was the Dale in our relationship, and I hated it."

"He was gaslighting you," Tank said angrily.

McKenna touched her nose, indicating he'd gotten it in one. "Thing is, I kept buying his answers. I wanted them to be true because I thought he was *the one*," she said. "I figured we'd live together for a couple years, get engaged, then married, then have kids. The whole shebang."

"That's what you want?"

She nodded. "More than anything."

Three months ago, Tank would have scoffed at anyone in their twenties wanting to tie themselves to one person for the rest of their lives. The twenties were for sowing wild oats, living life to the fullest. Marriage and kids were what you did when you got too old to have fun.

Now, though, the idea of McKenna wearing his wedding ring, her stomach round with their baby was...

Tank froze, his brain locked on that image.

And it locked *hard*.

He didn't even try to dismiss it or call himself an idiot or anything, because now that he'd seen it...

He wanted it.

Her.

Them.

"Finally, a colleague at work, an older woman I respected, pulled me aside and said it was time to open my eyes. Apparently, everyone at the company knew he was having an affair with Lisa. The woman said I was too good of a person to let a man cheat on me. It was hard to hear, but I was grateful to her for saying it. I confronted Eddie. He accused me of being jealous. Said he couldn't be with someone who was always so suspicious, and we broke things off."

"So he continued to deny it. What an asshole," Tank grumbled. "Good riddance."

McKenna nodded in agreement. "He couldn't deny it for long, because within six months, he was engaged to Lisa. I'd started looking for a new job a couple months after we split, but I wasn't having much luck finding one that paid as well. I had to cover my rent and living expenses. In the end, I stopped looking in Columbus. I decided I needed to completely clean the slate—and not just at work but a total overhaul. I applied for the job with the Stingrays, got it, and moved to Baltimore."

"So it's a happy ending."

"Yeah," she said. "I love it here. Which is why I won't do anything that'll risk what I've found—a great job, new friends, cool townhouse with sweet neighbors."

McKenna hadn't just thrown a roadblock in his path. She'd erected an entire fortress.

Awesome.

She tucked her legs under herself once more, and he could see she was cold. He used that observation to his advantage, sliding closer to her.

"You look like your mom," he observed, nodding toward the photos on the shelves, changing the subject to something less painful—for her *and* himself.

McKenna glanced over. "She calls me her mini-me. I've seen pictures of her when she was my age and it's kind of uncanny. How about you? You take after your mom or your dad?"

"Looks-wise? I'm actually a pretty good blend. Got my dad's hair color and complexion, my mom's eyes and nose—thank God."

McKenna laughed. "And personality-wise?"

Tank shrugged. In a lot of ways, he took after his dad—they were both competitive and ambitious, and they both possessed more than their fair share of arrogance—but it didn't bring Tank much joy to admit that. He and his dad had been estranged ever since his mom—who had been the glue—

passed away. "Another blend," he said, hedging. "Got my dad's drive to succeed, my mom's sense of humor. How about you?"

"I am *nothing* like my mother. She always joked that if not for our identical looks, she would have taken me back to the hospital years ago, certain they'd sent her home with the wrong baby."

Tank shifted slightly on the couch, closing the distance between them even more. He felt a bit ridiculous sitting in a jersey and boxers. Or at least, he did until McKenna's gaze lowered, taking in his muscular legs. Resting his arm along the back of the couch, he brushed his fingers along the side of her neck, enjoying the way she shivered.

He half expected her to call him out for his intimate touch, so he was pleasantly surprised when she didn't. Instead, she did one better, shifting toward him another inch or two, so that her knee rested against his thigh.

"Are you cold?" she asked, gesturing toward the fleece blanket hanging on the couch. "The windows in the townhouse are as old as the place is, so it tends to be drafty in here, no matter what time of year."

Tank didn't answer but reached around her, grabbing the blanket and flipping it open, then covering both of their laps. "We can share heat this way."

McKenna's teeth tugged on her lower lip, but again, she didn't reject his offer.

Tank had just decided to push his luck and go for broke, leaning toward her for a kiss, when another bright flash of lightning lit up the room before there was a crash outside and a fizzling sound that caused the lamps to flicker and go out.

They waited a good fifteen seconds, but the lights remained off.

"Damn," McKenna said, jumping from the couch. "Power's out."

Tank rose as well, grabbing his phone from the coffee table at the same time she reached for hers, both of them clicking on the flashlight app.

McKenna opened the single drawer in one of the end tables, rummaging around until she found a lighter. He watched as she made her way around the living room, lighting at least half a dozen candles he hadn't even noticed until that moment.

"Fan of candles?" he asked.

"Love them," she admitted, lighting the last. "Especially scented ones. I try to match smells with the holidays or seasons."

"What does March smell like?"

"March is a tough one. It's straddling the line between end of winter and beginning of spring. Since it also marks the end of the hockey season, which I'm discovering is a stressful time, I went for lavender because it's a soothing smell and is supposed to promote relaxation."

"Might have to hit the store tomorrow for some lavender candles because you're right, this month is a killer."

Once she finished lighting her candles, they returned to the couch, and he tucked them back under the blanket. This time, he didn't bother with personal space, wrapping his arm around her and holding her close.

McKenna stiffened briefly, then—thank God for lavender— she relaxed against him, even going so far as to rest her head on his shoulder.

The rain was still pouring outside, the storm raging. Tank wouldn't mind a flood if it meant he could stay here with her, just like this.

"Why didn't you go home for the holidays?" McKenna asked. "You're from Buffalo, right?"

He nodded.

"That's not a terrible drive, is it?" she asked.

"Little more than six hours. I didn't bother because Christmas isn't the same without my mom," he said, shocking himself by admitting that aloud. He hadn't talked about his mom since…

Tank sighed. Since her funeral.

It hurt too much.

However, now, as he sat in McKenna's cozy living room, he was reminded of his mother, who was also a fan of candles and fleece blankets, and who decorated their entire home with framed family photographs. He realized none of those things were that unusual, but it had been a long time since he'd hung out in a living room that wasn't his own, which was sparsely decorated and, yes, a pigsty. Or in a friend's, which was always filled with other people, all playing games or watching sports on TV.

McKenna turned, her face close to his, her gaze filled with empathy. "She made the holidays nice?"

He smiled sadly. "The best. She loved to bake, so the house always smelled like bread or sugar cookies or turkey. She decorated every inch of the place, the couch covered in at least a dozen holiday pillows, mistletoe hanging in every doorway, and lights strung pretty much everywhere. She started playing Christmas music in November and kept it rolling right through the New Year."

"Oh my God," McKenna exclaimed. "That sounds incredible."

"She also broke the bank on gifts because she had a memory like a steel trap. I could mention liking or wanting or needing something in February, and I swear the next Christmas, it was wrapped and under the tree. It took us ages to open all the gifts on Christmas morning."

Tank chuckled, recalling the mountain of presents that always awaited him and his dad when they came downstairs Christmas morning. Then, he recalled with a bit of guilt how small Mom's pile had always been in comparison. Not that she ever complained. She always swore she preferred seeing them open gifts over receiving anything for herself.

"God," he breathed. "I haven't thought about all this since..." Tank waited for the pain that accompanied any memory of his mother to strike. Strangely, it didn't. Instead, it felt nice to talk about her. "She was the best mom in the world."

McKenna reached out and grasped his hand, squeezing it. She didn't say anything. Her smile and kind eyes were enough.

"How about your holidays?" he asked. "Crazy like ours or low-key?"

"Low-key," McKenna replied. "But still fun. It was just me and my mom, so we didn't fool with cooking a big dinner. We went out every year to a Chinese restaurant. My mom loves the movie *A Christmas Story*, so she adopted that tradition when I was in elementary school. We always went to the same restaurant, and the family that ran it, the Changs, got to know us. By the time I was in high school, it felt like we were going to a relative's house for the holiday meal. We even started taking them gifts, and Mrs. Chang always sent us home with a tin of her almond cookies. Mom and I used to fight over them, they were so good."

"Sounds like fun."

McKenna nodded. "It was. We're an open-presents-on-Christmas-Eve family, though."

Tank put his other hand over his heart as if struck. "Sacrilege. What about poor Santa?"

"My mom never wanted to lie to me…about anything. So while I got money for lost teeth, candy on Easter, and presents for Christmas, I knew it all came from her."

Tank frowned. "That kind of takes the magic out of it."

McKenna shrugged. "I mean, I was still getting the cash, candy, and gifts. Though, I think I'll do it different with my kids. Because you're right. The magic part would have been fun. How about you? What would you do differently with your kids compared to the way you were raised?"

Tank wasn't sure how to answer that, because he hadn't even considered kids a part of his future until a couple months ago. Then…he realized exactly what he'd do differently. "I wouldn't push my kids into anything they didn't want to do, and I wouldn't give a shit if they were the best at everything."

McKenna frowned, and he sighed.

"Jesus, that came out bitter, didn't it?"

She tilted her head. "Your dad?"

Tank leaned his head on the back cushion of the couch. He never talked about his parents. Ever. Yet tonight, it was as if he couldn't keep the words in. "You know he played hockey, too?"

She nodded.

"He never made it out of the minors. Never got his shot to play professionally. He was thirty-three years old when an injury took him out for good. He holds the distinction of being one of the oldest players to never make it to the NHL, not that he brags about it. That's not one of those records anyone wants to hold."

McKenna grimaced. "Couldn't have been easy to be that close for so long and never make it."

"It wasn't. Which was why he was determined the same thing wouldn't happen to me. He had me on skates three minutes after I learned to walk, and drilling was more important than homework in my house."

Tank tried to temper his tone, but his father's determination to see his son succeed where he'd failed had destroyed any chance that the two of them might've had a close relationship. His father had been more coach than Dad.

"My dad was pissed about not getting his shot, so he turned full-on cliché, living vicariously through me. He took credit for my victories to anyone who would listen. Then, when we got home, he'd diminish and downplay any success I had by reassuring me—*all* the fucking time—that there were at least a thousand other players in the world who were better than me, and that I needed to work harder."

"Jesus," McKenna murmured.

"When I first went pro, my dad was always in the stands, always making sure the cameras found him, so he'd finally hear his name on TV. It used to drive me fucking nuts how he'd give interviews to absolutely anyone, trying to make it sound like we were one of those famous 'hockey father/son duos,' like the Howes or the Hulls or Nylanders or Domis."

"I'm sorry, Tank. That couldn't have been easy for you."

Tank lifted his head from the couch, turning toward her. "I dealt with it through the first season because I always tried to keep peace for my mom's sake, but then she had a stroke and died. Dad and I had it out right after her funeral. A lifetime of hate spewed out of me, and I told him I never wanted to see him at another one of my games."

"You were grieving," McKenna said, as if she thought he felt guilty and needed comforting.

"No. Everything I said to him that day had been bottled up inside me for twenty years. I don't regret saying it because I didn't say anything I didn't mean. My dad is a narcissistic asshole who's never loved anyone more than himself. Mom knew that, but she stayed. For me. I really think her stroke was the result of living with such a hate-filled man. He never hit us with fists, but trust me, words can wound even worse."

McKenna cupped his cheek with her hand, her thumb lightly caressing it. "I'm glad you cut ties with him. He doesn't deserve to have you in his life."

Tank wasn't sure what he'd expected her to say, but it sure as hell wasn't that. "Mouse," he whispered.

For the first time, McKenna initiated the kiss…and damn if hers didn't blow his out of the water. Because this one wasn't driven by horniness or even passion. It was one of caring, compassion, and, while he knew it probably couldn't be—could it?—even love.

Tank had never, not once, felt love in a kiss, but this one sure as hell stirred that emotion inside him.

She broke the union too quickly, and he was about to pull her back toward him when she slipped off her glasses, tossing them to the coffee table before diving in for seconds.

Her hands traveled from his face to his shoulders, gripping

him tighter, and Tank followed suit. All traces of softness and gentleness vanished, giving way to a hunger that was downright ravenous.

The kiss lasted for minutes, hours, days. When they finally needed air, they broke apart, staring deeply into each other's eyes.

He didn't need her to say that she wanted him. He could see it, could read it clear as day.

"You're so beautiful."

She smiled, the look one of genuine happiness. "Always the charmer."

He shook his head because he didn't want her to think that was a line, just him trying to get into her pants. That wasn't what it was. He must have given away his concern, because she cupped one of his cheeks while kissing the other.

"Thank you," she whispered, her breath warm.

Tank drew his lips along her face, down her jaw, to the side of her neck, while McKenna's fingers threaded through his hair.

Keeping his lips on her, he reached under her thighs, tugging until she slipped down to her back. Tank moved over her, caging her beneath him, groaning when she parted her legs and wrapped them around his waist.

This was the single greatest moment of his life, and he knew it.

Now, he just needed to savor it.

And find a way to make it last.

Forever.

CHAPTER EIGHT

MCKENNA TENDED to be the queen of overthinking things, but this moment didn't require thought. For once, she was throwing logic out the window and giving herself over to feelings.

Her mind was definitely going to kick in later and start listing all the reasons why this was wrong, but for now, she didn't care.

Didn't care about being smart or practical or any of those boring things.

For once, she wanted to throw caution to the wind and just... be.

With Tank.

With this sexy, surprisingly dear, and maybe even a little bit broken man.

McKenna closed her eyes as a sound she'd never made in her life—something between a whimper and a moan—came out when Tank sank his teeth into the crook between her neck and shoulder.

She'd had three lovers in the past, and all of them had been gentle, easygoing in bed. She'd thought their touches sweet and romantic, but Jesus, had she been selling herself short. Tank stroked the spot he'd just bitten with his tongue before kissing it all better.

He slipped his hands under her pajama top, roughly yanking her bra down so that he could cup her bare breasts. He pinched and rolled her nipples until she groaned.

"God," she exclaimed, her eyes flying open just in time to catch Tank's too-pleased smirk. The guy was playing her like a violin, and he knew it.

"I like those sounds of yours," he murmured, pinching her nipples again. She whimpered, her pussy clenching in response. Apparently, Tank was well-versed in pressure points, aware that pushing and prodding one part of the body would produce a reaction in another.

Before that moment, McKenna wouldn't have even considered her nipples an erogenous zone. The light kisses and sucks of past lovers had actually bored her.

"Are you going to scream for me, McKenna?"

Two responses popped into her head at his question at the exact same time. One, while she'd never screamed in bed in her life, she was damn sure she was going to for *him*.

And secondly, he'd called her by her name for the first time.

After a lifetime of being Mickey, Mac, Kenny, and Mouse, she couldn't recall the last time someone she was close to using her full name. She liked hearing it from him…a lot.

She'd done more than her fair share of fantasizing about what it would be like to sleep with Tank. The worn-out batteries in her vibrator could attest to that, but she'd paired him with her past sexual experiences and completely missed the boat on what to expect.

Fantasy Tank said silly things while being playful. She'd imagined tickles, soft strokes, even laughter. Probably because that was how they were when they were together. Things were always easy, fun, friendly.

So much for that assumption.

Because the real Tank?

He was a conqueror, the type to take what he wanted without asking or apologizing.

"Answer me, McKenna."

She blinked a few times, fighting to focus and remember the question. When she did, she felt her face grow hot, though not from embarrassment. She'd never been this aroused in her life, and they were both still dressed.

"Yes," she replied, certain if anyone could make her scream during sex, it was Tank.

Pleased by her answer, he lowered his head, kissing her cheek before placing his lips against her ear. "Good girl."

Jesus. H. Christ.

She was a goner.

While she'd had an amazing time with him tonight at the pub, she truly hadn't seen the date ending this way. The entire way home, she'd been debating whether or not it would be wise to let him kiss her good night on her front porch.

Boring McKenna had decided it wouldn't happen.

Thank God that stupid bitch wasn't here right now.

Rising to his knees, Tank reached for her hand, prompting her to sit up as well. "I have no idea where your bedroom is," he said, as he tugged her pajama top over her head. "But I know it's too far away."

McKenna didn't have time to consider his actions before he was tossing not only her shirt but her bra to the floor.

Her hands instinctively rose to cover her breasts. She hadn't even had time to prepare herself mentally for being naked in front of him. While he was a Greek god, all chiseled muscles and no fat, she was leaner, bonier.

Tank grasped her wrists, pulling them away and lifting them so he could kiss her palms. "I don't ever want you to hide from me," he said, lowering her hands to her lap. "I love everything I see."

McKenna knew he was talking about her tits, but the lonely woman, the one whose confidence was still wobbly from the last breakup, wanted to believe he was referring to more than just her body.

Then Tank kissed her again, and every bad, insecure feeling vanished in an instant.

She gave in to instinct, drawing his jersey over his head so she could lean toward him, taste and stroke and even bite. Tank growled when she sank her teeth into his pec, the sound low and guttural and so fucking hot.

"You're going to be my wildcat," he murmured, pushing her to her back once more.

She didn't have time to wrap her head around how much she liked that nickname most of all, before Tank took one of her nipples into his mouth and sucked…hard.

Her back arched as she cried out his name. Her hands found their way to his hair, and she gripped it. It felt as if she was at the very top of the roller coaster about to plummet back to the ground. She was terrified and thrilled at the same time, and she didn't want this ride to end.

Tank played with her breasts for way longer than any of her past lovers, driving her arousal up inch by inch. She wasn't sure why she'd expected him to just get right down to business. Maybe because he seemed to live his life in fast-forward, constantly accelerating from zero to sixty, always pushing things to the limit quickly.

Instead, Tank acted like a man with nothing but time on his hands. Time he intended to use to drive her out of her mind.

She was gasping for air when he finally lifted his head, his chocolate-brown eyes dark with something she'd never seen on a man's face.

Hunger…and a burning desire so powerful it made her dizzy.

"I want you," she whispered, shocked by the admission and then by how true it was.

Tank cupped her cheek. "I want you too."

McKenna had to blink a few times to clear her vision, hating the tears that accompanied his confession. Not that she hated the words. Just the fact that they proved how much Eddie's rejection had knocked her down.

Because despite the way Tank was looking at her as if she hung the moon, she couldn't stop herself from doubting the sincerity of his admission. After all, he could have any woman he wanted.

While it was hard for her to admit, the only real thing tonight would be the sex.

Mercifully, Tank didn't give her too much time to wallow in those negative feelings.

He shifted off the couch, rising to stand beside it.

She started to sit, but he held her down with a strong hand on her shoulder. "Don't move."

McKenna relaxed back into the cushions, drawing in a shaky breath when he slipped his fingers under the elastic of her silly Mickey pajama bottoms. He tugged them and her panties off in one go, drawing them down before tossing them to the floor.

She resisted the urge to cover herself again, closing her hands into fists by her sides. Tank rewarded her efforts with a smile, one finger traveling from the base of her throat, through the valley of her breasts, and over her stomach. It stopped just short of where she really wanted that finger to be.

"Good girl," he murmured again, acknowledging her efforts.

As he turned toward the coffee table, she watched as he opened his wallet and pulled out a condom.

Her body shivered, goose bumps forming. Because they'd reached the moment of truth.

It spoke to her level of trust in this man that she knew if she said stop, he would.

Not that she had any intention of saying that.

As far as she was concerned, the words "stop" and "no" didn't exist in her vocabulary tonight. She wanted everything Tank was willing to give.

Because, while she was too far gone right now, tomorrow she wouldn't be.

Tomorrow, she would tuck this—and any wayward emotions—into the proper box, before locking it away.

This was going to be a one-night stand.

Her first.

Of course, when Tank shoved his boxers down, adding them to the pile of clothing on the floor, she reconsidered…briefly.

Because *holy shit*.

"Um," she whispered, taking in his long, thick cock. For a fleeting moment, McKenna chastised herself for being a reckless fool because that model in the hot tub, the one from Turks and Caicos, had warned her—and every other woman in the world—that he was hung like a mule.

Tank sank down on the side of the couch, his bare ass pressing against her hip.

His smirk was back, but it didn't bug her anymore like it used to. If anything, it lightened the moment and, yes, while she wasn't proud of it, that smirk dared her, just as he intended it to.

The man had become too adept at reading her thoughts and responding in exactly the way she needed.

"Touch me," he demanded, twisting his hips so she knew without words where he wanted her hands.

She grasped his cock without hesitance. Just as she knew he'd stop, she also knew he wouldn't hurt her, and that gave her the freedom to explore without fear.

The way Tank groaned low in his throat encouraged her to tighten her grip, to stroke him from root to tip, up and down. Precome beaded on the head of his dick, and she started to lift, curious, wanting to taste.

Tank's hand landed on her shoulder again, pressing her down.

"You use that pretty mouth on me and this ends way too fast," he said, his admission making her ridiculously happy. She'd never questioned Tank's ability to make her come hard and fast. It might not have happened yet, but she didn't doubt for a second he was going to give her the best orgasm of her life.

However, the thought that she might be able to drive him out of his mind as well was a heady one. Because, unlike her and her pitiful sexual history, Tank had taken many lovers to bed—probably all gorgeous and well-versed.

McKenna squeezed her legs together, her pussy reminding her that it was still there and waiting none too patiently. "I want you," she said again. Those seemed to be the only words her hormone-drowned brain could think to say.

Tank tore open the condom wrapper. He pulled the condom free and started to roll it onto his cock, but McKenna took over quickly, finishing the task for him as he murmured praise under his breath.

From there, things moved both quickly and in slow motion.

Tank resumed his place above her as she parted her thighs, linking her ankles at the small of his back when he lowered his hips.

He gripped his dick, guiding it to her pussy. She gasped when the head of it brushed her clit. She expected him to put it inside her, so she was surprised when he let go, letting it ride high against his stomach, resting between them.

"Let me hear you gasp again," he said as he stroked her clit, getting exactly what he asked for.

He smiled, but it wasn't a cocky or self-satisfied one. Instead, he looked like a little boy who'd just gotten a puppy for Christmas.

"Beautiful," he murmured, and for the first time, she was genuinely starting to believe he meant that.

Tank pushed two thick fingers into her embarrassingly wet pussy, and her eyes drifted shut, her body flashing and sparking as if she was made of electricity.

"Fuck," he muttered. "You feel so good, Mouse. Tight and wet and perfect."

Her hips began to rise and fall in time with his fingers, which were moving faster, deeper. When his thumb grazed her clit, she jerked as she came.

She hadn't realized just how close she was.

Tank withdrew his fingers instantly, despite her crying out. He'd stopped too soon, leaving her pussy quivering and clenching around…nothing.

It felt wrong.

But only for a split second.

Because Tank filled the empty space again, with something much larger.

She screamed—literally screamed—when he pushed his cock inside her as she came.

McKenna wasn't sure if he'd prolonged the orgasm or prompted a second right on the heels of the first, but her body jolted as if she'd been hit by a semi. Her back arched almost violently under the impact.

It hurt.

It was bliss.

It was blinding white lights and blue heat.

Every bone in her body melted as Tank took her, fucked her hard through whatever number orgasm that was and into the next.

She'd been right.

He was a conqueror, and she was the spoils of war.

That was her last thought before things went black.

"Mouse?"

McKenna's eyes fluttered at the sound of Tank's voice, and when she managed to open them and focus, she found his face close to hers.

"There you are," he murmured.

She smiled. She felt drunk, even though she hadn't had more than two glasses of wine at the pub because they'd spent nearly the entire time out on the dance floor.

God, she felt more than drunk.

She felt wasted. Her body heavy, her thoughts sluggish, her emotions wildly out of control.

Because all she wanted to do was giggle.

So she did.

Tank grinned, shaking his head. "You scared me there for a second," he said, though she couldn't understand why.

"What?"

"You passed out, Mouse. Screamed, then went limp."

The thought of that should have sobered her. It didn't.

Instead, she laughed harder. "Guess there's no recovering from that," she said in gasping breaths, as she continued laughing. "No way I'll ever look cool now."

Tank laughed with her, placing a sweet kiss on her forehead. "You're wrong. Because, despite scaring the shit out of me, that was the coolest thing I've ever seen. And I want to see it again."

Her body trembled as she fought to get her mirth under control. "I've never… That was… Holy shit, Tank."

He laughed louder, then kissed her hard. "You make me feel so fucking good, Mouse."

His words were so sincere, she wasn't sure how to respond. Because she didn't think he was merely talking about her stroking his ego.

Then, she realized she knew exactly how to reply. "You make me feel good too."

They stared at each other for a full minute before McKenna became fully aware of her surroundings again. At some point, the power had come back on; the room lit once more not just by the candles, but by the living room lamps.

And Tank was still inside her.

"Did you—" she started, stopping abruptly.

Tank chuckled, reaching down to hold on to the condom as he withdrew. "Yeah. I came so hard I didn't realize you'd blacked out until I landed. That was when I freaked out a little. Mercifully, you were only out of it for a few seconds." He rose from the couch. "Kitchen back there?" he asked, pointing.

She nodded, letting him explore on his own. Under ordinary circumstances, she would have offered him a tour, but her bones were still mush, so she couldn't move if she tried.

He was obviously throwing the condom away, and then she heard the faucet in the sink running. He was only gone a minute or two, but he was still amused when he returned to find her exactly as he'd left her. Any shyness she might have had about being naked in front of him was long gone as she lounged there, not even bothering to pull a blanket over herself.

Tank lifted her feet, resuming his spot on the couch. Reaching for her hands, he pulled her upright, though he'd had to supply most of the strength. He lifted her to his lap, and she curled into his arms, resting her head on his shoulder.

Neither of them sought to fill the quiet with words at first. McKenna didn't have a clue what he was thinking, but as for her, she was replaying what had just happened because she was determined to commit every single second of that to memory.

"The rain stopped," she observed after several minutes.

"Mm-hmm."

They fell silent again, as Tank's cheek rested against the top of her head, his steady breathing and gentle beating of his heart creating a peace inside her she'd never experienced.

McKenna's mind rarely shut down, always thinking at a million miles an hour, but right now, it was filled with nothing. No thoughts, worries, plans. Just quiet.

She realized the same must be true for Tank, because she'd never known him to be so still.

She lifted her head. "Okay?"

He nodded. "Yeah."

Then it occurred to her that maybe he was giving her time to get her shit together so he could leave. She'd never done the "just sex" thing, so perhaps she was supposed to give him some signal that it was okay to leave or something.

"I suppose you want to get home now," she said, wishing her tone sounded as easy and breezy in reality as it had in her head.

Tank frowned. "No. I'm not going home."

She blinked. "You're not?"

He shook his head, lifting his chin toward the coffee table. "I've got three more condoms in that wallet, and we're going to blow through all of them tonight."

The comment was so Tank, so arrogant and confident, that she couldn't help but laugh and say, "Okay."

* * *

McKenna sank deeper into her pillow, shocked she was still conscious. Typically, she was an early to bed, early to rise kind of girl, so she wasn't sure where these second and third and fourth winds had come from.

A glance at the clock told her it was just after three a.m. The fact she had work in the morning should have had her in a state of panic, but instead, she simply wrapped her arm around Tank's waist and sighed contentedly.

"I can't believe we did this," she mused, still amazed by everything that had happened. After announcing they were going to blow through three more condoms, Tank had put his money where his mouth was. He'd carried her—and those condoms—upstairs, then used the first one while taking her doggie style in her bed. From there, they'd moved to the bathroom, taking a sexy shower together. When they got out, Tank dried her off, then turned her away from him, bent her over the bathroom counter, pulled on the second condom, and got her all dirty again.

They'd fallen asleep after that, the third condom forgotten until half an hour ago, when McKenna was roused from a deep sleep by the feeling of Tank's fingers sliding inside her. She'd never had someone fuck her awake, and she had to admit, she was a big fan.

"I wondered when your brain was going to kick in," Tank murmured.

"What?" she asked, groggy from too little sleep and too much sex. No, strike that. There was no such thing as too much sex when it came to Tank. What they'd done felt like the perfect amount.

"I honestly thought you'd need a looooong conversation before we made it to bed," he said.

McKenna snorted. "Yeah. I'm definitely that type. Usually."

"Any regrets?" he asked.

She considered his question, then shook her head. "Not at the moment."

"Tomorrow?"

McKenna could live to be a thousand years old and never regret what happened between them. Sure, there were a million reasons why they shouldn't have, and she was going to have to pay the piper on all of those, but she still wouldn't regret this.

"Technically, it is tomorrow. So no. Not then either."

Tank smiled widely. "Good." Then, he kissed her softly. "Good night, Mouse."

"Good night," she said on a yawn, sleep reclaiming her quickly.

* * *

Buzz.

Buzz.

McKenna slowly opened her eyes, blinking a few times because damn, she was tired.

The reason for her exhaustion was currently serving as her pillow, and McKenna resisted the urge to pinch herself when she felt the steady rhythm of his heart and the peaceful rise and fall of Tank's chest beneath her.

She remained still for a moment longer, waiting for panic to kick in.

Apparently, she was more exhausted than she realized

because nothing came. No self-recrimination. No desire to kick her own ass.

She didn't even bother to minimize the damage by referring to last night as a momentary lapse in judgment.

Because she wasn't sorry.

She'd never had a one-night stand before, explaining that away by saying she wasn't the type. She was rethinking that stance, realizing the reason she'd never indulged in one was because she'd never been presented with the opportunity.

Last night, she was.

And holy fuck, was she happy about that. Because the entire evening had been hot and amazing and…perfect.

Her phone buzzed again. She'd plugged it into the charger last night after stripping out of her wet clothing and putting on her pajamas.

Slowly extricating herself from Tank's warm embrace, she rolled over and somewhat blindly reached around on her night-stand, searching for her glasses before recalling she'd left them on the coffee table in the living room.

Unplugging the phone, she held it close to her face and saw it was a text from her mom.

"Who texts you at six a.m.?" Tank asked, his voice gruff from sleep and very, very sexy.

"My mother. I'm usually up by this time, getting ready for work. I forgot to text her last night." McKenna quickly replied with a simple, "Good morning," not bothering to read her mother's messages.

"You text her every night?"

"Not every night, but she knew I was going to the pub with you to see Hunter perform. I'm guessing she expected me to call and give her all the details."

"Is she a Hunter fan too?"

"I'm pretty sure every woman with eyes and ears is a Hunter fan, Tank."

He shifted toward her, wrapping a strong arm around her

waist so he could pull her flush against him. "If you wanted a morning quickie, Mouse, all you had to do was ask. No need to try to make me jealous."

She laughed, trying—and failing—to swat him away. "You used all the condoms."

Four. Of. Them.

In one night.

Tank had told her they would, but she hadn't truly believed him. At least not until he'd roused from a deep and dreamless sleep. Tank's fingers had been slowly sliding in and out of her soaking-wet pussy. She didn't know how long he'd been playing with her, so she didn't know if that arousal was the result or if drenched-and-ready-to-roll was just becoming her permanent state around him.

She had half-heartedly grumbled about being sleepy. Mercifully, he'd ignored her, slipping on the last condom and taking her hard and fast, both of them coming within minutes.

Her phone pinged again.

"Was she worried about you getting home okay?" he asked.

McKenna shook her head. "Nope. She's got my location on Find My Friends, so she probably knew the second I got in last night."

He chuckled. "Your mom stalks you?"

McKenna twisted to her back, loving the way Tank's hand casually lifted, cupping her breast as if they'd been in this position a thousand times before. "I'm a twenty-four-year-old woman who lives alone in a big city. I prefer to think of it as she's looking out for me. The same way I look out for her. Because I have her location, too."

"Do you have to check up on your mom a lot?"

"Not really, but I miss her. So there's some comfort in clicking on her location a few times a day, just to feel connected to her. Not that there's ever any big surprises as far as where she is. During the day, she's at work. On Thursday afternoons, she's at a local pub for happy hour with the girls from her office. One

Saturday a month, she's at Melanie Johnson's house for her monthly book club meeting, and then there are the times when she goes out on dates. Those nights I *do* stalk her, just to make sure she gets home okay."

"That's sweet," he said, and she could tell he meant it. "It's nice that you look out for each other."

"Oh, I'm way easier to keep track of than her. Unlike me, my mom goes on dates all the time. She's just got one of those personalities."

Tank tucked his arm under the pillow, his hand drifting down to rest on her stomach. "What do you mean?"

McKenna placed her hand on top his, toying with his fingers. "Mom is vivacious, the life of every party. Men tend to flock around her because she's intelligent, fun, and she's got a wicked sense of humor."

"And you think you don't have that kind of personality?"

McKenna snorted. "You've been out with me, Tank. You know perfectly well I'm not the life of any party. I'm more likely to blend in with the wallpaper."

Tank lifted his upper body, supporting it on his crooked elbow. "Mouse, we could be in a room with a thousand people right now, and you'd be the only person I'd see."

She froze for a moment, searching for a response to that because…wow. Finally, she just gave him a grin. "Smooth," she teased.

Tank didn't smile, his expression too serious. "McKenna. I know you think I'm a player, and I get that you would assume every word from my mouth is just a line I use to get into a woman's pants. But I've never said a thing to you that wasn't true, and *nothing* I say is just because I want to take you to bed."

McKenna bit her lower lip, the damn thing suddenly wobbly. Probably because that was the sweetest, most amazing thing anyone had ever said to her. He looked at her, waiting for some sort of reply, but all she could manage was a nod because her throat was suddenly tight.

Her phone buzzed once more. Mom was famous for sending countless texts without waiting for a reply in between.

Tank loosened his grip so that she could look at her phone.

Sure enough, Mom was firing off one text after another.

> Don't keep me waiting in suspense, Mickey.

> Need details about the concert.

> And your date with Tank.

He didn't even pretend not to look at her screen, kissing her shoulder as she read her mom's texts.

"She wants to know how your date went with me?" he asked, sounding slightly surprised.

"My mom is my best friend. So she knows everything I'm doing. We talk on the phone at least once a day and our texting is out of control."

"You really tell her *everything*?" It was obvious Tank found that odd, though she wasn't sure why.

McKenna rolled her eyes. "I'm pretty much all work and no play, Tank. It's not like I'm going out and doing scandalous things with dangerous men every night."

"Until now." He tightened his grip again, giving her another one of those highly addictive love bites of his. She was going to have to wear a turtleneck to work today.

She giggled. "I stand by my original statement," she joked, swatting his hand away when he started to tickle her. This morning, unlike last night, was more in line with Fantasy Tank, who was more playful and sweeter.

"Are you going to tell her about us?"

McKenna hesitated because, to be honest, she wasn't sure. She'd told her mom the night she lost her virginity. Her mom had been the one to point out Dale's emotional abuse, though it had taken lots of conversations—and a hell of a lot of pointing—before McKenna would admit she was right. And her mom sat up with her all night after Eddie broke things off, holding her as she cried.

But this…this, she wasn't sure how to share. Probably because her logic and her emotions were at odds, and while her mom was the best when it came to helping her sort through stuff, McKenna was afraid of what advice she might offer.

And that fear ran both ways, since she wasn't ready to hear her mom tell her to take a chance with Tank any more than she wanted to hear her say she should walk away.

"I already told her about the fake dating," she hedged, aware that wasn't really what he was asking.

"Thought we were keeping that a secret."

"We are, but I know she won't tell a single soul. In fact, she's the type of person who'll milk it for all its worth with her friends. She loves a gag. No doubt, the girls at work will go gaga over me dating a hockey player and Mom will fan the flames, just because it amuses her."

"I'd like to meet your mom."

She laughed. "This isn't that kind of relationship." As soon as those words slipped out, McKenna wished she could pull them back in.

Because Tank didn't look like he agreed.

And she really needed him to.

She started to slip out of his arms, but he held on tight.

"It's too early," he grumbled.

It was, but suddenly she was starting to see the truth in Tank's comment.

He was dangerous.

"I have to get ready for work." She wiggled until he relented and released her so she could scooch to the edge of the mattress. She hastily covered herself with the robe hanging over the foot-post of her bed, suddenly feeling self-conscious as her brain slowly started to reengage. "I need to get my glasses," she said. "I'm blind without them."

Tank let her go without comment, so she was surprised when

she returned and found him still in bed. He was sitting, his back propped against the pillows, his bare chest so fucking gorgeous, it stopped her in her tracks.

It honestly wasn't fair for a man to be that perfect.

Tank patted the mattress beside him.

It took everything she had not to accept that invitation.

"I really do need to get ready," she said. "And you guys have workouts, right?"

"Not until later this morning. Come cuddle with me for a little while."

McKenna couldn't help but giggle, because the word "cuddle" coming from Sex God Tank's mouth sounded all kinds of wrong…and right.

"Nope. Unlike you, I have to be at the office by nine."

Tank sighed, then threw his legs over the side of the bed. "Fine. Tell you what. You get ready and I'll make us breakfast."

"I thought you didn't cook."

He ignored her statement. "Do you have bread and eggs?"

She nodded.

"Then get ready for work, Mouse, and let me work my magic. I'll start the dryer too. I doubt my clothes dried before the power went out."

"Oh," she said. "I should have done that last night."

Tank wiggled his eyebrows. "You were distracted." He walked next to her, slapping her on the ass, the impact—unfortunately—muted by her robe. "I'll forgive you."

She swatted him on the arm, then watched as he unabashedly walked out of her bedroom and downstairs completely nude. Not that he had a choice, considering his only dry clothes were down there. She enjoyed the show until he was completely out of sight.

"Wow," she breathed. "Good morning to me."

Twenty minutes later, McKenna came downstairs to find Tank back in his jersey and boxers, buttering a pile of toast. He grinned when he saw her, taking in her work outfit.

The Stingrays organization subscribed to the casual Friday concept. Actually, the rest of the week was pretty casual, too. Benny had explained when he hired her that unless she had a meeting with the bigwigs, she was fine to work in jeans and tees, which was a big perk of the job as far as she was concerned, because she hated business attire.

Her mouth started watering when she saw the pile of fluffy scrambled eggs Tank had put on a plate for her. Then he slid a glass of orange juice next to it and gestured for her to sit down at the counter.

"Dig in," he said, joining her. They ate in companionable silence, dining together now a familiar thing, given all the meals they'd consumed together on the road.

They'd just finished eating when the dryer buzzer sounded. Tank walked upstairs to grab his clothes, looking way too at home in *her* home.

When he came back down, he was—sadly—dressed in his jeans and shirt from last night. "I threw my jersey in the washing machine, so it'll be clean for you to wear to tonight's game."

She considered telling him that she had a million other Stingrays shirts in her wardrobe, but he'd been very vocal and insistent about her wearing his jersey to the games.

She didn't bother picking the fight, because as this morning wore on, she started to recall all those reasons why she shouldn't like how nice it was having Tank in her personal space.

Tank took both of their dishes to the sink and rinsed them— something she knew he never did in his own kitchen—before returning to the counter.

"Okay, well," she started, wishing she knew what the hell she was supposed to say now. Did she thank him for the casual sex and countless orgasms? Did she just say "see you around" without making a big deal of it all?

"I'll see you tonight," Tank said, as he leaned toward her, giving her a soft, sweet but practically platonic kiss, when compared to last night's.

"Yep," she said, following him through her apartment, watching as he stopped to grab his car keys and phone from the living room. He must have reclaimed his wallet when he got dressed.

He gave her another quick kiss at the door, and then he was gone.

McKenna stood still, staring at the closed door, hating that he wasn't there anymore.

Which was completely the wrong way to feel.

She shoved all thoughts of Tank from her head, pretending it was just another Friday and mentally going over her daily agenda at work. She had a couple of meetings this morning. She usually hated meetings, but today, they would be a welcome distraction.

Grabbing her things, she locked her townhouse door and walked to her car.

It wasn't until she was halfway to work that her hormones vanished completely and her frantic brain finally kicked back in.

That was when she realized just how bad this was.

The piper had arrived. And he wanted payment in full. Because she only had two hard-and-fast rules she'd sworn to live by since leaving Columbus.

No hockey players.

No one from work.

God, hadn't she even said those words to Tank during their first meeting at his house? She'd sworn to him she would never date either.

Well, it looked like *never* had arrived.

And she was fucked.

CHAPTER NINE

TANK RUBBED HIS EYES WEARILY, as he dragged himself to yet another boring-ass team meeting.

It had been one week since he'd driven McKenna home from the pub, taken her to her bed—and her couch and her bathroom sink—and had the greatest sex of his life.

He'd woken up the morning after feeling like a million bucks, because McKenna had said she didn't regret what they'd done. More than that, he genuinely believed she felt the same things he did. That what they'd shared hadn't been "just sex."

Or at least that's what he *had* believed.

Clearly, the morning after had revealed different things to McKenna, who'd taken avoiding him to the next fucking level. The woman must have been a CIA operative or jewel thief in a previous life, because she was damn good at disappearing whenever he was nearby.

He'd sent countless texts and left an embarrassing number of voicemails asking if she wanted to get together to "advance their fake relationship," but her responding texts—what few there had been—were brief and all business, claiming everything from "too much work" to "headache" to "Mom in town." He didn't think that last one was a lie, because she told him that her mom visited once a month.

The only excuse she hadn't hit him with was the "staying in to wash my hair" crap.

She'd even managed to avoid their last road trip by convincing Benny to take some intern to their away game in L.A. so the woman could get travel experience.

It had been seven days—and Tank had hit his limit. If he'd felt a little more confident about where she stood, he might have caved and broached the subject about what the sex meant over a text thread, but he decided his only hope for navigating whatever came next was if he waited until they were together, alone, and he could read her expressions and hear her words in person. Interpreting tone of voice in a text was fucking impossible. Too many nuances in word choice and punctuation.

They hadn't said enough the morning after, and a lot of that was his fault because he'd pulled his punches, stupidly thinking slow and steady was the way to go.

She'd made a couple comments in bed that morning that indicated she still considered things between them to be fake. Unsure how to convince her otherwise, he'd decided to see how things played out the next time they were together. He didn't realize the next time wasn't going to happen for a full fucking week.

Today, he was putting his foot down. Even without words, she'd made it perfectly clear she was avoiding him because she regretted sleeping with him.

That hurt. But it wasn't all that surprising, either. McKenna had only ever slept with men she was in love with, and obviously, the two of them weren't at that level...yet. Add that to the fact that up until six weeks ago, she viewed him as a manwhore who fucked with reckless abandon, and it was no wonder she was probably kicking herself.

Tank wasn't sure how to convince her she was NOT another notch on his bedpost, but his history wasn't working in his favor.

Which was why he'd decided to stay the course as far as allowing her to think this was a fake relationship. Actions spoke louder than words, so he needed to show her that he'd changed rather than simply telling her.

Earlier in the week, when she refused to take his calls, Tank had worried that McKenna would convince Benny to drop the fake dating thing. However, as the week wore on and the team's social media pages made a point of pushing their relationship to the foreground, he started to relax. He didn't know if those posts were McKenna's or Roger's doing, but photos and short snippets about them had appeared almost daily.

There'd been pictures of her with the other wives and girlfriends, cheering in the team box. Several of the photos snapped by the paparazzi outside Pat's Pub had made their way to the team's Instagram and Facebook pages. The team had also tagged themselves on the Peewee mom's video of him chasing McKenna around the ice rink, and the comments accompanying it had been mostly favorable, a lot of people agreeing they were a cute couple.

Of course, there'd been too many cruel ones from catty women claiming he could do better. Trolling comments like that usually rolled off Tank's back, but that was when they were directed toward *him*. Hearing people disparage McKenna had him seeing red.

Now, Tank leaned against the wall just outside the large conference room, waiting for his prey. He grinned when he spotted her walking between Benny and Roger. He imagined her purposely placing herself there, fashioning them as her bodyguards.

She'd chosen wrong.

"There's my favorite Stingrays department," he said, when they approached. Benny rolled his eyes as Roger chuckled. McKenna looked leery, which bothered him a lot.

"Wanted to walk in with my girlfriend." Tank moved toward McKenna, leaving the other two men no choice but to take a step away as he wrapped his arm around her shoulders, tucking her close.

"Tank," McKenna said softly. "That's not appropriate at work."

Benny nodded. "She's right. Although," he leaned closer, his voice lower, "you two should probably sit together. The more people who notice and start talking about you as a couple, the better."

Tank smiled when Benny gave him the green light he'd been waiting for. He lowered his arm but didn't step away, worried she'd take off running if he gave her the opportunity. He placed his hand lightly on her lower back, guiding her into the room.

The conference room was the one the team used for press conferences, so it had auditorium-style seating. Today's meeting had been called by HR, so McKenna wasn't required to stand in the front with the presenters. Instead, she could sit with him.

He led her to two free seats near the rear of the room. McKenna sighed but sat without argument.

Kendra Kingsolver, the head of HR, called the meeting to order, clicking on the mouse to begin what was sure to be a mind-numbingly boring slideshow.

McKenna shifted uncomfortably in her seat after a minute or two, when he started toying with one of her Mouseketeer buns.

"Tank," she murmured under her breath, chastising him for staring at her and not listening to a word being said.

He leaned toward her. "You can run, but you can't hide," he whispered, enjoying the way she blushed.

He'd missed her this week, dammit. And not because he was dying to get her back into bed—which he was—but because she added a brand of fun to his days that he'd never experienced.

"I'm not running," she murmured back.

Tank sighed softly. "Bullshit. You realize we can't sell the girl-friend thing if you keep avoiding me."

McKenna narrowed her eyes, never failing to respond to his challenges.

If the only way to get her to hang out with him was to perpetuate the fake relationship, he'd pretend his ass off right into old age with her.

"Listen," she whispered.

"Something you'd like to share with the class, Tank?" Coach Fields said loudly, calling him out. The man had it out for Tank these days, and he just couldn't figure out why.

"No, Coach," he said, turning his attention back to Kendra, who continued the presentation.

McKenna bit her lower lip, face flushed, and her leg bounced nervously until he reached over, placing his hand on her knee.

She glanced at him, then sighed, settling down.

When he flipped his hand over, wiggling his fingers, she gave him a half grin, then slipped her fingers through his, allowing him to hold her hand.

It was ridiculous how fucking happy that simple concession made Tank. The two of them kept their attention on the screen, but Tank doubted McKenna was hearing much more than he was. Instead, he was focused solely on her, enjoying the delicate scent of her perfume, the soft skin of her hand, the feeling of his knee pressed tight to her thigh. He even matched his breathing to hers.

When the meeting was finally over, the two of them stood. McKenna tried to reclaim her hand, now that they were no longer shielded by their seated positions, but he held on tight.

Several of his friends gave him knowing grins. McKenna's presence in the team box, as well as the way the two of them were always together nowadays, hadn't gone unnoticed by his buddies. It was just a matter of time before Blake or Victor pulled him aside to ask what the hell was going on. He was sort of surprised Blake —the nosy ass—had held off *this* long, but he figured the fact they were fighting their asses off to land a wildcard spot in the play-offs, combined with Blake always racing back home to Erika and their beloved, spoiled puppy, Corky, was working in Tank's favor.

So far, he'd only said that he and McKenna were testing the waters, and they'd gone out on a few dates. As things progressed, his friends were going to want more details. Because Tank didn't date. Ever.

"Some of the gang are going out for dinner," Rook said, pointedly grinning at their linked hands as they walked out of the conference room, all of them headed out of the building.

"Where are you going?" McKenna asked, obviously spying a way to escape him.

"No clue yet. We're meeting in the parking lot to decide. I think Kostya's hoping to talk everyone into Moe's for seafood."

"Who's going?" Tank asked, even though he had no intention of joining them. He needed to get inside McKenna's head and see what the hell was going on, try to figure out a way to get them back on track, and he couldn't do that in a big crowd of people. Besides, he'd already made plans for the rest of their evening.

"Kostya, Andrew, Anatoli, and Victor. I think I convinced Preston, Chelsea, and Ally to come too. Chelsea's mom is watching the baby."

He smiled when he said Ally's name. The guy had it bad for Chelsea's best friend, something everyone—with the exception of Ally—could see clear as day.

Rook hesitated, then added, "And a few of the puck bunnies."

Victor walked up next to them, overhearing the last bit and growling, "What puck bunnies?"

Rook sighed. Victor was not fond of the team's groupies, so there was a good chance he was about to change his mind about joining them for dinner.

"Mindy, Elle, and maybe Kristie. I'm not sure who else." Rook shot a look in Tank's direction, a sure indication that he *did* know of at least one or two others.

They hit the parking lot, which was clearing out quickly,

since the HR meeting was the last thing on everyone's calendar for the day.

Sure enough, Lara was standing there, hanging out with Elle and Mindy, all three women chatting with Andrew, Kostya, and Anatoli next to Lara's Porsche, which she had—of course—parked right next to Tank's Audi.

"She's relentless," McKenna muttered.

"Yeah," he agreed. "I think the issue is that no one's ever said no to her. You know, as my girlfriend, it's your job to keep me from going astray."

"Tank—" she started.

"Come with me. We'll grab some dinner and I'll drive you back to your car after." He was aware she expected him to drive her to the restaurant where everyone else was going, but he wasn't about to squander this time with her.

"Fine. But just dinner," she said, pointing her finger at him.

Tank crossed his heart, not caring if he went to hell for telling a lie. Because if tonight went the way he hoped, they'd be indulging in dessert as well.

"Hey, Tank," Lara said, as they approached his car.

He nodded at her, annoyed when she closed the distance, claiming his free side as if he wasn't holding McKenna's hand.

"Long time, no see," she murmured, curling closer.

Tank tried to shift away, but Lara was tenaciously clinging to his arm.

"We're all going to Moe's for dinner," Kostya announced, happy that they'd gone with his choice.

"Cool," Tank said, finally managing to shake Lara off. "McKenna's riding with me."

Lara frowned, but before she could offer a complaint, Tank disengaged the locks on his car, quickly leading McKenna to the passenger seat.

Crossing in front of the hood, he waved to his buddies. "See you."

He intentionally didn't add the word *later*. He'd text Rook when they got to his place to let him know they wouldn't be joining them for dinner.

Lara was shooting daggers at McKenna when Tank pulled out of the parking space.

"She's still delightful," McKenna said dryly.

Tank laughed, because he could deal with a sarcastic McKenna better than a skittish one. "A real peach, right?"

She rolled her eyes, and Tank literally had to force himself to concentrate on the road before he popped a woody. He had no clue what it was about her eye rolling that got him instantly hard. If things weren't so up in the fucking air with them, he wouldn't give a shit about her catching him with a hard-on, but until he found a way to get them back on track, it was probably best to hold his arousal at bay, lest she run for the hills.

They drove in silence for the first few minutes, but it wasn't the easy, companionable quiet he'd gotten used to with her. Instead, this was stilting and awkward, making it clear neither of them knew what to say.

Or at least, McKenna didn't...until she figured out they weren't going to Moe's.

"Moe's is the other direction," she pointed out, when he turned down the street that led to his condo.

"We're not going to Moe's."

"But you said—"

"Nope," he interjected. "Just said we were going to grab some dinner. I didn't say where."

McKenna huffed an impatient breath, letting him know she'd intended to use their friends as a buffer. "So where are we going?"

"My place. I'm going to cook for you."

She quickly shook her head. "No. I don't think that's a good idea. Besides, the whole point of fake dating is to be seen."

And with that statement, Tank knew *exactly* where McKenna stood on this thing between them. She was still determined to play make-believe.

He wasn't thrilled about that, given how incredible that night between them was, but Rome wasn't built in a day, so he'd go along with it.

For now.

"I get tired of the cameras, Mouse. Tired of always putting on a show. I haven't seen or talked to you in a week, and it's obvious we need to get things straight between us. So tonight, I just want it to be us. Okay?"

She hesitated for just a moment, then conceded. "Okay."

He smiled, reaching over to place his hand on her thigh. He gave it a quick squeeze, then left it there. He waited for her to pull her leg away, so he was pleased when she didn't.

"I thought you said you couldn't cook," she said.

"I said I *didn't* cook, not that I couldn't. There's a difference."

"Guess I should have realized that. Those scrambled eggs of yours were light and fluffy and tasty. Mine are always the consistency of rubber."

He winked at her. "The secret is butter."

McKenna giggled, and they fell silent again. This time, however, it felt easier, less stressful.

Tank parked outside his condo, then reclaimed her hand, holding it as they rode the elevator up to his place.

McKenna's eyes widened when they walked inside. "Your cleaning lady clearly came today."

He shook his head. "Nope. She was here yesterday. I tidied up this morning after I grabbed groceries for our dinner tonight."

"Really?" she asked, her tone the perfect blend of surprised, suspicious, and maybe even touched.

Tank booped her nose. "Really."

"You realize I'm only here because you tricked me."

"You've seen me on the ice enough to know I don't always play fair. Just to win." Tank's condo was an open floor plan with the one great space containing his living room, dining room, with the kitchen separated by an island rather than a wall. He pulled out one of the stools by the island for her and she sat.

Walking to the fridge, he pulled out a bottle of Chardonnay. He noticed that seemed to be her favorite. "Wine?"

She nodded eagerly. "Yes, please."

He poured them both a glass, then tapped his against hers. "Hope you like stir-fry. I make a killer fried rice."

"That sounds great."

Tank fired up his wok, then pulled out the ingredients he'd prepped earlier, tossing the onions, carrots, and mushrooms in when the oil was hot.

He gestured to the Bluetooth speaker sitting on the end of the counter. "Why don't you pick out some music for us?"

McKenna connected her phone, scrolling through until she found a playlist she liked.

Tank didn't recognize the first song, but he liked it. Especially, when McKenna started humming along, swaying in her seat.

"Who's singing this?" he asked.

"The Jonas Brothers," she replied, as the brothers sang about some woman loving them to Heaven. "It's got a fun beat."

He agreed, pulling the wok off the heat and crossing to her. She laughed when he grabbed her hand and started spinning her around the kitchen. McKenna kicked off her shoes, so she could slide in her socks, the two of them pulling out their most ridiculous moves as they tried to one-up each other. McKenna gasped when he dipped her—the big ending—placing a quick, hard kiss on her lips.

He lifted her slowly, stroking her flushed cheek with the back of one finger.

McKenna pressed her palms to her face, *Home Alone* style. "I'm red, aren't I?"

"You're gorgeous," he replied.

McKenna grinned in that way that told him she didn't quite believe what he was saying, but she liked it anyway.

She returned to her stool, and he put the wok back on the heat, sautéing the vegetables and rice, scrambling a couple eggs off to one side of the large pan before heating the chicken and shrimp he'd cooked prior to the meeting. Once that was ready, he tossed in the jasmine rice and seasoned with soy sauce.

"It smells delicious," McKenna said, as he placed a large bowl of it in front of her, before grabbing Yum Yum sauce from the fridge.

Joining her at the counter, they discussed what little they'd heard in this afternoon's meeting while eating.

"This is so good," she said, praising his stir-fry after they both polished off a second helping. "Do you think you would have chosen hockey as a career if you hadn't been pressured by your dad?"

Tank had never thought about that. "Wow. That's hard to say. I mean, hockey is all I've ever known, and honestly, I love it. But now that you ask…"

She gestured toward her empty bowl. "You could have been a world-famous chef."

Tank snorted, then tilted his head toward the kitchen counter, covered with dirty dishes. "I think there's a clean-as-you-go standard for chefs and there's no way in hell I'd pass muster on that."

She laughed as she acknowledged the pile of dishes in the sink and on the counter. "Your poor housekeeper. I swear it looks like you used every dish and utensil in your kitchen, just to make the stir-fry."

Tank was very fond of Maria, and he paid her well because he really did put her through her paces, not that she ever seemed to mind. "She claims she has job security with me because she's never shown up and been surprised by a clean house—with the exception of the nights I'm on the road with the team."

"You're lucky to have her."

"I am. Why don't we go sit on the couch? It's more comfortable."

"Aren't you going to rinse the dishes?"

Tank didn't reply. Instead, he just grasped her hand and tugged her toward the living room, while she snickered.

"You're a heathen."

They sank down on the couch together, Tank not bothering to keep a proper distance. He'd missed her too damn much this week.

"It's getting kind of late," she said, glancing toward the clock on his wall.

"No, it's not," he countered. Hell would freeze over before he let her leave without some assurances that she wouldn't spend another week hiding from him. "You want to tell me what was going through your head this week?" he asked.

McKenna leaned back against the couch, blowing out a slow breath. When she didn't reply right away, he said the one thing that had kept coming back to him, day after day.

"You said you wouldn't regret what we did. Have you changed your mind on that?" He would hate knowing she regretted the single greatest night of his life.

"Yes and no."

He frowned. "Explain."

"The sex was incredible," she admitted, her cheeks flaming bright red. "I mean, like, *wow* incredible. It's hard to regret something that came with that many orgasms."

He laughed, then sobered. "Do you want to give up on the fake dating idea?" Tank kicked himself the moment he asked the question, because he wasn't sure what he'd do if she said yes.

She sighed. "That would be the easiest solution, but I don't think we should. We've already established ourselves as a couple, pushing it hard. Roger even got one of the network guys in the press box to zoom in on me sitting in the front row with Ainsley and Erika at the last home game, the announcer making a comment during a time-out about you, Blake, and Coulton being cheered on by girlfriends. FYI—I'm glad I didn't know that camera was pointing at me at the time, or I would have thrown up."

Tank wrapped his arm around her, giving her a quick kiss on the side of her head. "You'll get used to the press eventually."

"I'm very sure I won't. On top of me getting splashed on network TV, the posts mentioning us as a couple on social media are lighting up with comments, and for the most part, they're very positive. If we suddenly drop the relationship, it's going to negatively impact all the work we've put in because it will reinforce the idea that you're…"

"Incapable of maintaining a relationship with a nice girl?"

She crinkled her nose. "Ugh. Nice girl is as bad as the way Benny described me."

"What did he say?" Tank asked.

"He said I give off girl-next-door vibes."

Tank tried not to laugh because she clearly wasn't a fan, but in the end, he couldn't *not*. Her boss had hit that nail on the head.

"Asshole," she muttered, with no heat.

"There's nothing wrong with being nice, Mouse."

"Yeah, whatever," she said, brushing him off. "The point is, it's too late to put the brakes on…" She paused, waving her hand around, searching for a word.

"TanKenna," he helpfully supplied.

"I swear to God if you say that stupid name to Benny or Roger, I'll key your precious Audi."

Tank held up one hand. "Hey now. Easy on the threats toward my baby. You know I'm protective of her. So we're staying the course on the relationship."

"Fake relationship," she said quickly, correcting him.

"Then it sounds to me like you've been working against us this week."

"Yeah, I know," she admitted. "It's just…"

"Just," he prodded.

"Just that I'm not a one-night stand girl. I've only ever slept with men I loved. I'm not good at separating sex and emotions."

Tank knew it wasn't her intention, but McKenna had just given him hope. Hope that she was feeling something for him.

But he also knew she was nowhere near ready to admit that —even to herself—given the way she kept insisting on calling this thing between them fake.

So, he would have to continue working that angle.

"What if I taught you how to separate it?" Tank wasn't proud of that offer, because God knew the line between sex and his feelings for her didn't even exist.

But she'd hidden from him for a *week*. He couldn't go through that again.

"What do you mean?" she asked.

"One-night stands don't have to literally mean one night."

"You want to have sex again?!" Her eyes were saucers, her question way too loud.

"You've spent the last couple of months teaching me how to behave. It might be fun to turn the tables for a little while. Because I can definitely teach you how to be wild. That sounds better than *nice*, right?"

Damn, he wasn't sure where the words were coming from, but the fact McKenna appeared to consider his offer let him know she wasn't fighting this thing between them as hard as he feared.

"It's just sex," he said, those three words composing the biggest fucking lie he'd ever told another person.

She bit her lower lip, her desire for him clear as day on her face. But...the practical, logical, professional side of McKenna was a powerful force to be reckoned with.

He could see her compiling a list of a million reasons why they should not have sex again, something he couldn't let her do.

Tank grasped the back of her neck in one large palm, pulled her toward him, and kissed her, working overtime to wipe every thought out of her head that didn't include him and a bed.

McKenna stiffened for only a second before responding the same way she always did. Hell, *better* than she usually did, because she was hardcore kissing him back, her fingers digging into his shoulders, her nails stinging the skin.

This past week had been hell on her libido, too.

"I want you, Mouse," he whispered, his lips brushing against hers as he spoke. "Sex between us can mean as little or as much as you want."

McKenna's brows furrowed.

Tank tried to figure out how to dial that offer back, but he couldn't. Or more accurately, he didn't want to.

He needed to play this a hell of a lot cooler, which should have been easy, since the Tank he'd been prior to McKenna's steady presence in his life was a master when it came to casual affairs. But somewhere along the way, he'd lost his mojo.

So, he kissed her again, deciding the best way to make it across this minefield was by shutting up and not saying a damn thing.

McKenna, mercifully, let his misstep slide, her hands slipping beneath his shirt, seeking out bare skin.

"God, I love your hands on me," he murmured.

"I want you too. More than I should."

He responded to that by drawing his lips along the side of her neck, his hands cupping her breasts. They were both wearing too many clothes.

He was about to rectify that when she said, "Just…one more time."

Tank paused, lifting his lips away from her skin so he could look her in the eye. McKenna fisted his shirt, trying to pull him back where he was, but he resisted.

"No." He'd already made one concession tonight, allowing her to believe this thing between them wasn't real. She wasn't ready to risk her heart yet.

He wanted to blame that solely on the men in her past, the high school boyfriend's cheating, Dale's emotional abuse,

Eddie's rejection, but Tank knew plenty of the responsibility lay with him too. Because of the way he'd acted this past season, revealing himself as a callous, immature man only capable of thinking with his dick.

Hell, hadn't he told her point-blank that he had no intention of settling down until after he retired from hockey?

Even if he took those words back, telling her he'd changed his mind, he didn't think McKenna would believe him.

"Tank," she said, her tone proving she was about to insist.

He wasn't moved. "This isn't going to stop after tonight." If she pushed him away, he'd have to let her, because he refused to make a promise he couldn't keep, refused to compound the lies.

McKenna fell silent, but this time, he didn't seek to shut down her thoughts with distracting kisses. It was going to take time to convince her that he wasn't like any of the men in her past, but he couldn't do that if she hid from him, avoided him.

"This is a mistake," she finally said, the slight grimace on her face letting him know she wasn't going to press the issue.

He hadn't won the war—not yet—but at least the battle was still ongoing.

"Maybe," he said, with a playful grin as he pulled her glasses off, placing them on the coffee table. "But we're going to have one hell of a good time making it. Over and over and over again."

Finally, at last, McKenna smiled, laughing softly. "You're impossible. I swear I'm an intelligent woman, and yet with you…"

"You're the smartest woman I know," he said, intending to reassure her.

"Yeah, that bar feels low."

Tank burst out laughing, tugging McKenna down onto the cushions and tickling her while she squealed and tried to break free.

Once he had her beneath him, he decided to put the position

to good use, holding his weight on his elbows so he could kiss her.

Given the way McKenna not only returned his kiss but lifted her legs, wrapping them around his waist, he assumed whatever doubts she had about sleeping with him again had passed.

Tank continued kissing her—obsessed with her lips—until McKenna turned her head, gasping for breath.

"Take me to your bedroom," she said, cupping his cheek with her small hand.

Jesus Christ.

Best words ever.

Tank rose from the couch, then picked up McKenna, her breasts crushed against his chest, her arms wrapped around his shoulders, while his hands cradled her ass. He carried her to his room.

McKenna took a quick look around, and it occurred to Tank she was the first woman he'd ever taken to his bedroom. He knew bringing one-night stands to his home would only spell disaster if he landed a stage-five clinger, so he kept his liaisons either to hotels or the woman's place. That afforded him the freedom to leave whenever he wanted.

Bringing McKenna into his room told him just how far gone he was for the beautiful woman, because he didn't have an ounce of doubt now that she was here…he'd want her to stay.

"Your room is clean," she observed, as he set her on her feet just inside the door.

"Would it make me sound too cocky if I said I cleaned because I was hoping this was where the night would lead?"

"Yes, but I've never known you to hold back on the cocky comments, so why start now?"

He wrapped his arm around her neck, playfully messing up her hair. "You're having a lot of fun at my expense tonight, aren't you?"

She grinned widely. "At. With. It all seems to work with us."

It was a simple statement that was just so McKenna. She was

open and honest about her feelings and thoughts, which was refreshing. He was too used to women acting the way they thought he wanted in order to capture his attention. With McKenna, what he saw was what he got, and he liked it. A lot.

"I have fun with you, too," he replied, hoping she knew how sincere he was about that.

"Do I want to know how many miles you've put on that bed?" she asked, somewhat hesitantly, her nose crinkled.

"Zero," he answered honestly.

McKenna laughed, thinking he was joking, but the sound faded when he didn't join in.

"Seriously?"

"You're the first woman I've ever brought home for dinner and the first to see my bedroom."

McKenna blinked a few times, and he got the sense she was waiting for him to hit her with some punch line.

He didn't.

"I…" She paused, then gave him a soft smile. "I'm…" Finally, she just gave up. "I have no idea how to respond to that. I mean, I'm kind of relieved, and also touched and honored that you trust me enough to let me in."

As far as responses went, that one was pretty awesome.

Tank drew her back into his arms, kissing her again because he was perilously close to saying way too many things that would make it obvious none of this was fake to him.

Things McKenna wasn't ready to hear.

Yet.

So he let his hands—and lips—do the talking for him.

As they kissed, they took turns undressing each other. He pulled her shirt off, then she tugged his over his head. Her bra was next, followed by his jeans, then hers plus her panties. The last article of clothing to hit the floor was his boxer briefs.

Tank pressed on McKenna's shoulder encouraging her to sit on the side of the mattress. She lifted her arms, clearly expecting him to climb atop her the way he had in the living room.

He had something else in mind.

McKenna drew in a soft intake of breath when he knelt before her on the floor, parting her thighs with his hands on her knees.

"Tank," she whispered, as he leaned closer, running his tongue along her slit. "Oh my God."

Her hands flew to his hair, and for a moment, he wasn't sure if she was going to pull him closer or push him away. He stroked her with his tongue again, then glanced up to see her flushed face and wide eyes.

"No one's ever..." she started, before nipping on her lower lip.

He knew plenty of guys who claimed they never went down on women because they didn't like it or it didn't feed their own arousal.

Those guys were fucking idiots.

As far as Tank was concerned, there was nothing hotter than a woman out of her mind with need.

Unable to resist, he gave her a wink, which had the desired result. She laughed, then rolled her eyes.

After that, it was game on as far as Tank was concerned. He lowered his head, sucking her clit into his mouth as McKenna gasped, falling to her back as her hips sought more from him.

Lucky for her, he had plenty more to give. He continued to lick and suck her clit, as he pushed two fingers inside her now-soaking pussy.

With his free hand, he drew one of her legs up, placing her knee on his shoulder. McKenna followed suit with the other. The position lifted her ass off the mattress slightly, giving him more room to work.

Tank slowly started fucking her with the two fingers buried deep inside her, gradually building speed, teasing her clit with the tip of his tongue until she was writhing, gasping...begging.

"God, please, Tank!"

He wondered if she was asking him to make her come or to

fuck her. It didn't matter. He was going to do both...multiple times tonight.

Last week, she'd made a comment shortly after they'd taken their sexy shower together that she'd never had a lover who'd made her come more than once in an evening.

He'd vowed right then and there, he would never leave his girl hanging with just one. McKenna deserved all the orgasms, and he was committed to being the man who gave them to her.

Crooking his fingers inside her, Tank stroked the self-destruct button he'd located last week, and it had the desired effect.

McKenna's back arched, her legs squeezing tightly around his head as she came loudly.

He loved how noisy he could make his quiet little mouse in bed.

"Jesus!" she cried, when he continued to tease her G-spot, dragging the orgasm out until she went limp, her legs falling heavily off his shoulders. She was short enough that—on his tall bed—her feet didn't touch the ground.

Tank turned his head, placing a soft kiss on the inside of her thigh before pulling his fingers out and lifting his head.

McKenna's eyes were closed, her face, neck, and chest all the same bright red, that color always such a strong contrast to her usual porcelain-white complexion.

Her eyelids fluttered open when he rose from the floor. She gave him a soft but oh-so-satisfied smile as she lifted her arms, inviting him to come to her.

Tank tipped his head back. "Climb in, Mouse," he said, as he pulled the duvet down.

She shifted gracelessly, looking a bit drunk as she tried to move.

Tank opened the drawer to his nightstand, pulling out a condom before joining her. He was slightly surprised to discover McKenna had already caught her second wind, because the moment he rolled the condom on his dick, she was there, pushing on his shoulder, encouraging him to lay on his back.

Tank's hands gripped her hips as McKenna threw one leg over him, her small hand guiding his cock to her pussy.

He groaned with relief when she sank down, taking him to the hilt, though he knew it was a tight fit for her.

"So big," she breathed, stilling for a moment. He gave her the time she needed to adjust, despite the fact his body was clamoring for friction and motion and *her*… God, all of her.

McKenna placed her hands flat on his chest, her face pure wantonness when she pushed upward, until just the head of his dick remained inside before dropping back down.

Tank moaned, resisting the urge to take charge. This was the first time McKenna had assumed the lead, and he loved the way she drove.

Her tits bounced as she rocked up and down on his cock, and his mouth watered for a taste.

"Bend forward," he demanded.

McKenna frowned, probably because that position limited her movement, but he didn't give a shit about that. He wanted more.

"Now, Mouse."

He'd learned quickly how well she responded to his harsher tone, his sharper demands. His mouse might be a powerhouse at work, but in bed, she submitted to him beautifully.

She bent forward, allowing him to shift her. She cried out when he sank his teeth into one of her tight pink nipples.

Tank followed that nip with a lick before he sucked it inside his mouth, treating her nipple to the same rough suction he'd just used on her clit. McKenna's nails sank into the fleshy part of his upper arm, no doubt leaving marks.

She'd scratched his chest last week, and he'd admired the red streak for two days, sorry to discover it healed the third morning.

"Mark me," he commanded. "Give me a souvenir of tonight."

McKenna didn't need direction or prodding. Instead, she

drew her nails down both arms, hard enough to give him the scratches he desired.

He turned his attention to her other nipple, giving it the same treatment as the first as McKenna squirmed on his dick, clearly seeking more.

When he released her nipple with a pop, she pushed upright once again, bouncing rapidly, furiously, greedily on his cock.

Tank added his own fuel to the fire, thrusting his hips upward on every single one of her returns until McKenna thrashed her head from side to side and then back, crying out as her orgasm struck hard.

He held her hips in place, kept a firm grip on her so that every inch of his dick was treated to the massage of her clenching pussy.

It took all his strength not to say fuck it and join her in the throes of passion, but he was a selfish fucker, and he wanted more. Hours and fucking hours of more.

McKenna had barely begun to come down when he flipped their positions, tossing her beneath him on the bed and pounding into her.

She screamed as a third orgasm rumbled through her, and once again, Tank stilled, buried deep, fighting the very devil himself not to let her sweet body milk him dry.

McKenna's hair was sweaty and plastered to her face, the temperature in the room roughly pushing that of the surface of the sun. Tank felt perspiration coating his own skin, the two of them now slick from their exertions.

Once they finished, he would draw them a bath and the two of them could soak in the soothing jets.

But not yet.

He wasn't ready to leave her body yet.

Tank didn't give her time to relax before he withdrew, McKenna's pussy tightening as if to keep him inside.

She flopped bonelessly to her stomach, his hands guiding her, moving her, because her strength was spent.

Regardless, she didn't complain or shy away when he lifted her ass until her knees were planted on the mattress beneath her.

Her head was pressed to the pillow so he could only see her in profile. Her eyes were closed, as if she was still riding that cloud of bliss from her last orgasm.

If he had his way, she'd look like that for the rest of the night.

For the rest of their lives.

Gripping her hips again, Tank thrust inside her, straight to the hilt, not bothering to give her time to adjust. She didn't need it anymore, her body molded to accept him—glove him— perfectly.

Her eyes flew open, and she lifted her head as her fingers clenched in the pillow. When that didn't provide enough purchase, she released it, her hands pressed flat to the headboard of his bed.

He fucked her hard and fast, calling out her name when her final orgasm triggered his own, the two of them clashing together like titans at war, breaking against each other until they were reduced to nothing but dust.

This was what she did to him.

Destroyed him the best possible way.

Every. Single. Time.

McKenna moaned when he slid out of her body, and he felt the slightest twinge of guilt for taking her so hard.

She was a tiny thing, and he was big…everywhere. He should have taken more care.

"That was fucking amazing."

Tank chuckled, his guilt miraculously wiped away by her words.

He placed a soft kiss on her shoulder. "Don't move. I'm going to go run us a bath. I want to introduce you to my big-ass Jacuzzi tub."

"Mmmm," she hummed, her eyes closed. "I love him already."

Tank grinned as he ran the water, adding some Epsom salts to soothe both of their aching muscles.

For the next hour, he dedicated himself to taking care of his gorgeous little Mouse, the two of them cuddling in the tub until the water started to cool.

Once they were back in bed, he tucked her against his chest, unsurprised when she was fast asleep within moments.

Sleep, however, came slower for him.

Because he still had one hell of a hill left to climb.

He wasn't sure if he'd been smart to let her continue to operate under the ruse that this was all fake, but until he could convince her he wasn't like every other asshole in her life, he wasn't prepared to risk losing the best thing that ever happened to him.

CHAPTER TEN

MCKENNA GRINNED as she looked around the table, filled with friends, at Pat's Pub. Sometimes she was overwhelmed by the desire to pinch herself, amazed by how incredible her life was these days.

Losing Eddie had impacted her in more ways than just breaking her heart. During their year together as a couple, she'd created a social circle of his friends. After four years away at college, McKenna's slate had been somewhat wiped clean upon her return to Columbus. She'd struggled to find things in common with her high school girlfriends, many of whom had already gotten married and started families. So she'd found new ones. When she started work at Pete's Sporting Goods, her colleagues and Eddie's friends became her new gang.

However, when Eddie dumped her and moved on with Lisa, she learned quickly just whose friends they *really* were. She'd stopped getting invited to happy hours and birthday parties and dinner. Even at work, it quickly became apparent her colleagues had decided Eddie's side was the smarter choice, considering he was Pete's son and their future boss. She found herself suddenly eating lunch alone in her office, no longer included in conversations in the common room or invited to join in whenever they ordered food.

In Baltimore, she'd found better friendships in the last ten months than she'd ever managed to form in her own hometown. She and Erika had become close since fall, and the addition of Ainsley, Ally, and Chelsea to their gang of girls had only made things more fun. They'd arranged for a standing Sunday brunch once a month and had recently signed up for one of those paint-and-wine classes.

Everyone was in high spirits tonight because the Stingrays had clinched the wildcard spot in the playoffs. Their season wasn't over yet, and they were thrilled because it had definitely been down to the wire. Tonight's game had been the deciding factor, and the win had come in overtime. Nail-biter much?

McKenna was flying high herself, but it had precious little to do with the hockey results—though she was thrilled the team was going on—and everything to do with the Stingrays' right winger.

It had been three weeks since Tank drove her back to his place, cooked her a delicious meal, then given her the greatest sex of her life. Which was saying something, because she would have sworn there was no way he could've topped the previous week…when he'd given her the best sex of her life.

Since then, she'd stopped using that descriptor completely because Tank topped himself every night.

Yep.

Every.

Night.

She wasn't sure how she went from playing it safe with the man and keeping their relationship professional to throwing caution to the wind, but here she was. Sexually satisfied for the first time in her life and dating—shit, *fake* dating—the hottest, sweetest guy she'd ever known.

So yeah, she should be covered with bruises from pinching herself.

Mainly, because the man was a goddamn artist when it came to bedroom play, and while her sensible, boring side continued insisting she needed to put the brakes on, she refused to listen.

Probably because it wasn't just the sex confusing her and causing her to forget this wasn't real. It was all the rest, as well.

It was the romantic dinner dates, which weren't always in public places and just for the press. The way Tank had started making her those yummy scrambled eggs every morning after she slept over. The way he spent the better part of a Sunday playing Mr. Fix-it Man around her townhouse, strapping on a tool belt to repair a wobbly stool in her kitchen, hang the heavy-ass mirror she'd found at a flea market, and help her paint her bathroom—with the permission of her landlord—because she literally couldn't stand the disgusting lime-green walls the previous tenant had preferred.

It was the way he'd joined her for her rewatch of *Bridgerton*, grumbling throughout, even though she could tell he was really into it. How he'd started dragging her to the gym, because apparently climbing the stairs to her bedroom every night didn't count as cardio, and he insisted it was important for her to exercise. Not because he gave a damn what she looked like but because he seemed to genuinely care about her physical health.

And it was in the way he made of point of finding her in the arena right before a game, grinning like a madman when he saw her sitting there in his jersey, looking at her like it truly mattered that she was watching him.

Three weeks in, and her fake relationship with Tank was turning out to be the best relationship of her life.

Which was a big fucking problem.

Because it wasn't a relationship at all. Something she kept forgetting when she really—REALLY—shouldn't.

McKenna glanced at her phone for the hundredth time in half an hour. The text she'd sent Tank earlier was still marked unread.

Blake said he'd thought Tank would be right behind them

when they showered and changed after their post-game workout.

"He'll be here," Blake murmured, when he caught her looking at her phone.

"You and Tank are so cute," Erika said to her. "I swear you're both the same, always looking around for the other whenever you're apart for three minutes."

That was the other part of this situation making it hard for her to remember what she and Tank shared wasn't real.

Their friends.

Tank continued to insist that they keep up pretenses for everyone, not letting anyone in on the "fake nature" of their relationship. Honestly, she thought he would have caved on that by now, because his teammates were constantly giving him good-natured shit for falling hard and fast, despite swearing off committed relationships for years. McKenna figured he would have slipped at some point and told them the truth, if only to get them off his back.

"Like you and Blake are any different," Ainsley chimed in. "Codependent much, Erika?"

"Pot meet kettle," Chelsea tossed at Ainsley, at which point they all cracked up laughing because all three women—and their Stingrays men—were definitely still in the honeymoon phases of their relationships.

And the other women assumed she and Tank were the same. Which made McKenna wish for the millionth time that they were.

When Erika poured the last of the pitcher of beer in her glass, McKenna hopped up, grabbing the two empties. "My turn to buy a round."

She laughed as everyone at the table cheered. There were going to be a lot of folks catching rideshares home tonight.

McKenna walked to the end of the bar, nodding when Padraig held up one finger, letting her know he'd seen her. A lot of the locals knew that the Stingrays occasionally celebrated wins here, so the place was hopping, which was impressive considering it was a Monday night.

"Hey, Mac. Two more pitchers of the same?"

"Yep. It's a Natty Boh night." She handed Padraig the pitchers, then waited as he carried them to the tap.

Glancing out the window, she smiled when she caught sight of Tank parking his Audi across the street, relieved he'd finally made it.

Her happiness faded considerably when Lara climbed out of the passenger seat.

She felt frozen in place as she watched the two of them walk toward the pub together, chatting amiably.

While Lara was constantly around, Tank typically ignored the other woman, always remaining glued to McKenna's side. She'd stupidly thought that meant whatever feelings he'd had for Lara were gone. But now…she wasn't so sure.

He'd said from the start he was committed to doing whatever the PR department deemed necessary to protect his career. Perhaps McKenna had overestimated just how committed he actually was.

Had he been avoiding Lara not because he was uninterested in her but because he was determined to play his role of doting boyfriend just long enough to get out of the doghouse?

McKenna's chest grew tight, her heart starting to race—and not in a good way—because it felt as if someone had just told her that Christmas was canceled. Try as she may, she couldn't think of any reason why Tank and Lara should be showing up together. Well, no *innocent* reason. Especially when Lara reached for his arm, clinging to it as if she was afraid of falling in her ridiculously high heels.

Because the bar was so crowded, Tank and Lara stopped at the entrance once they walked in, seeking out the team's table. Even though they were standing relatively close to her, neither of them spotted her near the front window, probably because of her short stature and the fact they were aware their party would be sitting toward the back in their usual area.

Tank said something to Lara, but McKenna couldn't hear him with his back turned toward her. However, she could hear when she raised her face to Tank, shifting too close to him.

"Thanks, lover," Lara purred. "It's always fun taking a ride with you." She winked before walking toward their table.

Tank remained a few steps behind, and McKenna wondered if that was on purpose. If he was trying to make it look as if he and Lara had arrived separately.

She'd spent the last few months of her relationship with Eddie, questioning his actions and the motives behind them, driving herself insane because he'd gaslighted her into feeling like a jealous, suspicious woman, seeing things that weren't there.

She hated that she was now doing the same thing with Tank.

God. She was the world's biggest fool. And literally the worst judge of character when it came to men. Her track record proved it, considering she'd dated two cheaters and an emotional abuser.

Now, she was standing here, her heart cracking in two... because she'd fallen in love with a man who saw her as nothing more than a means to an end. A tool he could use to save his career. The worst part was, she'd *volunteered* to be that tool, then promptly let herself forget that's exactly what she was.

Tank wasn't the bad guy in this. He had agreed to a fake relationship and sex without strings. Nothing more, nothing less. And she'd let him believe she could handle that. Hell, she'd told *herself* she could handle that, because she was a stupid idiot, drunk on orgasms.

The fact that she was standing here, feeling as if her heart was being ripped to shreds, proved just how wrong she'd been.

She'd fallen in love with the wrong man.

Again.

"Here you go, Mac," Padraig said, loud enough to capture Tank's attention.

He grinned when he spotted her, walking over.

"There you are." He wrapped his arm around her, giving her a curious look when she stiffened uncomfortably.

She pulled away under the pretense of reaching into her back pocket for her credit card, which she handed to Padraig. The bartender took it but hung around for a minute to congratulate Tank on the big win.

McKenna listened with half an ear as Tank chatted with Padraig about the game, her thoughts and emotions creating too much havoc for her to follow along.

"That goal in the first…" Padraig continued, describing how Tank got the momentum rolling within the first five minutes of play.

"…wouldn't have known it from the way Coach just ripped me a new one over that high-sticking penalty in the…" Tank complained.

"…just part of the game…" Padraig commiserated.

"…couldn't have pulled off the win without Coulton…" Tank discussed how amazing their goalie had been, stopping shot after shot.

"…might be the year the Rays go all the way…" Padraig gushed excitedly.

McKenna stood there, fighting to regulate her breathing, trying to act normal despite the fact it was taking everything she had not to fall apart.

Finally, Padraig went to run her card.

"Did you save me a seat?" Tank pressed a kiss to the side of her head. He was an affectionate man, always finding ways to touch her, always giving her those sweet kisses. She could almost convince herself the pain she was experiencing was *his* fault, because he played this game too fucking well.

Unfortunately, the anger didn't land, because she knew the fault for this agony rested squarely on her shoulders.

"Actually," she said, clearing her throat, which had grown tight. "You can have my seat. I, uh, I've got a killer migraine coming on. I think I'd better head home."

Tank's happy expression morphed to one of concern. "We don't have to stay. In fact, I'll drive you home and—"

"No," she quickly interjected. "No. You stay here and celebrate. All I'm going to do is take some medicine, crawl into my bed, and sleep it off."

"I don't like the idea of you being alone if you don't feel well."

It was Tank…saying sweet things like that, that was fucking her up.

She gave him a forced smile. "It's just a headache, Tank. All I need is a good night's sleep in a dark, quiet room."

She realized her words had come out with a bit too much bite when Tank's concern switched to something else. The *right* something else…because he glanced over his shoulder, toward where Lara was standing near the other end of the bar with Emily, Mindy, and a couple other Stingrays groupies.

"Is this about Lara?" he asked.

She hastily shook her head, which was clearly a dead giveaway.

"Coach held me back to ream my ass for a penalty," he said. "When I came out, most of the parking lot was empty. Lara was standing next to her car. Apparently, she'd forgotten her purse in her uncle's box and security let her in to get it. When she came back out, someone had slashed a couple of her tires. She was alone in a dark parking lot, Mouse. She called a tow truck, and I gave her a lift here. She's planning to bum a ride home tonight with Emily."

It was a perfectly acceptable story. Just like the ones Eddie used to feed her.

And Tank told it with such conviction, she found herself believing him. Because she was a gullible idiot, always managing to fall for the man who only wanted to stay for a while but never forever.

"You don't owe me an explanation, Tank. Nothing between us is real, remember?"

McKenna took a small step back at the dark scowl that comment earned her, confused by his reaction. Shouldn't he be relieved by her words?

In the end, it didn't matter how he felt, because she really couldn't do any of this right now.

Talk to him.

Pretend she wasn't dying inside.

Act as if she believed him.

None of it.

"It was nice of you to make sure she was safe," she added for good measure, even though those words tasted like shit.

Tank studied her face way too closely, trying to decide if she was as cool as she was pretending.

"Honest, Tank. Everything is fine. I just have a headache."

Padraig returned with the slip for her to sign, so she turned away from Tank, drawing in a breath she hoped would steady her. Instead, it was shaky and shallow.

"Do you mind taking these back to the table?" she asked, picking up the pitchers and practically thrusting them into Tank's hands so he had no choice but to grab them. "And tell the girls I'll talk to them tomorrow?"

"Mouse—" Tank started.

"I'm fine," she repeated. "I just need sleep." She feared Tank was going to continue to fight her. "You need to celebrate with the team," she added, desperate to make her escape. "It was a great game."

He nodded but didn't smile. Then he pressed a soft kiss on her forehead. "If you're sure—"

"I am."

"I'll text you in the morning," he said.

"Okay. Have fun tonight," she said, those words sending a

piercing pain straight to her heart, as she considered the fact she was leaving him here with Lara.

Time to cut and run, because the tears were coming.

She stepped around him, giving him a quick wave over her shoulder. She crossed the street to the parking lot, feeling his eyes on her the entire way. She didn't look back because there was no hiding the utter devastation on her face.

She climbed into her car, carefully averting her face from the pub as she pulled out of the spot and onto the street. She didn't manage to start breathing again until she was a full block away.

She'd only made it one more block before she said, "Call Mom."

McKenna listened as the phone started ringing through the car's speakers, aware she probably shouldn't have initiated this call before she got home. She was only just managing to keep the tears at bay, and she feared the moment she heard her mother's voice, she'd lose it completely.

"Mickey, what a nice surprise. I figured you'd be out late celebrating with the team."

"I left early." She thought she'd done an okay job replying, her voice surprisingly steady.

It didn't matter. Her mother knew her too well. "What's wrong?"

She quickly swiped at the bastard tear that escaped its confines, sliding down her cheek. "I fucked up."

"It's Tank, isn't it?"

McKenna was surprised her mother had immediately jumped to the right reason, because while Mom knew all about the redemption tour and the fake dating, she hadn't told her about the sex or her feelings. It was the first time in her life that McKenna had ever kept a secret from her mom.

"Why do you say that?" McKenna asked.

"Mickey—I follow you on Find my Friends. I can see how many nights you haven't made it home...at all."

Jesus. McKenna really *had* been drunk on lust and orgasms.

She hadn't even considered the fact her mother could see her location. "Why didn't you say anything?"

"Because I knew you'd tell me when you were ready. You've fallen in love with him, haven't you?"

"I…" McKenna paused. She knew the answer to that question, but saying it out loud would make it too real. "I can't be in love with him."

"Why not?"

"So many reasons," McKenna said, the list forming in her mind. It was a long one.

"Like?" Mom prodded, sounding more like someone who needed to be convinced instead of someone who agreed.

"Tank isn't looking to settle down."

"He told you that?" Mom asked.

"Yes. He told me exactly that in very plain, easy-to-understand words."

"When?"

McKenna didn't understand why that mattered, but she replied anyway. "The first morning I went to his place after that video went viral. He said he wasn't even thinking about marriage until after he retired from the game. He's a player. He loves the whole 'rock star' kind of lifestyle attached to being a professional athlete."

"That was months ago, Mickey. Don't you think he could have changed his mind?"

McKenna shook her head, even though her mother couldn't see her. "No. Because none of this is real. I told you the whole relationship idea was just an act, part of our attempt to clean up his reputation. It's all been fake to him."

Mom fell silent for a moment, then pointed out the two words McKenna probably shouldn't have tacked onto the end of that last sentence. "To him? But not to you?"

She sighed. "I have a knack for picking the wrong guy. It seems to be my superpower. Always falling for guys who can't love me back…at least not for the long term."

"Every woman in the world has a list of duds, of fish they threw back. It's very rare for anyone to find the perfect guy right out of the gate. You had to go through those idiots to learn what you don't want in a man. And what you do."

"So you're saying Tank is just another one of my duds?" Even as McKenna said it, she knew he wasn't. If what Mom said was true, and Camden, Dale, and Eddie had taught her what she wanted in a man, then the lesson she'd learned was that she wanted Tank.

"No. I'm not saying that, because I'm still waiting to hear a good reason why you think you fucked up."

"He's a commitment-phobic hockey player. Sound familiar?"

Now *Mom* sighed. "Are you talking about your dad?"

"Of course, I am! You can't help but notice some pretty big similarities between him and Tank. Swaggering, cocky professional hockey players. More interested in scoring on and off the ice than settling down. Commitment isn't in their vocabulary."

"I'm disappointed in you, Mickey."

McKenna hadn't expected that response. She was clearly upset. Why wasn't her mom comforting her. "What? Why?"

"You're waiting for Tank to walk away because your dad did. That's not fair, because they're two very different men, and they were two *very* different situations."

"How?"

"Mine was a summer romance," Mom started. "Your dad made it clear from the outset that it wasn't going to last beyond August."

"Yeah, but you fell for him anyway, didn't you? Isn't that why you didn't tell him about me right away? Because you were hurt?"

"I think I was more hurt about losing the sex than the man."

"Mom!"

She laughed. "I've had twenty-four years to reflect on that time, and believe me when I say, your father and I would not have worked out as a couple. We were always better suited to be friends."

McKenna could see that. Mom had stayed in touch with Dad over the years, sending him pictures and updates on her. McKenna's childhood had been a roller coaster of phases, her feelings for her father fluctuating between extremes. Sometimes she was angry at him and annoyed because Mom's updates made her feel like one of those children people "adopted" from third world countries, who received photos and letters in return. Other times, she was sad, wondering why he didn't want to be with her. Then there were the days when she felt gratitude for the money he sent.

She experienced genuine happiness when he'd shown up to her high school graduation to watch her get her diploma. She'd invited him, thinking he'd just send a gift, so she was shocked when she ran across the football field afterward to hug her mother, and found him standing next to her.

It was the first time they'd ever met face-to-face, if she didn't count the one time he'd shown up right after Mom told him about her. Which McKenna didn't, considering she'd been six months old at the time and didn't remember it.

Of course, she felt as if she knew him, because she'd grown up watching him play hockey. His team, the Stingrays, became her and mom's team, the two of them huge fans. When he hung up his skates and started coaching at Vancouver, they'd briefly changed—well, added—allegiances, rooting for the Canadian team as well as their beloved Rays.

Complicated didn't even begin to come close to describing her feelings for her dad, and they were continuing to evolve even now. Especially with them living in the same city for the first time ever.

"Tank was never going to be a one-night stand or a summer fling for you, Mickey. I know you. You don't sleep with someone you don't have feelings for."

"Maybe not. But tonight, I found out Tank doesn't share

those feelings. He…" McKenna's voice broke slightly, and she wiped her eyes, aware it was stupid to drive while crying. "He showed up tonight at the pub with Lara, one of the women from the video."

"*Okay*," Mom drawled. "Why?"

"Tank said she was stranded in the parking lot outside the arena because someone slashed her tires. He gave her a ride to the pub because that's where her friends were."

Mom was silent, clearly waiting for more. "That's it?"

"Yes. Doesn't that sound kind of familiar?" McKenna pressed.

"Familiar?" Mom asked, confused.

"Eddie always had very reasonable explanations for why he was spending so much time with Lisa. Hanging around her desk because she needed help learning the job. Showing her around town because she was new."

"Okay, so basically, you're walking away from Tank because of things your dad and Eddie did. Am I hearing that right?"

McKenna blinked several times.

Could her mom be right?

Was she overreacting because of past trauma?

"No," she said, more to herself than her mother. "It's not because of those things. Not really. It's just…this has all become real to me. And to Tank, it's just pretend."

"How do you know that?"

"Because that's what we agreed to," McKenna replied.

"Correct. You both agreed to do this fake dating thing. But over the past few weeks, your feelings have changed. How do you know *Tank's* haven't? Have you asked him?"

She hadn't. Because she was too afraid to hear the answer.

"I'll take your silence as a no," Mom added. "I didn't raise a coward, Mickey. The way I see it, you have the opportunity to right not just one wrong tonight but two."

"What do you mean?"

"Go see your dad."

"Why?" McKenna asked.

"Because Tank isn't the only one you've been holding at arm's length. Part of your reason for moving to Baltimore was so that you'd have the chance to forge a relationship with your father. You haven't done that. Not really. And I'm concerned that until you address things with your dad, you'll always hold part of yourself back from others out of fear of rejection."

McKenna blew out a long, slow sigh. "You're really smart," she finally said, begrudgingly.

Her mother, her favorite person on the planet, laughed loudly. "Damn right. I've waited a lifetime to hear you admit that. Now call your dad."

Before McKenna could say okay to that, her mother told her she loved her and hung up.

And for the second time tonight, she dialed the phone before she could think better of it.

Dad answered on the second ring. "Hey, Kenny. What's up?"

"I'm sorry for calling so late. I was, uh…I was wondering if I could come by."

"Of course, you can."

"Okay. I'm in my car now. I'll be there in ten minutes."

"I'll be waiting."

They disconnected the phone. McKenna's thoughts were so chaotic now, she feared her brain would implode. She was stressed enough about the Tank thing, so why in the hell did she think opening the whole dad can of worms was a good idea?

McKenna had been to her father's place in Baltimore a handful of times since moving to the city, each time for dinner, except once just before the holidays when they exchanged gifts.

Ever since that initial face-to-face meeting at her graduation, her father began reaching out regularly, the two of them talking on the phone weekly, and he'd visited her at college at least once each semester for four years.

Mom wasn't wrong about McKenna continuing to hold him at arm's length, however. While she longed for a real father/daughter relationship, she honestly wasn't sure how to get there, and it was clear her dad didn't, either.

She had hoped the move to Baltimore would help, since they'd be in close proximity, but so far, the two of them had remained in the same "holding pattern," where they both walked on eggshells around each other, keeping things casual and friendly.

Her dad was standing in the open doorway of his house when she parked in the driveway. It was clear from his face that he was concerned, which wasn't a surprise, because she never dropped by like this.

She wasn't sure what she expected tonight to bring…but she knew what she needed.

So when she climbed the porch steps, it felt like the most natural thing in the world to simply walk into his outstretched arms and sink into his warm, comforting embrace.

"Dad," she said, her voice breaking as the tears she'd done a shitty job of holding back finally broke free in a torrent.

"Kenny," he said, holding her tightly, his own voice a bit wobbly as it hit both of them that was the first time she'd ever called him Dad…instead of Dean.

Dean Fields was just twenty-one when he'd gotten the call from her mom about having a daughter. To his credit, he'd immediately come to see her. However, he'd been at the very beginning of his hockey career, playing for the Baltimore Stingrays. While he'd admitted he wasn't prepared to be a father, he'd done as much as he could at the time, which was to help support her financially.

Dad rocked her gently, shushing her in a soft voice. "It's okay," he reassured her. "Whatever it is, we'll make it okay."

They were the perfect dad words and exactly what she needed to hear. They calmed her, and she lifted her head.

Dad wiped the tears from her cheeks with his thumbs. "Tank?"

She nodded, half expecting him to lose his shit toward his

player. After all, she'd spent the past few weeks listening to Tank bitch, as well as wonder, about why the coach was riding his ass.

McKenna was damn sure she knew why her father was giving Tank a hard time, but since she was the one who'd insisted on keeping her relationship with Dad a secret at work, she couldn't tell Tank.

It was Mom who'd suggested McKenna call her father after she'd quit her job at Pete's Sporting Goods, explaining that she wanted to start over in a new city. Mom hadn't been thrilled about the idea, but claimed she'd feel a hell of a lot better knowing that at least in Baltimore, her dad would be nearby.

Dad was thrilled when McKenna told him she was thinking about moving to the city. So much so, he'd talked to Hugh and Benny about the possibility of his daughter with the marketing degree coming to work for the Stingrays. Benny had been in the process of expanding the PR department, so he agreed to interview her.

Benny had assured her countless times that it was her interview that landed her the job, not nepotism, but she wasn't sure she entirely believed that. It was why she worked her ass off. It was also why she'd asked if Hugh and Benny would keep the nature of her relationship to the coach a secret—at least for a little while. She wanted the time to prove herself capable of doing the job.

Dad was disappointed about not being able to introduce her as his daughter, but he understood, and because they were doing all that eggshell-walking, he agreed.

He always agreed, always held his tongue, always proceeded with caution.

She was grateful to him for letting her take things at her own pace. But she was also kind of fucking done with that.

She just wanted a dad. Wanted *her* dad.

"Come inside," he said, when she realized they were still standing in the open doorway.

He led her into the kitchen, putting a kettle on to make hot tea as she sat at the dining room table.

"Do you want to tell me what happened?" he asked, joining her at the table while they waited for the water to heat.

She nodded. "Yes, but before I start, I want you to know none of this is Tank's fault."

Dad's expression said he was withholding judgment on that.

"I know you have some reservations about me and him."

Dad had cornered her at the charity gala, concerned about the fact that McKenna had shown up on Tank's arm. His reputation had been a big sticking point for Dad, who'd gently tried to insist Tank wasn't right for her, and that she shouldn't get involved with him. It was the first crack in their eggshells, the first time Dad had asserted that someone wasn't good enough for his daughter.

McKenna had been touched, and she'd quickly reassured him there wasn't anything going on between her and Tank. Because at the time, there wasn't. She'd been directed to attend that gala with him as his keeper, and when she told Dad that, he was visibly relieved.

Or at least he *had* been…until she'd nearly fucked up and let Tank kiss her on the dance floor.

Then a week later, they launched the fake dating scheme. Dad hadn't approached her again about Tank, something that actually stressed her out, because she was afraid he thought she'd lied to him at the gala.

And his silence on the subject definitely couldn't be construed as acceptance. Because shortly after the gala, Dad started riding Tank's ass—who didn't have a clue that the only thing he'd done wrong was date her.

"Kenny," Dad said, using the nickname that had just sort of appeared during one of his college visits. It slipped out by accident one day during lunch, and that was when Dad admitted he'd always thought of her as his little Kenny, ever since she was a baby. She told him she liked the nickname, and from that point on, he continued using it. Now that she thought about it, perhaps that was the first eggshell cracking. "I know guys like Tank. Hell, I *was* a guy like Tank. He's only looking for a good time, not forever. I don't want to see you get hur—"

He stopped mid-word, taking in her puffy eyes and tear-streaked cheeks. Obviously, she'd already been hurt.

"Tank didn't hurt me."

Dad crossed his arms, tilting his head in obvious disbelief.

"I mean, I *am* hurting, but that's on me. I know it looks like Tank and I are in a relationship, but the truth is, that was Benny's doing. He thought it might help repair Tank's reputation if he appeared to be in a committed relationship with…" She sighed. "A nice woman. So we've been fake dating."

Dad scowled. "I'm going to have a word with Benny. I don't think forcing you to date a hockey player is part of your damn job description—"

McKenna held up her hand to cut him off. "I agreed to do it. He didn't force me. He asked and I said yes."

"Kenny," Dad said, shaking his head. He'd made a couple of comments, just in passing, over this season about her working too hard. He knew why she did it, so he didn't usually push the envelope. "I think we both know you have a hard time saying no to Benny because you're determined to prove you deserve the job. You've proven that, kiddo. A million times over."

She appreciated him saying that. Not that it would stop her from feeling otherwise, but that was simply because it was in her nature to worry.

"Maybe so, but I still agreed."

"So what happened? Why are you here tonight?"

"A bunch of the guys went to the pub to celebrate tonight's win."

Dad's nod told her that he knew that.

"I was there too. Tank was late."

Dad grimaced. "I held him back after the other guys left."

"I know," she said. "You're giving him a hard time because of me."

He shrugged, not bothering to deny it.

"Anyway, Tank showed up later...with Lara. She's one of the women from that video."

"I know who she is," Dad said.

"He said he was just giving her a ride because someone had vandalized her car, but seeing them together..." Her throat started to close again.

"You realized you have feelings for him."

"It's not fake to me anymore. Actually, I'm not sure it ever was," she confessed.

"But it is for Tank." Dad's words weren't a question, but McKenna felt like maybe they should be. Mom seemed to believe —though it was probably wishful thinking—that Tank's feelings might be genuine, too.

"I don't know," she said. "Neither of us has admitted it's not fake, but when we're together..." She felt her cheeks heating, knew without a mirror she was blushing.

Dad blew out a hard breath. Mercifully—for both of them— the kettle began whistling. He got up and made them both a cup of tea, delivering them to the table and resuming his seat.

"The two of you are sleeping together," he said, as McKenna bit her lower lip, flames erupting on her face.

"Yes," she whispered. "I know it was stupid, but..." There wasn't anything to say after "but." It *was* just plain stupid. She wasn't a casual-sex girl, and she knew that going in. The problem was, nothing with Tank felt casual. It just felt... wonderful and right.

"When he walked into the pub with Lara, I realized I'd let it all go too far. And while Tank assured me it was perfectly innocent, that he'd only given her a lift, I couldn't help but remember all of Eddie's lies when I confronted him about Lisa."

Dad knew about Eddie, the two of them discussing her ex when she called to tell him she was considering a move to Baltimore, and he'd asked why. She hadn't gone into a lot of the emotional details, merely stating that it was hard working with her ex-boyfriend and the woman he cheated on her with.

"I'm sorry, Kenny," Dad said, reaching over and patting her hand consolingly. "Have you talked to your mom? What does she say?"

"She thinks I should talk to Tank about my feelings."

Dad grinned crookedly. "Of course, she does. Your mother is the queen of talking out feelings."

McKenna was slightly confused by that response, mainly because while *she* knew that, she didn't know how her *father* did.

Dad answered her unspoken question. "I've called Ellie quite a lot over the years," he confessed. "Your mom's been helping me deal with…"

"Me?"

"No. Not you. Me," he replied. "And my feelings."

"*About* me," McKenna added, surprised to know Dad had been talking to Mom about her. Although, she wasn't sure why. The conversations Dad just mentioned were right up Mom's alley.

"Our communication when you were younger was mainly just through email, though we did chat on the phone a few times a year. I called her after I got the invitation to come to your high school graduation. If it had just been a generic announcement thing, I probably wouldn't have come. Simply because I didn't want to take any of the attention away from you and your accomplishments. But you'd added a handwritten note that said you really hoped I could attend."

McKenna recalled doing that. She'd addressed the envelope, and she had truly planned to just shove in the standard announcement. But at the last minute, she'd included the note, uncertain what was driving the request. "Mom convinced you to come?"

"She said she thought it was time. Past time, is what she actually said. I hope that was the right thing to do. Showing up, I mean."

"It was," McKenna said, flipping her hand over to grasp Dad's. "I was glad you came. And happy when you showed up that fall during my freshman year at college to take me out for that big steak dinner. I was so over cafeteria food at that point. I guess I'm just glad that you kept calling and visiting."

"Kenny, I'm not proud of the decision I made when I was twenty-one. I was a young, stupid, arrogant, selfish idiot. I thought hockey was the most important thing in the world. I was wrong. And your mother was too good to me, letting me walk away without cutting me out. I can't tell you how much I loved getting those letters and photos."

"The money you sent every month meant she could work less and spend more time raising me. We lived in a much nicer house in a safer neighborhood than we ever could have, if it had just been us on our own. And I mean, come on, some of those birthday and Christmas gifts you sent… I was the first kid in my class to get an iPad and a phone."

"Your mom was *less* good to me after those gifts," Dad joked. They shared a short laugh before he sobered up again. "Money was the least I could do. And I do mean the very least."

"No, it's not. You could have walked away completely and never looked back."

"I have so many regrets about the way I handled things all these years."

McKenna pushed her chair closer. "I don't want you to see me and feel regret. That would just be," she shrugged, "totally shitty."

"You're right," Dad agreed. "It would be."

"You told Mom you felt like this?"

He nodded.

"What did she tell you to do?" she asked.

Dad chuckled. "Talk to you."

McKenna laughed as well, because Mom had hit them both with the same advice.

"Don't screw things up with Tank because of what I did," Dad said after several moments. "I fucked it all up. I'm not sure…" He rubbed his beard, leaning back. "I'm not sure Tank will."

"What makes you say that?"

He toyed with the handle on his mug. "He's different lately. Not quite the same swaggering idiot he was before that video."

"I think he was scared straight by the possibility of losing his contract," she muttered.

Dad shook his head. "No, it feels like more than that. Listen, I don't have a lot of experience giving parental advice, but I'm going to give it a try. Don't assume Tank will let you down just because I did, and because that asshole Eddie did. Maybe he'll surprise you…in the best possible way. Wouldn't you rather take a chance on finding love instead of hiding behind a lie because it's safer?"

McKenna blew out a long breath, leaning back in her chair. "Damn, for someone with little experience, you just nailed that one."

Dad grinned, then rose slightly so he could bend forward to give her a kiss on top of her head. It was the most affectionate Dad thing she'd ever experienced, and tears filled her eyes again. This time, though, they were happy ones.

"Thanks, Dad," she said, her voice wobbly as she used that word for the second time. With each repetition, it felt better, more natural, right.

"And if the guy fucks up and lets the most gorgeous girl in the world slip through his fingers, just know that I will make his life a living hell on that ice."

McKenna laughed, even though she was pretty sure from his tone and expression, he wasn't joking around. "If he picks Lara over me, I'm going to let you do that."

"You got my bloodthirsty nature," Dad said, looking very

pleased. "That's good. It'll serve you well. Do you think…" He paused, visibly uncertain. "Do you think we could start to let people know you're my daughter? I understand if you still want to keep it on the down—"

"I'd like to start telling people." She hadn't lied about wanting the chance to prove herself, and she felt like she had, so it might be nice to be able to talk about her dad without having to measure every word in case she slipped up.

Dad's smile was brighter than the sun. "Good. Because I've been wanting to brag about you."

She laughed again, and then the two of them continued to talk, consuming four more cups of hot tea as they covered every topic under the sun until nearly three in the morning. She emailed Benny somewhere around one a.m., to let him know she'd be taking her first ever "sick" day.

In the end, she spent the night in Dad's guest room, because he didn't want her driving home alone so late. And in the morning, she came downstairs to discover her dad making her pancakes and sausage links—her favorite breakfast. She was thrilled to learn it was his favorite, too.

By the time she got home, it was just after noon, and when she turned her phone back on—she'd turned it off as soon as she parked outside Dad's house—she discovered several missed calls and half a dozen texts from Tank. All of them expressing concern for her headache.

Which was fitting.

Because damn, did she have one now.

An hour after returning from Dad's, McKenna went to straight to her bed…and she didn't leave it again for two days. Struck down by a killer flu—high temperature, headache, chills, fatigue, the works.

So, instead of figuring out what to do in regard to Tank, she simply slept. And when the headache and nausea got to be too much, she occasionally prayed for death.

CHAPTER ELEVEN

TANK SAT in the locker room late Friday evening, leaning against his locker, Blake sitting next to him on the long bench.

Tonight had been the first game in the wildcard playoff. Because they were pitted against top-seeded Washington, their away game was only a short bus ride. As such, they'd returned to Baltimore right after a soul-crushing loss.

Rather than talk to them in D.C., Coach Fields had taken the bus trip home to compose his thoughts, gathering the entire team in the locker room upon their return.

While Tank was devastated by tonight's loss, his sadness was overshadowed by his anxiety regarding McKenna.

He hadn't seen her since Monday night at Pat's Pub, and he'd spent too much of the past few days stressed out that McKenna hadn't believed him when he'd said nothing happened between him and Lara.

To be honest, Lara persistently texted him enough that Tank had harbored a bit of suspicion, wondering if the woman had slashed her own tires to create a situation where he'd need to save her. But even if she had, he couldn't in good conscience leave a woman stranded alone outside the arena at night, no matter what their history was.

So he'd dismissed the thought, offered her the lift and, in the end, it had been a short, painfully awkward ride from the arena to Pat's Pub, as Lara tried to convince him to skip the celebration with the team to do a victory lap or three in her bed. That hadn't been a hard invitation to turn down. One, because he wasn't the slightest bit tempted, and two, because he was pissed as shit with Lara for even making the suggestion.

He was dating McKenna, and they'd made that fact very public. Whether or not it was real was inconsequential, because as far as Lara knew, it was. And yet she was still offering to sleep with him.

For three weeks, he and McKenna had put on a strong dating show—going out for dinner, her sitting in the team's box wearing his jersey, lots of public hand-holding and kissing.

Of course, they'd done even more in private.

While McKenna had been resistant to continue a physical affair at the beginning, that pushback didn't last long. Once they'd decided to explore their sexual attraction, she'd been all-fucking-in.

"That was a tough loss," Coach Fields began, his words drawing Tank out of his head and back into the moment. Ordinarily, after a loss like tonight's, Tank would have been in a foul mood as he analyzed his every play and penalty, trying to figure out what he'd done wrong and what had to happen to improve for the next game.

Right now, he was too busy analyzing another game, the one taking place off the ice with McKenna, to spare even a second thought to tonight's shit show.

The coach continued to talk, and Tank found himself pulled into the speech, impressed and even comforted by the words. Tank had run the gamut as far as his opinions toward Coach Fields were concerned. At first, he'd reserved judgment—doing the old "wait and see." Then around the holidays, he'd started to respect and like the guy. Lately, all good feelings toward his coach had morphed to resentment and annoyance as the man continually singled him out, berating him for basically every fucking little thing.

If he wanted to listen to *that* kind of shit, all Tank had to do was call his dad.

"So tonight's over and done. Wipe the slate clean. Okay?"

Several of the guys yelled out okay; a few others clapped. Coach Fields' pep talk had been a good one, and while Tank would continue to kick his own ass over too many missed shots on goal and a couple stupid penalties, he felt better—and even pumped—as they approached game two.

"Good," Coach Fields said, after wrapping things up. "I'll see you guys bright and early tomorrow morning for workouts. Be prepared to put in a long day. We've got some shit to work out on the ice, too."

Tank rose with Blake, both of them reaching for their duffels. It had been a hell of a long-ass week, and it was about to get even longer, because Tank wasn't going home until he saw McKenna. Three days without laying eyes on his gorgeous girl had been three too many.

"Tank," Coach called out. "You mind staying behind a minute."

Tank's growl was low enough that only Blake and Victor, who were standing next to him, heard it. Both of his buddies gave him consoling glances, because none of them could figure out why Coach seemed to have singled out Tank to continually harass.

"I'll see you guys in the morning," he said, waiting until the rest of his teammates filed out of the locker room.

Once they were alone, Tank sank back down on the bench, preparing himself for another of the coach's dressing downs. His leg bounced impatiently, hating this delay. His plan for tonight was to go to McKenna's house and beat on the door until she let him in—flu or not.

Tank wasn't proud of himself for initially questioning whether she'd truly been sick. The problem was, he couldn't forget how she'd avoided him for a week following their first night together. So now, he couldn't shake the feeling that something had changed between them Monday night, and he was worried to death about her breaking things off.

By the time Wednesday arrived, his imagination had gone wild, and he was certain she was lying about the flu because she was angry and hurt by him showing up at the pub with Lara.

Those fears were alleviated when Blake's girlfriend, Erika, who was an E.R. doctor, had stopped by to check on McKenna. According to Blake, McKenna had caught some bug that was going around, and the only thing she could do to combat it was sleep and drink plenty of fluids, while knocking the fever down with over-the-counter medications.

Knowing she really was sick, however, hadn't made him feel much better. Since then, he'd texted constantly, offering to stop by to bring her soup or medicine or just to hang out with her. She'd forbidden him from coming anywhere near her place, saying she wasn't about to give him the flu right before a playoff game. And while he knew she was right to keep him away, he hated knowing she was sick and alone, and that he was unable to help her.

So tonight, he was going to her place and laying his damn cards on the table. He was tired of pretending this relationship was fake. It was the most real thing he'd ever experienced in his life. It was time for him to stop being a fucking coward and tell her how he felt.

But first, he had to endure another lecture.

"You were distracted tonight," Coach Fields said.

Tank nodded, because there was no point denying the obvious. His head hadn't been in that game. Instead, he'd been focused on what came after. "I know, and I'm sorry about that. I've had some things on my mind this week and—"

"Some *things* or some*one*?" Coach interjected.

Tank paused for a moment, because ever since his suspension, any friendly repertoire he and Dean Fields had shared evaporated. Which was why his question seemed too pointed and personal for their current coach/player relationship.

"Someone," he begrudgingly admitted.

"McKenna?"

Tank wasn't sure how to reply to that question, since he wasn't sure how much his coach knew. Apart from him, McKenna, Benny, and Roger, he didn't think anyone else had been told their relationship wasn't real. Well, except for McKenna's mom, whom she'd told in confidence.

Had Benny filled the coach in on the true nature of their relationship? Or at least, what Benny thought to be true?

"Yeah. McKenna." Tank didn't add anything more, because this wasn't a conversation he wanted to have with the man. Obviously, the coach wasn't a fan of his. Earlier in the season, Tank might have considered sharing personal concerns, but no more.

"She's different from your usual type," Coach observed.

Again, Tank wasn't sure what to make of this conversation. "She is."

"And she's the distraction?"

Tank nodded. "I fucked things up with her, let some shit go too far, but I'm going to take care of it tonight," he said, hoping that would be enough to reassure his coach. "I swear by the next game, I'll be back on track."

"You're going to take care of it?" Coach Fields didn't seem as relieved by that answer as he would've hoped. In fact, he looked downright furious, though Tank couldn't figure out why.

"Yes."

Tank wasn't sure what to make of the coach's scowl, but he wasn't in the mood to hang out any longer. He'd hit his limit on Coach Fields.

Besides, Tank had been away from McKenna for three whole days—days when she'd been sick and he couldn't care for her, days when she may or may not have been upset with him over

Lara, days when she continued to believe that this thing between them was fake.

"I need to go, Coach," he said, rising. "I'm going to talk to McKenna, set things straight, and I swear by tomorrow, I'll be fully focused on the playoffs." That was a lie, because regardless of how tonight went, Tank was finding it harder and harder to get McKenna out of his mind.

He grabbed his duffel, heading toward the door of the locker room, intent on getting out of there. Now that he'd made up his mind to talk to her, he was anxious to get to the next part.

He'd made it to the open door when Coach Fields caught him by the arm, swinging him around with more force than Tank expected.

He found himself face-to-face with his now-furious coach. "I don't know what you intend to say to her, but I swear to God, if you do or say *anything* to hurt Kenny, I will—"

"Kenny?"

Coach released his arm, his resigned expression making it clear he hadn't meant to say that.

Coach Fields was McKenna's father.

That revelation hit Tank like a ton of bricks, too many things crashing in on him at once.

He considered all the things McKenna had told him about her dad, how he'd been an absent parent, contributing only money to her upbringing. Then he recalled his coach admitting he'd been a lot like Tank when he was young, how he'd been a skirt-chaser, swaggering and cocky at the beginning of his hockey career.

Now, he understood her two dating rules.

And how fucked he was.

She wasn't just avoiding a workplace relationship because of her asshole ex. She was avoiding a relationship with a hockey player...one who was exactly like her dad.

"McKenna's father is the only one who calls her Kenny," Tank said.

Coach looked surprised to discover Tank knew that. However, before the man could reply, Tank turned when he heard someone else calling his name.

McKenna was at the end of the hallway, walking toward him. "Tank. I was afraid I'd missed you," she started, pulling up short when Coach Fields, who'd been hidden from her view, stepped out of the locker room.

"Oh. I, um…" She glanced at the coach—her father—then turned her gaze back to Tank. "I didn't mean to interrupt."

"That's all right, *Kenny*," Tank said. "We were talking about you."

McKenna's eyes flew to Coach Fields, who sighed.

"I slipped up on your nickname," her dad said quietly.

McKenna nodded, peering back at Tank cautiously. "I was going to tell you," she started. "Tonight, actually."

"He's your dad?" Tank asked stupidly. Because of *course* he was.

She bit her lower lip. "Yeah."

"Guess that explains why you've been riding my ass lately," Tank murmured to his coach.

The matching guilty looks the father and daughter duo sent him might have been funny, if Tank wasn't still reeling from the disclosure.

"No one knows?" he asked McKenna. "About the two of you?"

"Hugh and Benny do," she replied. "I asked them to keep it a secret because I didn't want anyone to think I'd been hired simply because my dad was the coach."

Tank now understood what drove McKenna to work so damn hard. Obviously, she was worried that people would think she only got her job because she was Dean's daughter. If that fact had been revealed when she'd first started working here, that was certainly what he and his buddies would have thought. But now, after seeing her do the job, there was no question McKenna had been the best candidate for her position.

"We agreed Monday night that we were finished keeping it a secret," Coach Fields said, "though I didn't mean to drop it on you like that."

"Monday night?" he asked.

McKenna sighed. "I might have lied about the headache... that night," she hastily added. "I really was sick the rest of the week though."

"You're feeling better, right?" Coach asked.

McKenna nodded at her dad. "I am. Much. I was glad you didn't get sick, too."

Tank watched as Coach stepped over to her, giving her a hug and a fatherly kiss on the head. "I was worried about you," he murmured. "You got the soup I left on your porch?"

She nodded. "I did. Thank you."

"Your mom told me it was your favorite." Releasing her, Coach Fields gave Tank a long, hard warning look, then said, "I'll leave you two alone."

Neither he nor McKenna spoke as Coach Fields walked back into the locker room, the door closing behind him.

"What are you doing here, Mouse?" Tank asked.

"I was hoping we could talk."

While Tank had been on his way to initiate a conversation of his own, he was now nervous, because he wasn't sure if it was good or bad that she'd decided to seek him out on her own.

"Okay. Wanna come back to my place?" Tank offered.

McKenna hesitated just long enough that his worries became full-blown.

"Or we could talk at your place if you'd prefer," he said, wondering if that would be a more amenable option to her. He hoped she'd go for that because he didn't want to have this conversation in public, preferring privacy as he bared his soul to her.

"I'd come here thinking we could just talk in my office but... maybe my place would be better," she said, looking as lost as he felt.

Her office?

Tank couldn't help but think that didn't bode well for him.

"Your place," he said, refusing to continue treating this thing between them like it was just part of their jobs.

"Sure. Meet me there?" she asked.

The fact they weren't riding together was another huge red flag, and Tank felt as if she'd punched him in the gut. She obviously wanted him to have his own car so he could leave after she said whatever it was she had on her mind.

Unable to speak, thanks to the weight now pressing on his chest, he merely nodded.

The two of them walked to the parking lot in silence.

"See you in a few," he said, as she climbed into her car.

Tank walked to his own vehicle, his heart lodged in his throat. Maybe never falling in love hadn't been such a bad way to live his life, he decided, as he drove to McKenna's townhouse. Because at least he'd never had to feel this heavy, agonizing, relentless pressure.

McKenna, who'd snagged the parking spot in front of her townhouse, was waiting at the door as he walked down the block toward her.

"Come on in." She led him to the living room. "Would you like something to drink?" she offered, as he took a seat on the end of her comfy couch.

He shook his head. "No."

She dropped down on the other end, leaving way too much space between them.

"So Coach Fields is your dad," he said, choosing to start with a safer topic. He was aware he was simply prolonging the pain, but he hadn't seen her, hadn't touched or kissed her in days. If she was determined to break things off with him, he was damn well going to steal every extra second he could sitting here next to her.

"Yeah. He was twenty-one when he found out he had a

daughter, right at the beginning of his hockey career with the Stingrays."

"So it was Dean who was sending gifts and child support all those years," he said, recalling that conversation by the waterfront.

"Yeah, and for most of my life, that was all it was. He'd hung up his skates and started coaching by the time I was in high school. On a bit of a whim, I invited him to my graduation, and he came. It was the first time we'd ever met in person."

Tank's eyes widened. "You invited him?"

"Yeah," she said, as if that shouldn't be so surprising to him. "I've experienced a million different feelings toward my dad over the years, but I've never hated him. Maybe that was because Mom never said a negative thing about him. And the money he sent…well, it was kind of a lot. I mean, he could have denied I was his and just walked away without looking back, but he didn't. He made sure I was financially cared for. And then, when I invited him, he showed up."

"So what's your relationship now?" Tank was still struggling to believe she was Coach Fields' daughter, but as he played through certain things—like the coach pulling her aside at the gala and then dragging them apart on the dance floor—it started to make sense.

"Evolving," she replied. "After graduation, we started talking more. Mainly just phone calls and the occasional short visit, never anything super heavy. When I was at college, he asked me about my classes, my friends, my hobbies. Eventually, he started telling me stories about his life, which I had to admit were super enter-taining. He's met all kinds of famous people, and he's a funny guy. When all that shit with Eddie went down, and I knew I needed to get away, Dad stepped up and made it happen, helped me find the job and this place to live. He's been great," she said, smiling.

Tank couldn't help but smile, too, because it was so her. McKenna was open and loving. There were probably plenty of kids who would have rejected Dean, would have resented him for walking away, but McKenna only saw the good.

Hell, once Tank had stopped acting like such a dick around her, she'd even started finding the positives in *him*, things he hadn't even managed to see in himself.

"I'm sorry I didn't tell you about our relationship sooner," she said. "I know he's been giving you a hard time."

Tank shrugged. "My biggest issue with all that was not knowing what I'd done. Now that I do...I get it."

"I guess you understand now why I've been so adamant about not dating hockey players and coworkers."

McKenna had told him from the very beginning what her lines in the sand were. He was both, and yet, he'd been arrogant enough to think those rules wouldn't apply to him. Maybe he hadn't changed as much as he thought.

Tank nodded. "I tick all the wrong boxes."

"I'm also sorry I didn't stick around on Monday. I..." She sighed. "I saw you with Lara, and some of the insecurities I thought I'd kicked after Eddie came roaring back to the surface."

Eddie, her prick of an ex, had chosen a Barbie Doll over her, while lying to her about his fidelity. Seeing Tank walk into Pat's Pub with Lara had hurt her more than she'd let on.

Tank reached out, taking her hands in his. "I swear it was just a ride from the arena to the pub. I'm not interested in Lara. At. All," he stressed.

McKenna squeezed his hands back. "I believe you, Tank. And even if I didn't..."

Tank wasn't sure where she'd been heading with that last statement, but he knew she wasn't going to finish the thought.

She released his hands, tucking hers in her lap, wringing them nervously. "I let things go too far, Tank."

Fuck. She was going to break things off.

He should have told her from the start that none of this was fake for him, but he'd been too afraid of losing her. Instead, he let her believe this was all a game to him, because his reputation had been working against him.

"Mouse, I need to say something—" he started, desperate to let her know how he really felt.

"Please," she said, cutting him off. "Let me go first."

He shook his head, unwilling to hear the words. He considered himself a tough guy, but he would fall apart completely if he had to hear her say the words "it's over."

"Mouse. McKenna," he added, hoping his use of her real name would somehow let her know how serious he was.

She turned toward him, refusing to give way. "Tank, I need you to know—"

"Dammit, Mouse!" he said, reclaiming her hands, tugging her closer, determined to make her listen.

In the end, neither of them gave way, each speaking over the other at the exact same time.

"It was never fake to me," he said.

"It wasn't fake for me," she said.

CHAPTER TWELVE

"WHAT?" McKenna asked, certain she must have heard Tank wrong.

He didn't reply to her question, however.

Instead, he just smiled, then he laughed as if she'd just told him the most hilarious joke ever.

McKenna drew her hands out of his, trying to figure out what was so funny. Her heart was racing a million miles an hour. It had taken every ounce of courage she could muster to get in her car and drive to the arena tonight.

Dad had texted her from the bus as they were returning to Baltimore to check on her, since she hadn't made it to the game. She'd turned the corner on the flu somewhere in the middle of last night, and by this morning, she'd felt much, much better. She'd even intended to go to work and travel with the team to D.C., but Benny had insisted she take one more day. Considering she'd wound up taking a two-hour nap this afternoon, she had to admit her boss had probably been right to tell her to stay home.

She'd discovered from Dad that he intended to talk to the team upon their return. Unable to let another day go without seeing Tank, she'd showered, gotten dressed, and driven to the arena.

She'd considering texting to invite him over but decided that was probably a bad idea. Given the fact she hadn't seen him in days, she had worried she would talk herself out of telling him about her feelings, simply so she could steal another night with him.

When she found him alone with Dad, she rethought that plan, deciding privacy was the better way to go. By coming to her place, he could simply leave if her feelings weren't reciprocated, and she could sob into the Ben and Jerry's New York Super Fudge Chuck she'd added to her Instacart delivery this morning.

Surely, she'd heard him wrong, so she went ahead and delivered the speech she'd been practicing since waking up this morning with an un-fogged brain for the first time in days.

"I've gotten my heart broken by every guy I ever cared for, and I guess, after Eddie, I let it cripple me. I know you're not a relationship guy, Tank. And sex is just sex for you, but this thing between us…" She drew in a deep breath, aware her cheeks were flaming red. "It was never fake for me."

"Are you kidding right now, Mouse? What you and I shared was not *just sex*, and it sure as hell wasn't fake." Tank cupped her cheeks, his smile so wide, it deepened the laugh lines by his dark brown eyes. "I'm so in love with you, I can't fucking breathe."

This time, it was McKenna's turn to smile, then laugh. Because holy crap!

Tank frowned. "That's funny?"

"That's wonderful," she gushed, wrapping her arms around his neck, hugging him with all her might. When she loosened her grip, she pulled away until their faces were mere inches apart. "The first few times I said those three little words, I said them to the wrong men. This time…I want to say them to the right man. I love you, too," she said.

Tank gave her a hard kiss. "I wanted to ask you out after the gala, but you kept saying you wouldn't date a hockey player or a coworker. So when Benny suggested the fake dating and you were clearly on board, I took advantage of the opportunity. I know my reputation leaves a lot to be desired, and I said a bunch of stupid shit when we first started working together about not wanting a relationship, but I was wrong, Mouse. You make me want *everything*—dating, marriage, kids, a lifetime."

McKenna had never heard anything more wonderful in her life. "I want all that too. With you."

They kissed again, but this time they went slower, savored it.

When they pulled apart, neither of them sought to move away. Instead, they looked deep into each other's eyes, grinning like lunatics.

"I was so afraid you didn't feel the same," she confessed. "When you walked into the pub with Lara, I realized just how deep my feelings ran. I was so jealous I couldn't see straight."

Tank lifted her from where she sat on the cushions, pulling her onto his lap. "I'm going to be a jealous boyfriend, too. I swear to God, I nearly threw a punch at Hunter Maxwell just because you blushed when you talked to him. I'm going to hoard those blushes of yours like a dragon with gold, Mouse."

She giggled. "God knows you make me blush more than anyone else."

He ran the back of his finger over her cheek. "You're so beautiful."

She started to roll her eyes, but Tank gripped her chin tightly between his thumb and forefinger.

"Don't roll your eyes, Mouse. I mean it. You're the most beautiful woman I've ever seen."

His eyes and tone were so sincere, McKenna had to swallow down the lump forming in her throat.

"I can't believe this is real," she whispered. "I've spent weeks lying to myself—and you—about this all being make-believe, trying to convince myself I could do the casual-sex thing. Turns out, I really suck at that."

"Thank God." He drew his lips along the side of her neck, placing a hundred tiny kisses there. "FYI. There's nothing casual about the way I feel for you."

McKenna turned toward him, her breasts pressed to his chest as she captured his lips with her own, drowning in his drugging, amazing kisses.

They parted briefly as Tank pulled her glasses off, placing them on the end table, before drawing her shirt over her head, his expert fingers flicking her bra open with ease. He wiggled his eyebrows as he dramatically tossed it over his shoulder and onto the floor.

"Such a slob," she teased.

Tank didn't laugh, but that was only because he'd already lowered his head, sucking one of her nipples into his mouth.

McKenna threw her head back, gasping. Tank had discovered early on that she liked the rough edge to his touches, loved the way he came at her like the world's sexiest, most ravenous beast.

He treated the other nipple to the same as she gyrated on his lap. His cock was thick and hard and oh so inviting. She rubbed against him like a cat in heat, so ready to move to the next part.

Tank, on the other hand, was in no hurry, now that he'd freed her breasts. He nibbled, sucked, licked, and kissed the taut tips, groaning against them as if she was feeding him some delicious feast.

"Tank," she said, gasping. "Please.

He lifted his head, giving her a quick kiss. "Patience, Mouse."

She narrowed her eyes. "It's been five days," she barked out. They hadn't shared a bed since Sunday, and it was now Friday. While the McKenna she'd been pre-Tank was capable of going months without an orgasm, this new version of herself was far more greedy and needy.

"And I can tell you right now, that's never happening again." He voiced those words with such conviction, she believed him.

"God, I missed you. For future reference, I don't give a shit if you come down with the plague, you're not keeping me away from you again. It killed me knowing you were sick and I couldn't take care of you."

She was touched by the thought that he'd want to care for her if she was sick.

"It's the playoffs," she reminded him.

"Refer back to the words 'don't give a shit,'" he said.

Best. Boyfriend. Ever.

Boyfriend.

McKenna repeated that word a few more times in her head, letting it sink in deep. "I want you."

He chuckled. "Soon."

When he returned his attention to her breasts, she groaned… then moaned. Because, fuck, he was good at that.

McKenna sought out her own relief, shifting her hips and dragging her slit over his cock, cursing the clothing barrier between them. When she couldn't take it any longer, she pushed him away, her hands flat against his shoulders.

He started to draw her back, but relented when she dropped off the couch, kneeling on the floor between his outstretched thighs.

"Jesus," he breathed, as she unbuckled and unzipped his jeans.

Tank lifted his hips, helping as she tugged the denim as well as his boxer briefs down to his ankles. He toed his shoes off, then finished shedding the pants on his own.

McKenna pushed on the inside of his knees, creating more space for herself as she reached for his dick, wrapping her hand around it. He really was extremely well-endowed, so managing to take much of him inside her mouth would be a challenge.

Her reticence must have shown, because Tank grasped the back of her neck, tipping her face up to his with his thumb under her jaw. "Just the head," he said.

She frowned, confused, until Tank shifted forward, sitting on the edge of the couch. He placed his large palm over hers on his shaft, guiding his cock to her mouth.

McKenna swirled her tongue over the head, tasting the precome there. Then she did as he said, taking the head of his dick inside. Even just that part was more than a mouthful.

Tank began stroking his cock, controlling her hand as well, jerking himself off as she sucked the head of his dick like he'd done to her nipples. The way he groaned, murmuring praise under his breath, gave her the confidence that she was turning him on, doing it right.

Tank started to stroke faster, so McKenna used her free hand to cup his balls, giving them a gentle squeeze.

"Fuck," he cursed. "You keep doing that and I'm going to come."

She didn't have a problem with that, but her mouth was too full for her to say so. Instead, she just moaned her approval and sucked him harder.

"Goddammit, Mouse," he said, releasing his cock and taking her ponytail in his fist. He used that grip to push her head lower on his dick, brushing against the back of her throat once, twice, three times before pulling her off completely.

"Hey," she complained, determined to push him over the edge with her mouth.

He pressed his thumb firmly against her lips, cutting off her argument.

"Climb on top of me," he demanded.

On second thought, they could always finish the blowjob later.

McKenna quickly scrambled from the floor. Before she could reclaim her previous position, Tank reached for the button on her jeans, managing to get her completely naked in seconds.

She climbed back onto his lap, reclaiming his cock. Lifting, she guided him to her opening, then slid down slowly, shuddering with pleasure as she took him all the way inside.

Tank gripped her hips, and his head fell back against the couch cushions as he moaned low in this throat.

She started to lift once more, needing all the friction, but Tank's fingers tightened and he held her in place, not allowing her to move.

"Tank," she complained, trying to peel his fingers away.

"Condom," he said, through gritted teeth. "We forgot the condom."

Oh.

"I'm on the Pill," she said.

"I've never taken a woman without a condom."

"If you'd prefer to—"

She didn't finish her sentence before Tank put his grip on her hips to use, lifting her and pulling her back down with enough force that she squealed, her pussy muscles clenching in a way that said her first orgasm wasn't going to take long to come.

"Yes!" she hissed, when he lifted her again. This time, she was the one slamming back down. They set their pace quickly, McKenna rising and falling, taking him deeper with each pass.

Tank pulled her toward him several times, stealing hard kisses as they fucked.

A dozen strokes in, McKenna fell apart, trembling in Tank's arms as she came.

"Tank!" she cried out, the pleasure so intense it almost hurt.

His hands found their way to her ass, cupping the globes while holding her in place, his cock buried deep.

"Fuck, that feels..." Tank was still talking through clenched teeth, and she could tell he was fighting hard to keep from coming himself.

"We have all night," she said, when she finally managed to catch her breath. She fell forward, resting her forehead on his shoulder.

"We have forever," he said, correcting her.

She smiled as she lifted her head. "You're right. We do. So you don't have to pace yourself."

Tank clearly didn't need to be told twice, and that was when she realized just how close to the brink he was. He grasped her hips again, dragging her up and down his cock half a dozen more times before he exploded, calling out her name, sheer bliss on his face.

She'd never really seen his expression when he came—primarily because she was always too blinded by her own pleasure.

"I honestly didn't think you could get any hotter," she murmured, blown away by how utterly sexy he was when in the throes of a climax.

Tank cracked one closed eyelid open, just a little bit, while giving her that cocky grin that used to drive her crazy, but now...

Well, it still drove her crazy, but in a much better way.

Tank closed his eyes again, tucking McKenna against his chest, the two of them cuddling in the aftermath. She longed for this part of their sexual routine as much as the physical act. She loved the way he always held her afterward, placing soft kisses on the top of her head while whispering the sweetest words she'd ever heard.

Words like beautiful, perfect, even sexy.

Tonight, he added the word *love*, and she swore if not for his arms holding her down, she could fly.

After a few minutes, Tank broke the silence. "I'm going to go too fast, Mouse. I see where this is going, and I'm going to be impatient as hell to get us there."

She lifted her head. "What do you mean?"

"I'm currently sitting here trying to decide if you should move in with me, or if I should come live here with you. I'm even planning a quick trip to the hardware store before workouts tomorrow to buy packing boxes and tape."

She giggled. "Yeah, that *is* too fast."

"I've spent a lifetime telling myself I didn't want this yet, but I can see now I just hadn't wanted it with anyone who came before. You've got me rearranging all my priorities and plans for the future."

McKenna didn't hate the sound of that. She'd dated Eddie for a full year, and every time she suggested they move in together, he insisted it was too soon. At the time, she'd thought he was being smart, making sure they were truly ready before they took the next step. In hindsight, she could see he'd always been hesitant about making a real commitment to her.

Tank wasn't suffering from the same problem. Which wasn't as scary as it should be.

"I like that you see me in your future."

"You're not just *in* it, Mouse. You *are* it. So what do you think? Your place or mine?"

She shook her head. "You're crazy."

"Never denied that," he shamelessly replied.

"Tell you what, why don't we use Benny's timeline? We'll keep dating through the rest of the season and the summer, and we can revisit the living-together idea when training camp starts next year."

"I'll agree to the timeline, if you agree that we don't revisit the idea. We enact it."

McKenna thought she should argue the point, but she didn't really want to. "Okay."

"Okay," he repeated excitedly. "Which place? Or should we just give up both and choose a new home together?"

She laughed. "Your place," she replied. "It's bigger than this one, with a hell of a lot better parking. It's on the waterfront. And we'd be paying a mortgage, not rent. That's a much smarter way to go."

"The condo's paid for," he said. "So it's already ours."

She loved the way he used the pronoun *ours*.

"I'm glad you want to live there," Tank continued. "I'd hate to move too far away from our boat."

She blinked a few times. "You have a boat?"

He chuckled. "*We* have a boat. It's docked at a marina a couple blocks down from *our* condo."

"Ours, huh? I like the sound of that."

Tank kissed her cheek. "So do I."

Then it occurred to her, they'd been having this whole conversation with his dick still tucked inside her.

She started to move, but Tank tightened his grip on her ass. "Hold on," was all he said, before he stood up. McKenna hastily wrapped her arms around his shoulders, her legs around his waist, giggling when he turned and carried her upstairs.

Of course, the giggling quickly gave way to moans, because Tank's cock grew harder inside her with every step they took toward her bedroom.

By the time they reached her bed, he was fully erect and stretching her oh so tightly.

Tank placed her on the mattress on her back, coming over her. He kissed her. Just one long, slow, sensual kiss. And then he took her again, thrusting into her like a man possessed.

Which suited her just fine, because she'd never felt this wild and wicked and wanton.

"God!" she cried out, her orgasm striking hard.

Not that Tank acknowledged it. He fucked her through that one and straight into the next as McKenna saw literal stars. She'd blacked out the first time they had sex, and idiot that she was, she figured that was just a fluke, the result of a too-long abstinence.

Now, she was starting to think the blackouts might become a regular thing.

She gripped his shoulders tightly, gasping for air. Her body was on system overload, her pussy clenching over and over, her clit tingling out of control as Tank reached down to stroke it. She wasn't sure she could survive another orgasm, but it didn't look like Tank was going to give her a choice.

"I can't...take..." she said, gasping. "Too much. Too goo—"

The last word was cut off by a scream—God, she hoped her neighbors didn't call the cops—as she came again.

Mercifully, Tank was with her this time, groaning out her name, his spine rigid as he pumped even more cum inside her.

Inside her.

And for a split second, she saw the two of them making a baby.

Not that motherhood was something she wanted right away. She was only twenty-four, after all. But there was something very exciting about the idea of having a baby with Tank, so she let that dream play out behind her closed eyes.

When her eyelids fluttered open, she realized Tank was watching her.

"You see it too," he said, his voice gruff. "Our future."

She nodded. "I do."

"So we move in together in August," he said. "And I'm thinking a Christmas wedding. My mother would have loved that. And then—"

"Next Christmas?" she asked, trying not to laugh at his child-like enthusiasm. Clearly, she was going to have to be the adult about this relationship.

"Of course. And then..." This time he paused, making it obvious he wanted her to fill in the next blank.

She knew she shouldn't encourage this, but damn if she wasn't just as impatient. She didn't have a clue why she was so certain this thing with Tank would last. Of all her past boyfriends, he should feel like the riskiest one to plan a future with. And yet, she didn't have a single doubt about him or them.

"And then," she said softly, "we make a family."

Tank smiled a lot, and McKenna seriously thought she'd seen all his smiles—the cocky ones, the smirks, the silly ones, and the softer kind he offered her after sex.

But the one he flashed at her when she mentioned their family was by far the brightest and best of all.

EPILOGUE

VICTOR LEANED back in the booth at Pat's Pub and watched the celebration unwind around him. The atmosphere in the pub was chaotic and loud and downright joyous, as his teammates, their significant others, and a shit ton of fans partied their asses off.

The Stingrays had made it through the first round of playoffs —by the skin of their teeth, beating Washington tonight in game seven. So, their season was going into overtime.

He stroked his chin, growling to himself. He sported a beard year-round, but he typically kept it well-groomed. Thanks to that no-shaving superstition, the goddamn thing was growing wildly out of control right now, and he looked like a fucking caveman.

"You suck at celebrating," his sister, Vivian, said, as she claimed the other side of the booth.

"I'm celebrating," he said, lifting his Guinness.

She tilted her head toward the crowd. "The party's over there."

Victor shrugged. "It's too fucking loud over there. I prefer to watch it unfold from the comfort of my own booth. Which was blissfully quiet until twenty seconds ago."

"Last of the original party guys," she teased.

He and his sister were polar opposites, so different it was hard for Victor to believe they were even related. Despite that, she was his best friend in the whole world.

The two of them had been through some shit in their lives, but they'd both come out on the other end, stronger. Because they were survivors.

"Listen, I've been wanting to talk to you about something, but I didn't want to bring it up until this round against Washington was over."

Victor frowned because his sister, who was usually smiling and easygoing, suddenly looked…nervous.

Vivian was never nervous.

"What's wrong?" he asked, his voice gruff with concern.

"Nothing's wrong. In fact, something's right. At least for me. Maybe. If, um…"

"What the hell is going on with you?" Vivian was the most straightforward, forthright person he knew, and she never minced words. "Stop hedging and spit it out."

"I need a favor."

Victor frowned harder. Vivian didn't have to ask for favors from him, and she knew that. There wasn't anything he wouldn't do for his kid sister.

"And it's kind of a big one," she added.

"Ask," he barked.

She toyed with the label on her bottle of beer. "What are you doing this summer?"

"Same thing I always do. Decompressing and relaxing at my house."

"Think you could do that with Pip?"

Victor laughed, because his adorable five-year-old niece was more chaotic than the whole group of people currently partying their asses off in this pub put together. "Fuck no."

Vivian stared him down. "Will you?"

Victor paused when he realized his sister was serious. There was only one thing that would pull her away from her daughter. One *big* thing. "You're finishing the book."

She nodded. "Pip starts school in the fall. I think it will be harder to leave then. You wouldn't be the sole caregiver," she hastily added. "Belle will come too."

Victor closed his eyes, not even bothering to hide his disdain. His sister was well aware of Victor's feelings toward Pip's nanny.

The woman was an annoying, cheerful fucking Mary Poppins ray of goddamn sunshine. She drove him fucking *crazy*.

"Vic," Vivian said, reaching across the table. "I wouldn't ask if it wasn't important."

He nodded because he knew that. Just like he knew he was going to say yes, because it was Vivian asking and she deserved this chance.

"Please," she said, squeezing his hand.

He grimaced, then shrugged.

"Yeah, okay. Pip and…Belle can come stay with me for the summer." And then because it was him, he added an angry "*fuck*" for good measure.

Be sure to check out the entire Stingrays Hockey series!

Restraint

Resist

Rematch

Release

Reclaim

Remain

Reaction

Return

And meet some former Stingrays players in these books!

Making His Play

Wild and Wicked

Calling all fans of Mari Carr AND Facebook! There's a group for you. Come join Mari Carr's Facebook group for sneak peaks, cover reveals, contests and more! Join now.

And be sure to join Mari's mailing list to receive a **FREE** sexy novella, Midnight Wild.

ABOUT THE AUTHOR

Virginia native Mari Carr is a New York Times and USA TODAY bestseller of contemporary romance novels. With over three million copies of her books sold, Mari was the winner of the Romance Writers of America's Passionate Plume award for her novella, Erotic Research. She has over a hundred published works, including her popular Wild Irish and Italian Stallions books, along with the Trinity Masters series she writes with Lila Dubois.

Follow Mari:
www.maricarr.com
mari@maricarr.com

Join her newsletter so you don't miss new releases and for exclusive subscriber-only content.

www.ingramcontent.com/pod-product-compliance
Lightning Source LLC
Chambersburg PA
CBHW032230050726
47591CB00001B/333

BIN TRAVERLER FORM

Cut By: Irene #23 **Qty** 46 **Date** 7/31/26

Scanned By: **Qty** **Date**

Scanned Batch ID's

_______________________ _______________________ _______________________

Notes / Exceptions

____